VOLUME TWO

THE FICTION COLLECTION
VOLUME TWO

From Legends to the current lore...

This volume features a collection of short stories that span many eras of the *Star Wars* timeline, telling tales that chronicle the exploits of assorted side characters along with some more familar names from the saga, including Obi-Wan Kenobi, Princess Leia, and Asajj Ventress.

This volume includes Legends stories—from the continuity pre-2014—such as a thrilling heist featuring Weequay pirate Hondo Ohnaka; a disturbing tale of the Sith featuring Darth Malgus; and the final action-packed frontline mission of Republic trooper Jace Malcom.

From the current lore—2015 to present—there is the tale of a squadron of TIE fighter pilots every bit as bold as their rebel counterparts; the story of an antiques dealer who must fight to protect Jedi artifacts he has kept safe since the Order fell; and a cat-and-mouse thriller that sees a reporter uncovering the truth about Orson Krennic and his sinister plans for the planet Jedha...

TITAN EDITORIAL
Editor Jonathan Wilkins
Managing Editor Martin Eden
Art Director Oz Browne
Senior Designer Andrew Leung
Assistant Editor Phoebe Hedges
Production Controller Kelly Fenlon
Senior Production Controller Jackie Flook
Sales and Circulation Manager Steve Tothill
Marketing and Sales Coordinator George Wickenden
Marketing and Advertisement Assistant Lauren Noding
Editorial Editor Duncan Baizley
Publishing Director Ricky Claydon
Publishing Director John Dziewiatkowski
Operations Director Leigh Baulch
Publishers Vivian Cheung & Nick Landau

DISTRIBUTION
U.S. Newsstand: Total Publisher Services, Inc.
John Dziewiatkowski, 630-851-7683
U.S. Distribution: Ingrams Periodicals,
Curtis Circulation Company
U.K. Newsstand: Marketforce, 0203 787 9199
U.S./U.K. Direct Sales Market: Diamond Comic Distributors
For more info on advertising contact adinfo@titanemail.com

First edition: September 2021

Star Wars Insider: The Official Fiction Collection Volume Two is published by Titan Magazines, a division of Titan Publishing Group Limited, 144 Southwark Street, London, SE1 0UP

Printed in China.

For sale in the U.S., Canada, U.K., and Eire

ISBN: 9781787737082

Titan Authorized User. TMN 3872

A CIP catalogue record for this title is available from the British Library.

10 9 8 7 6 5 4 3 2 1

LUCASFILM PUBLISHING
Senior Editor Brett Rector
Creative Director Michael Siglain
Art Director Troy Alders
Art Department Phil Szostak
Story Group Leland Chee, Pablo Hidalgo
Asset Management Chris Argyropoulos, Jackey Cabrera, Gabrielle Levenson, Bryce Pinkos, Erik Sanchez, Sarah Williams, Jason Schultz

Special Thanks: Erich Schoeneweiss, Christopher Troise, Kevin Pearl, Eugene Paraszczuk

CONTENTS

LEGENDS

The following stories are from Legends continuity, originally published from 2011 to 2013.

™

INCOGNITO

WRITTEN BY **JOHN JACKSON MILLER**
ART BY **CHRIS SCALF**

"You, there! Leave her alone!" Dewell Bronk's entreaty was barely more than a whisper, and it was no surprise that the toughs didn't hear him. He looked urgently across the aisle of the transport at the delinquents, a pair of young, horn-headed Devaronians. They'd been hassling the poor old Twi'lek woman since she'd boarded. When they had first yanked at her satchel, she had resisted briefly, but now she looked on meekly as the youths pawed through her belongings.

Dewell wanted to tell them to stop. Louder, this time. He could: he had an authoritative voice, one he was famous for. But that was in a different world, one where his small stature meant very little. No one was going to listen to a meter-tall, pudgy Kedorzhan in the lower hold of a passenger transport.

He looked around in desperation. The Tallaan Clipper had no security personnel on this level, just the frightening-looking first officer that Dewell never wanted to talk to again. He missed his bodyguards, who could have sorted this out in an instant. But he hadn't seen them since he hurriedly left his apartment on Coruscant. He expected he would never see them—or the apartment—again.

No, for the first time in ages, Dewell Bronk was alone and without help. And worst of all, he was unable to help—a new experience for the three-time recipient of the Coruscant Benevolent Society's Good Neighbor of the Year Award.

Life had changed. And he already hated it.

One of the Devaronians looked directly at him: an angry stare. Feeling his public-spiritness flee with his courage, Dewell instantly looked away. His whiskered jowls sagged, and he sank low in his seat. He was being foolish. How could he be anyone's rescuer now, when he was trying to avoid attention?

Worried, he felt again for the weight by his feet. Everything he owned was in a sack, tied with a small rope that he had looped around his ankle. Since leaving on the first leg of his odyssey, he had kept the bag mashed between his heels; he didn't want to wake from sleep to find it stolen. Not that there was anything much to take. The credits he'd planned to use in his escape were already gone: spent, to pay for his seat on this transport and the next one, and for the single meal a day that was supposed to come with the fares.

It was a sad predicament for someone who had lived his life close to the bright spots of the galaxy, traveling at will and, occasionally, in style. That moment had passed—and might never return again. Now Dewell, someone who had fought for justice his whole career, was reduced to doing nothing as thieves harassed an elderly fellow being. He could hear it: they were pulling rudely at her head-tendrils now. Dewell's heart ached. There was nothing he could do.

"You don't want to disturb that woman," a nearby voice said. Its tones were warm and confident. A human voice, Dewell thought, but he didn't dare to look up. Some poor hero was about to be thrashed.

"We don't want to disturb this woman," a gruff Devaronian voice responded.

Puzzled, Dewell leaned over and peeked across the aisle. The two hoodlums had dropped the Twi'lek's pouch and were walking to the ladder leading to the upper level. The person who had spoken first was the human who had boarded at the previous stop—the one Dewell had mentally labeled "the Young Father."

Dewell didn't know if the human was father to the child. Nor did he really know how young the man was. Kedorzhan eyes were sharp in the dark, but most other species lived in the light. Kedorzhans seldom opened their eyes beyond a crack in daylight. Dewell had always refused to wear a visor, feeling it better to be able to look directly into the eyes of his listeners, even if it meant he often had trouble telling one person from another. To Dewell, people tended to become shapes, happy and sad, cruel and innocent. In the harshly lit cabin, the Young Father was a kindly blur, his face obscured by a brown hood as he cradled the bundled infant.

Dewell looked left and right. No one else had seen or heard what had happened with the Devaronians; everyone else had moved away, fearful to get involved. And now the Twi'lek moved, too, grabbing her bag and rushing off to the rear compartment. The Young Father sighed and sat in her vacated seat.

"That's telling those punks," Dewell said reflexively. He knew it was a mistake for a fugitive to speak to a stranger—even a chivalrous one. Who knew how many

people were searching for him, and what tactics their agents might use? But the human barely turned. Beneath the man's cowl, the Kedorzhan made out two shining blue-gray dots in a hairy face.

"Just some high-spirited kids," the human said.

"I know young spirits," Dewell said. His broad nose twitched disdainfully. "Those were criminals." He cleared his throat. "You should report them to the captain."

"It's really not necessary."

Dewell sighed, embarrassed. So brave, volunteering someone else to do the right thing. The Young Father had taken one risk but would go no further. Seeing the child fussing in the man's arms, Dewell couldn't blame him.

The human checked and rechecked the child's wrappings. Even with his poor eyesight, Dewell could tell the man was puzzled.

"Your child is hungry," Dewell said.

"He just ate a little while ago," the Young Father replied. "I didn't think it was time again."

"The child decides when it is time again," Dewell said, feeling a little more comfortable. He grinned as the human went fishing in his backpack for a bottle. New parents were amusing. Dewell had only had time for seven children in his life: not many for a Kedorzhan, but there had been so many more important things to do. Now, squinting at the infant, Dewell found himself wishing that he'd spent more time with his own children—and wondering where all of them were today.

Well, he knew where one was. Poor Tyloor was dead, his body lost somewhere out on the battlefield. Dead, like so many other children of the Republic, in a conflict that had never made any sense to Dewell. And, while the Clone Wars were thankfully—and suddenly—over, the main battle of the Kedorzhan's career seemed lost too.

The Kedorzhans were a small people in height, power, and numbers. Short-legged with four fat fingers on each hand, they had migrated everywhere underground work was to be found. Most worlds had welcomed the the pleasant, plump-faced people; they kept to themselves and caused

Forgetting his size—and everything else that concerned him—Dewell charged into the secluded area.

few problems. When the Kedorzhans had finally obtained Republic representation and a Senate seat, many had assumed that the diminutive beings would conduct themselves just as Dewell was now. Certainly, they would mind their own business, taking the lead of other species while trying not to be noticed.

But Dewell and his illustrious predecessors had defied expectations, using their newfound power to fight for the weakest of the galaxy. They had lived underfoot, that experience had driven them to help others.

That fact—and Tyloor's death, among so many others—was why he had signed the Petition of the 2000 without question. Supreme Chancellor Palpatine had overstepped his bounds, clawing for government rights that had been reserved for the people. And not simply important powers of use in an emergency. No, many of the new measures were simply arbitrary, undoing protections for the weak for no reason at all.

His advisors had told him not to sign the petition. Now, with the Jedi gone and the Empire declared, many of his colleagues had already withdrawn their names. Dewell would not. But he feared that would be the last act of bravery he would ever perform.

The wretched first officer appeared in the doorway, as drunk as he had been before. "Station stop," he called into the hold. "Cross over to Pad 560 to reach our line's connector flight for the Outer Rim. Everyone else, thanks for..." Dewell didn't hear the rest, reaching down for the bag of belongings at his feet. It was time to move again.

Dewell didn't know what planet he was on, except that the sky was a bright green, and that, again, he was having trouble seeing. He was glad to get off the Space Slug, in any event.

He had waited for the Devaronians to disembark first. He hadn't seen where the Young Father had gone. That was too bad; the human had seemed a decent sort. This was how it was going to be, Dewell realized. Going from one place to another, never forming a relationship that lasted more than five minutes, never mind a friendship. It was hardly a life worth living, much less fighting for.

Slouching as he walked across the grungy spaceport, his bag tightly in hand, he looked around at the crowd. He felt eyes on him, and while he couldn't see any faces clearly, he imagined the rest. He spotted a lonely passageway leading between two of the maintenance buildings, and headed toward it. That way he could get to the landing pad while avoiding most of the foot traffic.

Walking down the tiled alley, he heard a bleating cry from around a corner. Instinctively, he stepped forward and looked. A long-trunked Ortolan janitor, still clutching his mop, was being shaken by two figures in white armor. Clone troopers, from the so-called Grand Army of the Republic. Dewell couldn't hear what they were saying, but the stubby blue figure howled as they shook him.

That was enough! Forgetting his size—and everything else that concerned him—Dewell charged into the secluded area. "Stop that!" he yelled. The troopers paid him no mind. The rope wrapped tightly around his paw, Dewell slung his bag of belongings forward. It struck the trooper holding the janitor on the shin.

He had their attention now, whether he

wanted it or not. The trooper dropped the Ortolan, who ran off through one of the side passages, abandoning his cleaning cart and bucket. Pulling a blaster rifle from over his shoulder, the trooper looked directly at the Kedorzhan. "Dewell Bronk?"

Dewell looked up, startled. "That is my name."

"Senator Bronk, you are under arrest."

"On whose authority?"

"Emperor Palpatine." The second trooper held up a datapad with Dewell's image.

Dewell's eyes opened to their full, enormous width. Of course, there was no Imperial interest in hassling janitors. At least, not yet. It was a trap, and he had walked right into it. His arms fell to his sides. "I guess I knew this was—"

Before he could finish, something astonishing happened. The janitor's bucket landed over the helmet of the first clone trooper with a loud clang, spilling sudsy water and completely obscuring the soldier's vision. The second trooper turned, raising his rifle; surely, it would have taken someone a Wookiee's height to shove the bucket over his partner's head. But there was no one behind him at all. Instead, there was someone to the side—wielding, of all things, a large spray can. As Dewell dove for the ground, he heard the loud spritzing noise and smelled the high-pressure cleanser foam.

Looking up, he saw the comical sight of the trooper, his eye ports and air intakes clogged with the thick goo, moving his rifle in an attempt to fire randomly. But his assailant was on him now, wresting away the weapon. The secluded area was shaded enough that Dewell could make out his rescuer's identity.

The Young Father!

In one swift move, the human smashed the trooper in the head with the butt of his own rifle. The armored figure stumbled backwards, bumping into his bucket-headed partner. The Young Father shoved at them both now—exactly how, Dewell could not see—pushing them into one of the side doorways. It was a maintenance pit, he realized. He heard the colossal clamor as the armored men tumbled down a staircase.

The Young Father walked over and closed the door, locking it. "They won't be bothering you again, Senator."

Dewell looked around. "But where..."

The Young Father nodded toward a spot behind him. Stepping forward, Dewell made out the shape of the baby, cradled and resting comfortably atop the Ortolan's janitorial cart. The man lifted the child.

"I believe they've been following you since the Space Slug," the Young Father said. "The Emperor has agents everywhere."

Bronk didn't ask how the man knew. "I don't understand. There are plenty of Kedorzhans—and we mostly look alike. My documents were perfectly forged. Was it the first officer?"

"The Devaronians, I think. Forgeries can get you far—but they knew your reputation for protecting the weak. I suspect they knew you were on the run, and were using that to smoke you out. There, and here." He nodded toward the locked door. "But it's early days for Palpatine's Empire.

"Your strength may surprise you," the Young Father said, squeezing the bundle he was holding. "Even the smallest among us could change the galaxy."

Next time, it might well be the victim—the Twi'lek woman or the Ortolan janitor—who's the informant."

Dewell shook his head. "It's not in my nature not to trust."

"Mine either," the Young Father said, pulling the child close. He turned and began walking away. "Your next flight is over here," he said. "I'll see you get there."

Bronk followed the short distance across to Pad 560, glad that no one seemed to have noticed the earlier commotion. The starship was little better than the Space Slug, but it was outgassing and ready to go, and that made it look quite heavenly.

Dewell stood near the landing ramp and looked back to the Young Father. "Thank you."

The man simply nodded and started to turn away.

"This is what it's going to be like, isn't it?" Dewell asked, looking down at the ground.

The Young Father paused. "How do you mean?"

"Life in hiding. In exile. I'll need to fear every stranger, every comm connection. I won't be able to touch a datapad without fear that Palpatine's cronies are looking in." Dewell looked up. "I'm exaggerating, right?"

"I'm afraid not," the man said. He nodded sympathetically. "It will be that way and worse. Things that are basic to your being, things that brought you joy and fulfillment, may become liabilities. Even the thing that defines you—the very desire to help others."

Dewell looked back at the starship, and then out at the milling blur of passengers, heading this way and that. Gesturing to them, the Young Father continued, keeping his head down. "You'll think crowds will offer security—but that only works as long as you offer nothing of yourself to anyone. And that's not the worst thing. Kind acts by others will have to be evaluated with skepticism, and suspicion." He smiled gently. "Present company excepted."

Dewell looked down. The man didn't look familiar—he saw so few human faces clearly that he remembered none of them. But he knew a companion in crisis when he heard one. "It sounds like you're in the same situation."

"Not exactly," the man said. "You have more choices available than I do."

Dewell stared at the ground for a moment, until he realized what the man meant. "I can't live in hiding." Taking a breath, the little Kedorzhan straightened. "I guess I go back."

The human nodded somberly.

"I'll have to recant, to declare support for Palpatine." The words made him feel nauseous as he stepped away from the ramp.

"You'll be in a better position to help people," the Young Father said. "That may be the place to be, until people of your strength are called for."

"Strength!" Dewell laughed. "I'm afraid of every bright light and loud noise."

"Your strength may surprise you," the Young Father said, squeezing the bundle he was holding. "Even the smallest among us could change the galaxy."

"Even your child."

The Young Father looked down and smiled. "Even he."

"I hope we don't have to wait that long," Dewell said.

"Agreed." The Young Father nodded. "But I'm prepared to."

He looked over his shoulder. Across the tarmac, another transport was readying to lift off. "That's my ride."

Dewell watched as the man turned. "I'm sorry," he called. "I don't think I caught your name."

"Who I am is no longer important," the Young Father said, not looking back.

Dewell nodded. "Maybe. But what you do is." He waved. "Keep doing it... if you can."

THE THIRD LESSON

WRITTEN BY **PAUL S. KEMP**
ART BY **MAREK OKOŃ**

A haze of smoke hung in the air, the black residuum of the Imperial fleet's pre-landing bombardment of Alderaan. Rage burned in Malgus, its seed grown from the word he kept hearing over Imperial communication channels: Retreat.

The Empire had lost Alderaan. Hours before Malgus had walked its surface as a conqueror, but now...

Now signal fires dotted its surface, rallying points for the Republic forces.

A counterattack was coming. Reports indicated a Republic fleet en route to Alderaan.

Retreat.

Retreat.

He clenched his fists so hard it made his fingers ache. His breathing sounded like a rasp over wood. His skin stung from burns. A Republic commando had exploded a grenade in his face, and combat with a Jedi witch had damaged his lungs. Lacerations and contusions made a grim mosaic on his flesh.

But he felt no pain. He felt only anger.

Hate.

A sense of frustration that made him want to shout.

His personal shuttle roared low over the scorched landscape. Below him, buildings and bodies smoldered in the ruins of an Alderaani town. Around him, Imperial ships prowled the sky, flying escort. He tried to unknot his fists, failed. He wanted—

The presence of a light-side Force user bumped up against his Force sensitivity, a sudden flare in his perception. He looked down and out the viewport.
He saw nothing but charred ruins, rubbled buildings, burnt out vehicles. He pinched the comlink he wore.

"Turn us around."

"My lord?" asked his pilot.

"Come about, cut speed to one quarter, and reduce altitude by one hundred meters."

"Yes, my lord."

As the shuttle wheeled around and slowed, Malgus overrode the safeties and lowered the landing ramp. Wind whipped into the cabin, carrying the smell of a charred planet, a planet Malgus had intended to kill, but instead had only wounded.

Someone had to pay for that.

He took the hilt of his lightsaber in hand and sank into the Force. The burned-out buildings below stuck out of the scorched earth like rotted teeth, crooked and black.

"Slower," he said to the pilot.

He reached out through the Force, probing for the light-side presence he had felt.

At first there was nothing, and he wondered if he had been mistaken, or if the light-side user had perceived Malgus and suppressed his power. But then...

There.

He felt it as an irritation behind his eyes, an itch only violence could scratch. He shed his cloak and stepped
to the edge of the landing ramp. The wind pulled at him. Anger swelled in him, buoyed him up. The Force anchored him in place. He pinched his comlink again.

"Hover above the ruins until I return."

"Return, my lord? Where are you going? You're seriously wounded."

Malgus deactivated the comlink and leapt

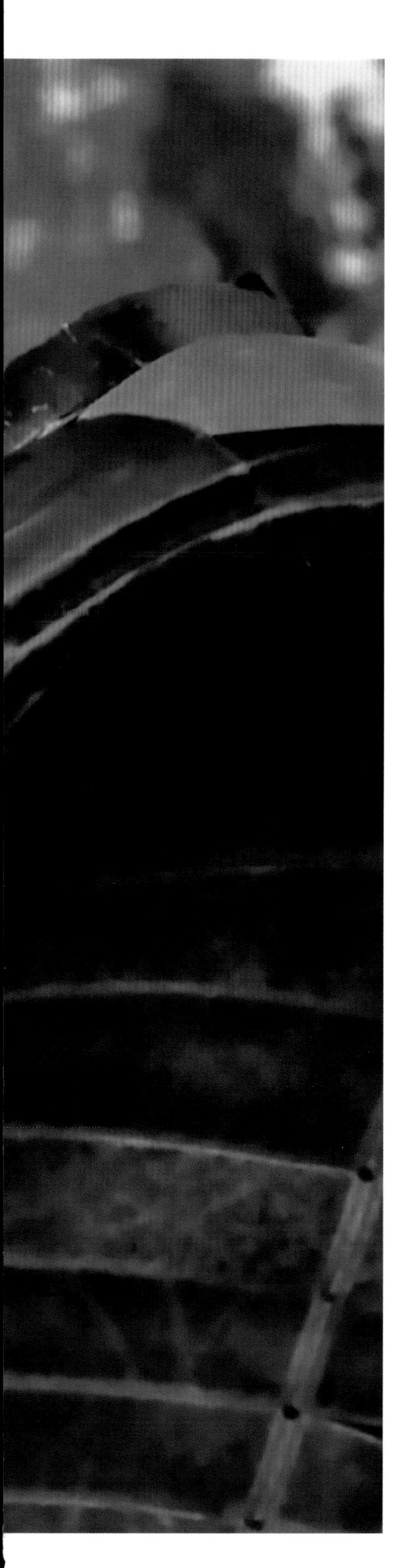

off the ramp into the open air. He ignited his blade as the ground rushed up to meet him. Using the Force to cushion the impact, he hit the ground in a crouch.

He stood in the center of a street pockmarked with craters and littered with broken glass and overturned speeders. An aircar burned 10 meters from him, vomiting gouts of black smoke into the sky. Somewhere, a wind bell chimed furiously in the gusts.

"I'm here, Jedi!" Malgus shouted, his voice booming over the ruins.

Behind him, he heard the hum of an activating lightsaber, then another.

He turned to see a male Zabrak, a Jedi, emerge from one of the burned-out buildings that lined the street. The blue line of a lightsaber glowed in each of his hands. He studied Malgus sidelong.

"Malgus," the Jedi said.

Malgus did not know the Jedi's name and he did not care. The Zabrak was merely the focus of his anger, a convenient target for his rage.

Malgus fell into the Force, roared, and bounded down the street, his anger lending him speed.

The Jedi held his ground. At twenty meters, the Jedi raised his lightsabers aloft to either side and drew them both down with a flourish.

Too late the rumble of the falling buildings penetrated the haze of Malgus's anger. An avalanche of duracrete and transparisteel crashed down on him from either side of the street...

The creases on his father's Imperial uniform looked sharp enough to cut meat, but his tone was as soft as the belly that overflowed his trousers.

"Come with me, Veradun."

Veradun followed his father to the enormous menagerie they kept on the grounds of the family's estate. His father, a biologist in the Imperial Science Corps, collected animals from countless worlds. The family had their own private zoo, financed by the Empire. Veradun had helped tend the creatures since he'd been a small boy.

Shrieks, chitters, howls, and a pungent animal stink greeted their entrance. His father's voice knifed through the noise.

"You know why I enjoy these animals so much?"

Veradun shook his head. He saw himself reflected in the lenses of his father's eyeglasses.

"Because we can learn from them."

"Learn what?"

His father smiled cryptically. "Come on."

Father put a hand on his shoulder and steered him through the maze of habitats, cages, and tanks, until they reached the transparisteel cube of the kouhun tank. A thick layer of sand, dotted with a few loose rocks and some loose fur, was all that was visible. The segmented arthropod, its body as long as Veradun's arm, lay hidden somewhere underneath the sand of the tank. Veradun walked around the tank, trying to spot any sign of the kouhun. Nothing.

Meanwhile, his father lifted a feeder rat from a nearby cage and held it over the kouhoun's tank.

"I fed it earlier," Veradun said.

"I know."

His father dropped the rat into the tank and it froze the moment it hit the sand. It sniffed the air, whiskers twitching.

The sand near it bulged.

The rat squealed with fear but before it could move, the kouhoun erupted from the sand under it, seized the rodent in its scissor-like mandibles, and bit it in half. Blood spilled, painting the sand red.

> **He turnd to see a male Zabrak, a Jedi, emerge from one of the burned-out buildings that lined the street.**

The kouhon crawled fully from the sand, its head all mandibles and dead black eyes. Dozens of pairs of legs propelled its segmented body over the bloody bits of the rat. But it did not eat, and after a moment it burrowed back into the sand, leaving the rat's carcass unmolested.

"Why do you think it killed the rat?" his father asked. "It was not hungry. As you said, you fed it not long ago."

"Instinct," Veradun said. "It's a savage creature."

"Good, Veradun. Good. Indeed, the kouhon kills for no reason. Does that make sense to you?"

"No, but... it's an animal."

His father kneeled to look Veradun in the face. "Right. And you're not. The kouhon teaches us that senseless savagery is the province of animals, not men. Savagery is useful only if it's controlled and put in service to an end. Do you understand?"

Veradun considered, nodded.

"The end is everything," his father said.

Malgus stood in a pocket under a mountain of rubble, legs bent, the power from his upraised hands preventing several tons of duracrete and steel from crushing him. Dust made his already troubled breathing more difficult. He coughed as the words of his father echoed in his mind.

He'd been sloppy, so lost in his need for revenge that he'd failed to properly evaluate the Jedi's power. He'd surrendered his reason to bloodlust. But no more. With an effort of will, he contained his anger, controlled it, made it a whetstone against which he sharpened his power. Using the Force, he blew the rubble up and away from him. It fell with a crash into the adjacent buildings. A Force-augmented leap carried him out and over the heap. The Jedi's eyes widened as Malgus hit the street. Malgus sneered and charged.

He closed the distance between them rapidly. The red line of Malgus's lightsaber moved so quickly it blurred into a red smear. The Jedi parried again and again, the sizzle of blade on blade resounding through the ruins. Malgus's onslaught—a blizzard of slashes, cuts, and stabs—allowed the Jedi no room for a counterattack. The Jedi retreated before the offensive, desperately intercepting Malgus's blows.

Malgus could have ended the Jedi in any of several ways, but he needed the satisfaction of a lightsaber kill.

"This is my favorite," his father said.

"The viirsun?"

Veradun had always found the avian boring. A small ground bird with drab, brown and black feathers, it did little of interest other than care for its offspring, a male that was soon to leave the nest.

"Not the viirsun, no," his father said.

"Then what?"

The viirsun's habitat—native plants, a single tree, a few rocks—was built behind a transparisteel wall. As they watched, the mother regurgitated some partially digested insects into the mouth of her nearly grown offspring. Veradun had seen the same thing a hundred times, but his father watched intently, as if he'd never seen it before.

"What are you looking at?" Veradun asked. He saw nothing unusual.

"Watch."

After devouring the insects, the offspring stood and strutted about the habitat, testing its legs. The mother watched, preening her feathers. In time, the offspring returned to the mother, stood over her, and began pecking at her with its beak. At first Veradun thought it wanted more food, but the pecking became more and more violent. Wings flapped, feathers flew. The mother attempted retreat but the offspring pursued, seized her neck in his beak and shook violently, once, twice. The offspring dropped her to the ground and began to feed.

Veradun had never seen anything like it.

"The offspring isn't a viirsun," his father explained. "It's a mimnil. In its immature state, it looks like a juvenile viirsun. It kills the original offspring and replaces them. When it's ready to molt, it attacks its adoptive mother. I've been watching this one for a while."

A mimnil. Veradun had never suspected.

"I... still don't understand."

"Often things that pretend weakness await only the right moment to show strength. Do you understand, now?"

Veradun considered, nodded.

You must trust no one," his father said. "Least of all those who appear weak."

"Often things that pretend weakness await only the right moment to show strength."

Malgus's lightsaber traced glittering red arcs through the air. He spun, slashed, stabbed, pushing the Jedi backwards. But always the Jedi parried. He seemed to be biding his time.

He was baiting him, Malgus realized. Feigning weakness.

Malgus relented in his attack, backed off a few steps, and reached out through the Force. Immediately he felt the faint, intentionally suppressed signature of another light-side user to his right. The Jedi's ally was hidden in the rubble, moving closer.

Malgus loosed a furious series of overhand strikes that forced the Zabrak to retreat rapidly. Sidestepping a stab from the Jedi, Malgus rode his motion into a Force-augmented spinning side kick that hit the Jedi in the ribs and sent him cartwheeling into the wall of nearby building. At the same time, he reached out with the Force for the hidden light-side user, brushed aside

the resistance he felt, and pulled the Jedi out of hiding.

A human male in his twenties rose up out of ruins, dangling like a fish on the hook of Malgus's power. His legs kicked futilely; the green blade of his lightsaber cut at empty air; he gagged as Malgus's power squeezed shut his throat.

"Vorin!" shouted the Zabrak.

"So much for your ambush," Malgus said, and closed his fist, crushing Vorin's windpipe. He let the body fall to the charred earth. A flash of anger, quickly suppressed, shot from the Zabrak as he bounded over the rubble at Malgus. Malgus watched him come, his red blade held slack at his side.

At 10 meters, Malgus extended his free hand and loosed veins of blue Force lightning. They struck the charging Jedi: swept through his defenses, swirled around him, and began to burn flesh.

Shouting with pain, the Jedi leaned forward into the lightning—teeth bare, blue blades held before him —and staggered toward Malgus. Despite his burns, he came onward. One step, another, another, but he was failing, wilting in the heat of the lightning. Malgus channeled more power and the Jedi fell to his knees, screaming. The lightning spiraled around the Zabrak, blasting dark holes in his body. The lightsabers fell from his hands and he writhed in agony, screaming his pain into the sky.

Malgus ended his attack. The Jedi, ruined, fell to the ground and rolled over onto his back. His breathing sounded even worse than Malgus's.

Malgus strode to his side and stood over him.

He found that he admired the Jedi's mettle.

He deactivated his lightsaber.

After watching the mimnil devour the viirsun, his father had taken him to a new cage that must have been a recent addition to the zoo, for Veradun had never noticed it before. A tarp covered it, concealing the contents.

"What's in it?" Veradun asked.

His father looked somber. "The third lesson."

Veradun's gaze went from his father, to the cage, and back to his father.

"I think you'll be a great warrior, Veradun," his father said. "A tremendous asset to the Empire."

Veradun heard the sadness in the words but did not understand them.

"Your instructors tell me they've seen few with your potential in the Force."

"I'm honored by their praise."

His father smiled distantly. "A shuttle arrives for you tomorrow, to take you to the academy on Dromund Kaas. I want you to know that I'm proud of you. Always remember that."

"I will. And I'm doubly honored by your praise, father."

His father kneeled, embraced him, stood, and walked away.

"Where are you going?" Veradun called. "What about the third lesson?"

"Look in the cage," his father said. "Perhaps you'll figure it out yourself."

Veradun watched his father go, then turned and unveiled the contents of the cage the way he might unveil a secret—slowly, carefully, and with a sense of trepidation.

He let the tarp fall to the ground.

The cage was entirely empty.

For a moment he wondered if his father had made a mistake.

But his father never made mistakes.

He stared at the empty cage for a long while, considering. Finally, he thought he understood.

The Jedi, his face twisted with pain, stared up at Malgus. One of the horns on his head had cracked from the heat of the Force lightning. The Jedi's eyes went to the deactivated lightsaber in Malgus's fist and he cocked his head.

Malgus read the question in his eyes.

Mercy from a Sith?

Malgus smiled. He stepped forward, activated his blade, and stabbed the Jedi through the chest.

"Sleep," he said.

The Jedi's eyes held the question for the few moments it took for them to go vacant. Malgus stood, deactivated his blade, inhaled, and walked away. The question in the Jedi's eyes was one he had asked himself countless times, the one his father had tried to help him answer those many years earlier.

The answer had never fully satisfied him, but he supposed that was the point.

Sometimes there was just an empty cage.

THE LAST BATTLE OF COLONEL JACE MALCOM

WRITTEN BY **ALEXANDER FREED**
ART BY **DAVID RABBITTE**

T-MINUS SEVEN HOURS.

The dying man's armor dripped with sweat in the fog, beads of moisture—not water, never water on this planet—forming on the white plastoid chestplate and dripping onto the ground. The dying man himself was propped against a rock, and Sergeant Immel crouched above him as she fumbled to resecure his helmet. "He's out, Colonel," she said. "Autodoc pegs him at critical."

Jace Malcom watched the horizon. Through his helmet's display filters, the fog seemed to dissolve before the yellow sky and rocky cliffs, then snapped back into place as the filter tech gave up with an electronic shrug. No further enemy presence. At least, nothing obvious.

"Your call," Jace said. "His tracer functional?"

"It works. What about vultures?"

"If the Empire has time to send vultures, it means we failed the mission."

Not true, of course. The black-suited troopers could flock to the battlefield at any time—death's own heralds, following med tracers to find their victims. But Immel knew the odds, so Jace could afford the lie.

"Why me?" Immel asked.

"Special Forces is here to advise, and I'm glad to be an extra gun. But in the field, the game's yours."

"You're lowlife scum, Colonel Malcom."

"SpecForce is nothing but."

Jace watched Immel. Her armored shoulders rose and fell as she took a long breath, then, silent, leaned over her dying comrade and thumbed a device on his belt. Her voice crackled through Jace's helmet comlink a moment later.

"All teams, we're pressing on."

Immel plucked her rifle out of the dust and started checking its readouts. Jace knelt beside the dying man and placed a hand on his shoulder.

"Corporal Amden vor Keioidian. You did the Republic proud. You did all of *us* proud. And we'll be back for you."

Jace stood, nodded to Immel, and they slunk off together into the fog, rifles cradled close. Immel didn't look back, and Jace smiled bitterly, feeling the expression blunted by the scars on his face. She'd made the right call. She might end up a decent leader after all.

Then again, he thought, *she'd better.* The troops were going to need someone to look up to, and he didn't have much time left.

T-MINUS FOUR HOURS.

The battlefield narrowed to a series of canyons, channeling the fog like a riverbed. Kalandis Seven's gravity—low enough to make stone-tossing a sport at base, high enough to ensure that a fall was still painful—made the march easier, but no less tedious.

Breaking the long silence came static-distorted cheering over Jace's comlink. Children shrieked and fireworks popped, each accompanied by a blast of white noise. In one motion, not breaking stride as they traversed the barren landscape, Jace and Immel lowered the volume level on their helmet comms.

The propaganda broadcast overrode all channels every hour, blared by Republic Strategic Information Service agents in orbit. This time, it was another news report on the Empire's withdrawal from Corellia and the Core Worlds. A genuine, unadulterated victory for the Republic, but one very far away from the Kalandis system, and not the first apparent victory Jace had seen in his career.

It was forty years now, he thought—kept thinking, every day at different times, when some private showed off

There were no tricks to fighting Sith, Jace had explained to more officers and grunts than he cared to remember. Sith were powerful, and fast, and they broke just as easily as anyone else.

her first scar in the mess hall or while reviewing specs for the hundredth variation of some starfighter—forty years since the Sith Empire had come to conquer the galaxy, and he'd been fighting ever since.

He supposed he wouldn't be fighting much longer.

Immel's voice cut through commentary on the Supreme Chancellor's latest speech. "Target in sight."

They had emerged from the narrow mouth of a canyon onto a cracked plain, where the silhouettes of dark spires stretched skyward behind the fog. "We've reached the spaceport," Immel continued, adjusting her comlink. "All teams, report in."

Jace listened to the crackling voices speak up, one by one, as he unslung a satchel and checked the contents. He knew the soldiers' names (Zenhai, Kayle, Min-Reva), had met most of them (Eron collected antique music recordings; Camur had a caf allergy), had even hand-selected a few for this mission (Yennir of the Green saw through fog like glass). They were young and stupid and brave, and he could think of worse men and women to serve with.

"Ready to go?" Immel asked.

Jace nodded and tossed Immel the satchel. "Beacons charged and ready. Plant them on the targets and the fog won't matter—our fighter wing will know exactly where to drop the payload."

"Assuming the pilots aren't making out with their droids back at base. You done this before?"

"Bomb a spaceport? More times than I can count."

"What're the odds they won't rebuild tomorrow?"

Jace shrugged his shoulders. "I can think of worse ways for the Imps to blow resources."

Taking out a spaceport would be a major step in securing Kalandis, even if it did get rebuilt. Even if there were a dozen other Imp bases on the planet. Jace had put together the plan himself.

But Immel wasn't wrong to wonder what good it would do.

Keep lying to her, Jace thought. *You have an example to set.*

The spaceport was a mixture of flat metal landing pads, squat command bunkers, and slender control towers. Jace and Immel made their approach together, silent, observing the enemy patrols—pairs of Imperial troopers clad in black and red. The fog made avoiding the enemy easy enough, until the heat of a landing starship blasted the fog away, whipping a scorching, misty wall across Jace and a nearby patrol.

The Imperials hadn't turned, hadn't noticed anything before Jace's blaster bolts burned twin holes in the backs of their suits. The roar of the starship's engines continued as Jace and Immel rushed to drag the bodies under a half-repaired Imperial fighter.

One of the bodies groaned as the engine roar began to fade. Immel pressed the barrel of her rifle to the back of the man's helmet and pulled the trigger before rolling the corpse into the fighter's shadow. "Mercy shot," she muttered.

Either way, Jace thought.

Immel withdrew a beacon and clipped it to a nearby power terminal as the fog rushed back in. Jace squinted and adjusted his helmet's filters, looking in the direction of the vessel that had just landed.

"Southern tower is fifty meters that way," Immel said. "Prime target—you plan to help?"

Jace didn't turn, continuing to stare toward the looming shadow of the starship through the fog. It was too large to be a bomber. Sleeker hull shape than most transports. "How are we doing for time?" he asked.

"Fighters are in the air by now. We've got at least two hours before they show."

Jace swore, then jutted a thumb in the direction of the starship. "All right—we're adjusting the plan. That thing that just landed? Pretty sure it's a planetary command ship on a refueling run."

Immel moved to Jace's side and knelt, gesturing for him to follow suit. "Another patrol," she said. "Keep talking."

"Ship'll be gone by the time our fighters arrive, but if we could capture that thing? Its navicomputer could point us to every Imp target on the planet."

Immel glanced at the power terminal where the metal disc of the targeting beacon hummed quietly. "Whole blasted world would be a blue milk run," she agreed. "But we're not equipped for a boarding action."

"We're not," Jace said, "and we don't have a lot of spare firepower, but we're not losing this chance."

Immel paused.

"Sir," she said. "I'm in command of these men, and I'm not sending them—"

Good woman, Jace thought, even as he interrupted her.

"You're not sending them anywhere. You finish the mission, and I go in alone. Won't draw attention that way."

And it's not a bad way to go out, either, he added silently.

T-MINUS ONE HOUR.

The sentry looked almost innocent without his helmet—young, sun-haired, a splash of a birthmark on his neck. He walked down the command ship corridor, sidearm holstered, eating a ration bar.

Three steps, and Jace was out of his hiding place, gloved hands bringing the butt of his rifle onto the sentry's head. The man crumpled to the floor with barely a sound. Jace gasped in pain.

"Are you all right?" Immel asked, the comlink barely carrying her voice.

"Fine," Jace said. "Took a bolt on the lower deck. Fused some skin to the armor, but I'm fine." It was true, and the kolto injections dulled the pain. What bothered him was that he noticed the pain at all. The gifts of old age.

"Beacons are all set, fighters are almost on-site. I'd join you, but you might have noticed that ship just took off."

"I noticed. I'll be okay." Jace followed the sentry's path toward a heavy blast door—the entrance to the bridge. "What do you think of Private Kayle?" he asked.

"Bad shot, can't read a label, probably poison himself one day. Knows his faults and takes orders."

"Could be your new forward on the null-racket team. Plays a mean game. Think about it."

Immel's reply was a long time coming. "You going somewhere?"

"Might be," Jace said. "Just keep him in mind. It's good to spend time with your squad."

Jace muted his comm and hit the control panel. The blast door irised open and the bridge came into view—black metal and blinking consoles, and a transparisteel dome looking out onto fog and sky. Only a handful of officers manned their stations; forty years of instinct and threat assessments told Jace they wouldn't be a problem.

The Sith overseer was a different matter.

The Sith stood in the center of the bridge, a black cloud of dark robes with a metal armor core and the face of an etched brass mask. Jace didn't wait for the mask to turn before running, boots slamming against the deck, directly toward his opponent.

There were no tricks to fighting Sith, Jace had explained to more officers and grunts than he cared to remember. Sith were powerful, and fast, and they broke just as easily as anyone else. You couldn't afford to fear them—not even for a moment. The rest was just smart fighting.

The robed figure narrowed and twirled like a dancer, evading Jace's

His body reached the broken dome as the ship pitched forward, starting to hurtle toward the planet surface. He looked out into the endless fog and readied himself for the fall. No chute, no jump pack, no grav unit.

blaster bursts as he closed the distance. She—was it a woman?—reached for the lightsaber at her belt even as Jace howled and crashed into her, letting the weight of his armor take them both down.

Jace felt something give beneath him—a robed arm twisted out of position or a rib broken somewhere—even as he slammed an elbow toward where the Sith's head seemed to be. The hard impact of the deck told him he missed, and a second later a hand closed over his helmet and his vision turned white.

Heat stabbed at his face, lancing into his temples and trickling down his nose like sweat. He rolled, and blinked away spots in time to see the last arcs of electricity jump from the Sith's hand toward him. Any longer, or without the helmet, and the Sith's sorcery would've charred his skull.

Somehow, Jace had held on to his rifle. He tried to stand, unable to feel his legs, as the Sith reached for her lightsaber again—only to find it gone, dropped to the deck barely a meter away.

Jace squeezed his rifle's trigger. This time, the bolts struck heart and lung, even as his helmet filters pixilated from the electrical damage. He heard a muffled sound from the Sith, some final command, as she died.

For an instant, as Jace heard the shouting, saw the officers run toward the exit of the bridge, he felt the rush of victory. The command ship was his. Kalandis Seven was going to the Republic. Immel and her team could win the whole blasted planet.

Then the voice came over the bridge speakers: "Self-destruct initiated."

The consoles ripped apart, metal and plastic and glass burning and streaking through the air. The transparisteel cockpit dome shattered, raining knives. Jace swore and fell, his body shaking as he tried to crawl forward over the trembling deck and away from the fire he felt at his back.

So damn close, he thought.

His body reached the broken dome as the ship pitched forward, starting to hurtle toward the planet surface. He looked out into the endless fog and readied himself for the fall. No chute, no jump pack, no grav unit. There was comfort knowing what had to come next.

The ship shook, and Jace rolled out into the fog, falling free, looking down onto a rising shadow. He hit surface fast—much too fast, much too close to be at ground level—and lay stunned for a few long moments. He realized he was hugging the wing of a Republic fighter, hovering near the plummeting mass of the Imperial command ship.

Painfully, he reached up to turn his comm back on. "Immel to Malcom," he heard immediately. "Thought we could spare one fighter for you. Would've mentioned it if you hadn't gone silent."

"Thank you," Jace said, and closed his eyes. He allowed himself to lie back on the wing and ache. "Mission status?"

"Spaceport's in burning little chunks. I'd feel pretty good if you weren't showing off up there, blowing up command ships."

"I was trying to capture it, Sergeant. We could've won the planet."

He could hear the smirk in Immel's voice, and he felt himself curl his lip in irritation. "Yeah, you really messed up—we'll buy you a drink back at base, Colonel, but only the one. Bottom shelf stuff."

Jace watched the fog drift around him, felt the surprisingly gentle thrumming of the wing beneath him, and crawled to the fighter's upper hatch. The distant sounds of fire and tearing metal came from far below. Immel still didn't understand, and this was his last chance to tell her. "No," he said. "You won't."

"Repeat that?"

"I've been recalled, Sergeant. Right about now, there's a transport arriving to take me to the Core Worlds."

Jace heard Immel swear.

Then: "You SpecForce boys are all scum."

T-PLUS FORTY MINUTES.

Jace watched the ochre dot of Kalandis Seven retreat through the viewport of the starship *Frontier Justice*. The ship's captain—a Jedi Knight whose name Jace hadn't caught, who had fought through half a dozen blockades just to arrive at Kalandis on time—hadn't complained when Jace arrived battered and late. It was one thing Jace liked about Jedi: They took things in stride.

"Any idea why they sent you?" Jace asked. The Jedi Knight didn't spare Jace a glance as he tore half-melted wires out from under an engineering console.

"The Supreme Chancellor thinks you're wasted out here," the Jedi said. "Beyond that, I don't know."

An electrical popping sound emerged from the console, and the Jedi shuffled out before continuing. "My guess is you're in for a promotion. Whole war is changing."

"Not the first time I've been told that," Jace said. He watched Kalandis Seven disappear into the star field, the ochre dot now indistinguishable from a thousand other distant worlds and distant suns.

"The troops down there won't last long, now," Jace added. "They don't have the training to hold the place." He rubbed at his cheek, rubbed at his scars, then spoke again. "They'll be overrun within the month. Casualties'll be heavy."

The Jedi stood and turned to face Jace. "You don't know that," he said.

Jace shrugged. "I don't," he agreed. They'd share the lie together. "Doesn't matter now. The Supreme Chancellor orders you back to the Core Worlds, that's where you go."

Still, blast her for taking him off the battlefield. Forty years of leaving soldiers behind and losing people was enough of a burden to shoulder. As for a promotion? More responsibility never made anything easier, it only changed t he scope of the job.

Jace excused himself and made his way to the guest quarters—a spartan barracks where he dropped onto a cot and took up a datapad, browsing over a list of his comrades on Kalandis Seven. Shanra Immel, Amden vor Keioidian,Vaskus Kayle, Yennir of the Green. Everyone he'd fought with. The team he'd been willing to die for. The team he'd done everything to save.

When he reached the end of the list, he deleted the names from his personal file and put the datapad away.

Time to move on to the next battle.

HONDO OHNAKA'S NOT-SO-BIG SCORE

WRITTEN BY **JASON FRY**
ART BY **CHRIS SCALF**

It was a summer's day on Florrum, which meant the plains were baking, the generators were overloaded, and the last place Hondo Ohnaka wanted to be was a messy office crowded with unwashed Weequay pirates. And on top of everything else, the holoprojector refused to work no matter how many times the pirate boss whacked it with his fist.

"Master, you're hitting the off switch," objected 4A-2R, attempting to squeeze between the leathery-skinned Finn Tegotash and Goru. Tegotash, annoyed, shoved the bug-eyed protocol droid into Goru, who threatened the hapless mechanical with immediate disassembly.

"Four-aye, as soon as you're done provoking the gentlemen we'll get down to business," Hondo said.

One of Hondo's blows connected with the activation switch, and the pirates hooted appreciatively at the glossy, needle-nosed liner that now hung in the air above his desk.

"Our target is the *Salin Mariner*, traveling from Lianna to Botajef," Hondo said. "A *C-One* liner with eighteen passengers in first class, enjoying the finest hospitality that Salin Excursions has to offer."

Hondo raised his goggles and grinned.

"Oh, the sights they'll see along the fabulous Salin! The Fire Rapids of Mazuma! The Carpastor Comet Swarm! And at the end, a few lucky ones will visit the plains of Florrum and get an up-close look at a real working pirate base!"

Most of the pirates laughed and cheered—only Hondo's hasty warning kept Dagu Flask from firing a celebratory pistol shot into the light fixture. But a few of the Weequays looked confused.

"The trip to Florrum will come after we kidnap them from the ship and hold them for ransom," Hondo said, more slowly this time.

Now everyone was cheering—including the Kowakian monkey-lizard Pilf Mukmuk, cackling merrily from his usual perch on Hondo's shoulder.

"Be a pleasure blowin' a hole in that pretty boat," the massive Goru grunted. "We'll stop her dead, then plunder her at our leisure!"

Hondo cut short the cheers.

"Whoa now—an operation like this requires subtlety and finesse. We shall select our guests through personal inspection during the cruise. Once we have them picked out, we'll arrange a diversion, bring the *Mariner* to a halt, and be in and out before sector law enforcement can arrive."

"But I wanted to blow a hole in 'er," grumbled Goru.

"Who's gonna pick the lucky passengers, boss?" asked Tegotash.

"Ah," Hondo said. "For that job we'll need someone sophisticated and cultured, a refined traveler who can blend in with the upper-crust of galactic society."

The pirates looked baffled.

"Hey, I'm talking about myself of course," Hondo said. "Behold Rondo Rosada, import-export magnate and art collector!"

"But boss, won't you need backup to take the hostages?" asked Flask.

"Our associate at Salin Excursions has arranged for three slots aboard the *Mariner*. Turk and Piit will be joining me on the cruise."

The pirates stared enviously at Turk Falso and Peg Leg Piit.

"Now that's some high-class piratin'!" Sabo said, then began to guffaw. "Imagine ol' Piit here decked out in the finery of a Sakiyan princess!"

Piit tossed her pigtail, offended. "I clean up jes' fine. Unlike a grimy spice-goblin like yerself."

Hondo whistled to cut short the resulting argument. "Alas! There is only one opening in first class. Turk and Piit shall be posing as crew, and assisting me—no doubt heroically—from belowdecks."

"Belowdecks?" Turk wailed, jowl frills drooping.

"Belowdecks," Hondo said. "Sanitation, to be specific."

Hondo straightened the lines of his black velvet doublet, buffed his crystal monocle on his sleeve, then stepped onto

the promenade deck of the *Salin Mariner*. Outside the transparisteel windows, the churning chaos of hyperspace swirled and seethed. But inside, a quartet from Far Dostany was playing a stately waltz, while liveried attendants hovered around the three tables, bringing cocktails and trays of dainties.

"Mr. Rosada?" asked a young human female wearing the ship's livery. "Your tablemates are already awaiting you, sir. And can I get you something from the bar? Perhaps a Corellian Reserve?"

"Splendid," Hondo said, blinking sleepily. Finding his well-appointed suite to his liking, he'd arranged for a pedicure—the better to show off his gaberwool slippers—and then enjoyed a long afternoon nap between shimmersilk sheets. "In fact, my blossom, let's make it a double! I'm celebrating!"

"A double it is," the attendant said with a smile, pulling out a chair at the center table. "And here you are, sir."

Hondo settled himself in his chair and beamed at his tablemates—a blue-skinned, near-human young Wroonian female and a fat older male in a maroon overcoat; a balding, bearded and horned Gotal; a grumpy-looking Siniteen with beady eyes and a bald head that looked like an exposed brain; and a salmon-skinned Bivall wearing jeweled clasps on his swiveling eyestalks.

"A fine evening to you all, gentlebeings," Hondo said. "I am Rondo Rosada, from—GREAT MOTHER OF QUAY, I AM BEING DEVOURED!"

Hondo hopped away from the table, one slippered foot in his hand.

"Got your toes licked, did you?," asked the older Wroonian, chuckling. "Higgs and Twiggs were just saying hello. Come out, you naughty boys!"

He lifted the tablecloth and two long, green-furred heads appeared, purple tongues flicking at the air.

Daddy loves his Kobarian swamp dogs almost as much as he loves me, simpered the Wroonian female. Higgsie and Twiggsie are show dogs—a wedding present for me and my fiancé

"Worth a fortune," her father said. "Part of my darling Pelf's dowry. The marriage is arranged, of course—we're not commoners."

Hondo sat down again, waving away the attendants' hands smoothing his doublet, and tucked his slippered feet safely behind the legs of his chair. His brandy arrived, and over appetizers he met his tablemates. The Wroonians were Pelf Pachoola and her father Fume, on her way

to Botajef for her nuptials. The Siniteen, Sibs Monchan, was an entrepreneur who designed HoloNet interfaces, while the Bivall was Usk Haffa, who proudly proclaimed himself the largest owner of commercial real estate on Protobranch. The Gotal, Dix Tarfait, grunted that he was a small businessman and resumed a truculent silence.

"And what do you do, Rosada?" asked Fume, making kissing noises as he fed giblets to Higgs and Twiggs.

"Oh, I dabble," Hondo said, signaling for another brandy. "Import-export, shipping and, ah, personnel acquisitions. It's not much, but it's enough to pay for the occasional pampering like this."

"Don't work myself," Fume muttered, brushing a speck off his long coat. "Grandfather's fortune spared me the indignity. Find the idea demeaning."

"Speak for yourself," grumbled Monchan without looking up from his datapad. "My firm, Monchantics, cleared half a billion credits in net profit last fiscal quarter. Our initial public offering hits the Mileva Stock Exchange next month. All the product of hard work and vision.

"I obviously haven't worked enough," Haffa said. "You may feel pampered, Mr. Rosada, but I am not impressed by our accommodations. The cabins are practically threadbare, the holos are last month's, and while the bottles say Corellian Reserve, what they're pouring is Vasarian."

"I like Vasarian," the Gotal grunted.

"Agree—this cruise is like camping," Fume grunted. "At least we're not losing the common touch."

His tablemates chuckled and Hondo glowered at his brandy as attendants appeared with covered dishes. He decided not to assess the jellied gherks until informed of their deficiencies.

Hondo realized his napkin was still on the table and swept it into his lap. It seemed like there were far too many forks—goodness, the table was *covered* with them—and he peered over at Pelf, waiting to see which utensil she picked up. But she was warbling at her father about floral arrangements, while Haffa and Monchan were arguing about Trade Federation excise taxes. Nobody was eating, or showing any signs of doing so. Hondo's stomach rumbled.

Clearly this called for another brandy, whatever the quality.

The next morning, his cabin spinning, Hondo staggered into the refresher's sanisteam, where he decided after some debate not to drown himself. He donned his green velvet doublet, searched half-heartedly for his missing monocle,and made his way tentatively to the *Mariner*'s Vista Walk, cringing at each shockingly loud greeting from various attendants.

Outside the viewports, hyperspace was bright and nauseating. He checked to see he was alone and extracted his combination comlink and locator. The device was top of the line, designed to send an encrypted signal to Goru and the trailer ships.

Goru answered at once, and at a deplorable volume.

"Louder—they might not have heard you on Coruscant," Hondo said. "We'll stop the ship tomorrow night—after dinner of course. Are the mass mines ready for deployment?"

"Yeah, boss," Goru said, more quietly this time. "They'll haul 'er right out of hyperspace. But we's having trouble finding suitable medic uniforms."

Hondo sighed. "Uniforms? Why do you need uniforms? Once you're aboard the ship you're allowed to be pirates! Paint one of the attack shuttles in emergency-response colors and memorize the script I gave you. You remember, the one about the quarantine on Phindar. Goru? Are you listening?"

"We could just blow a hole in the ship," Goru said plaintively.

Hondo sighed and leaned against the viewport, thinking he'd rest his eyes for a moment. Then something hit him in the chest, sending him staggering into the path of an exuberantly fleshed Ruebeqni matron who honked in alarm.

"HIGGSIE! BAD HIGGSIE!"

"Am-Shak's mattock! What fresh hell is this?" yelped Hondo, as the Kobarian swamp dog leapt on him again, leash trailing uselessly. His comlink flew out of his hand and Higgs snatched it from the air as Hondo fell on his backside.

"Higgsie! Sit this instant!" commanded Pelf.

Higgs belched and obediently settled on his haunches, while Twiggs began to lick Hondo's face with long swipes.

"Twiggsie! Sit!" Pelf said. "The boys are just glad to see you, Mr. Rosada! And so am I! You were so funny last night! You kept pinching my cheeks and saying I was precious!"

Hondo rose shakily, offering the comlink-devouring Higgs a murderous glance. "Well, so you are, my little blue dumpling."

Pelf tittered and shook a finger at Hondo. You said you wanted to kidnap me and hold me for ransom! I don't think my fiancé would like that very much, Mr. Rosada!

"Ah," Hondo said. "Heh. You shouldn't listen to dinner-party chatter—it'll go to your pretty cerulean head."

"Over dessert you announced you adored the entire table and planned to kidnap us all!" Pelf said. "That was before you decided it was time to speak to the band."

"Speak to the band?" Hondo asked.

"Oh yes! You announced that if you had to suffer through another dull minuet you'd seize the helm and fly us into the nearest sun. Then you threw a stack of credit chips at the band and ordered them to play nothing but scrak and smazzo. You never said you could dance, Mr. Rosada!"

"I have been known to cut a rug or two," said Hondo, wandering over to give Higgs an experimental smack in the ribs.

"I'll say! You put on quite a show—well, at least until you catapulted Dame Malitikis into the dessert cart. But the surgeon says her shoulder will be good as new."

Higgs, tired of being thumped, growled at Hondo.

"Easy, Mr. Rosada—Higgsie isn't a drum!" Pelf said. "Well, I have party appetizers to pick out. See you at lunch!"

Hondo arrived as lunch was ending, his thunderous headache reduced to a dull throb by a late-morning nap and a carafe of caf. The banquet hall fell silent as he walked in, and the quartet missed a cue. Then the chatter picked up again and the musicians pivoted into a sunny waltz. Glowering, Hondo stalked to his seat. The Pachoolas were arguing about invitations, while Higgs and Twiggs snored contentedly in the aisle.

"Ah, Mr. Rosada," Monchan said with a smile Hondo found slightly mocking. "Usk and I were just discussing union troubles. We figured a cultured businessman such as yourself must have an interesting take on employee relations."

Hondo decided two things right then and there: He wasn't in the mood to be mocked, and he was doubling the ransom on Monchan and Haffa.

"Get yourself a gundark," he growled. "You want an established matriarch—as in every culture, they're the meanest. Take the troublemaker with the least talent and throw him in the hole with her while everyone else watches. After she's torn off his arms, complaints will magically cease."

"You're speaking metaphorically of course," said Dix Tarfait.

"Metaphors, bah—I am a man of action!" Hondo said, bringing one fist down on the table and making the excess forks jump.

The surly Gotal smiled, showing his flat yellow teeth.

"I distribute liquor and spirits—my territory covers five sectors. A gundark would prove useful on sales calls."

The female attendant appeared at Hondo's side. "Mr. Rosada! What an eventful cruise you've had so far, sir!"

"Eventful? Heh! I'm just trying to keep things interesting,"

"We've arranged a surprise—a holographic exhibition of Saffa paintings over dessert. Now don't be bashful, Mr. Rosada! You did say on your passenger questionnaire that you were an expert on Saffa paintings!"

A waiter tripped over one of the swamp dogs, sending a tureen flying.

Monchan stared at Hondo. "Saffa paintings? Really? You don't seem the type, Mr. Rosada."

"Oh, I hate to brag. Humility is a virtue—that's what Mom taught me."

"I'm sure," Monchan said. He whispered something to Haffa, who smirked.

Three attendants guided in levitating terminals displaying shimmering paintings, all slashing lines and whorls and colors that made Hondo's head hurt worse.

"Ooh, pretty," Pelf said, peering at the paintings.

Hondo cursed whatever whim had brought Saffa paintings into his brain when confronted with the empty spaces of the questionnaire. But then the talk of art reminded him of an annoying Nouane philosopher Sabo had grabbed off a passing liner.

"Swamp dog got your tongue, Mr. Rosada?" asked Monchan. "Please, enlighten us about what we're looking at."

Sabo had looked stunned when Hondo explained that fancy talk didn't mean a being had two credits to rub together, while the philosopher's babbling had proved so annoying that he really had wound up in a gundark hole. But what had been his name? Hondo couldn't remember.

"Mr. Rosada?" Monchan inquired. "I asked if you recognized the period of this Saffa painting."

Hondo decided to triple the ransom on Monchan.

"Your question, Mr. Monchan, reveals the difference between looking at art and understanding it," Hondo harrumphed. "What period is this? What medium is that? These annoying little facts are not knowledge, or wisdom! They are just noise! Which is the opposite of appreciation! Pelf, look at this painting here. Tell me what you see, my delectable azure cupcake."

"Um, it's red? Red and green and squiggly! Is it a deek-pa-neek out for a swim?"

"Ha—there you have it, Monchan," Hondo said. "A what-she-said out for a swim. *That* is artistic sensitivity – not your scavenger hunt for facts. You asked me to explain Saffa paintings and I cannot—for no one can! But I'm afraid Saffa paintings have done an excellent job of explaining *you*."

Monchan blinked at Hondo, who folded his arms and leaned back in his chair, smiling.

Then Pelf began to shriek, arm extended, mouth a horrified O.

"Who is that?" she squeaked, pointing at a woman on the other side of the room in an elaborate orange dress that reminded Hondo of a carnivorous night-flower from Forlonis Minor.

"Why Miss Pachoola, that's the *Mariner*'s apprentice pastry chef," the attendant said. "She's just bringing in the new dessert cart."

"DADDY!" wailed Pelf. "HER DRESS! IT'S THE SAME DRESS AS THE BRIDESMAIDS'!"

The sleeve of Fume's maroon coat was instantly wet with tears. He whispered something consoling to his daughter.

"NO, IT WILL NOT BE ALL RIGHT! A PASTRY CHEF ON A THIRD-RATE LINER IS WEARING THE SAME DRESS AS MY BRIDESMAIDS!"

"Apprentice pastry chef," Hondo said helpfully, signaling for a brandy.

"MAKE IT STOP, DADDY! MAKE HER GO AWAY FOREVER!"

Higgs and Twiggs roused themselves and began to howl. Hondo plugged that ear with a finger and leaned across the table to Dix Tarfait. "Liquor distributor, eh?"

With Pelf still in distress, Hondo volunteered to take Higgs and Twiggs for their afternoon constitutional around the Vista Walk. The swamp dogs alternated snuffling at things and leaping on Hondo, who fended them off with Huttese imprecations while waiting for the steward to arrive.

Hondo decided not to kidnap Pelf—the thought of her shrieking in a cell on Florrum made his head pound all over again. But Tarfait would make a fine substitute. A liquor distributor, a Wroonian aristocrat, a HoloNet magnate and a real-estate mogul—yes, those four would do nicely. Now if only the idiot steward would shake a leg and—

"Mr. Rosada?" asked a young, goggle-eyed human in *Mariner* livery. "I heard your animal companion needs an emetic?"

"Urgently," Hondo said, taking the vial and slipping the steward a credit. "Always eating things he shouldn't! Higgs, you rascal— didn't I tell you your tummy would get you into trouble?"

He wasn't sure how one convinced a Kobarian swamp dog to take medicine, but the two beasts spotted the vial and started to yip eagerly. Hondo tried to remember which was Higgs and which was Twiggs, then threw up his hands.

"What am I, a veterinarian?" he asked, uncapping the vial and emptying it on the floor.

Higgs and Twiggs lapped up the emetic, then wagged their tails and licked their chops. Nothing happened for a minute or so, but

then the two swamp dogs stopped swishing their tails, looking more puzzled than usual. A moment later, Hondo had retreated to the end of the leashes, eyes squeezed shut, while the other passengers were fleeing the Vista Walk as if a gang of Merson slavers had just smashed through the viewports.

Hondo opened one watering eye wide enough to spot his gleaming comlink in the mess regurgitated by Higgs and Twiggs, who hung their heads apologetically. He took a step forward, one hand fumbling in front of him, then began to gag.

"What do those people feed you?" Hondo gasped. "Mynock knuckles marinated in speeder lubricant?"

That was it: Fume and his valuable swamp dogs were staying behind too. Higgs and Twiggs' digestive fluids might render half of Florrum uninhabitable.

Hondo spotted the horrified-looking steward on the other side of the Vista Walk, plotting his getaway.

"Don't stand there like a stunned nerf!" he yelled, snapping his fingers. "Call Sanitation!"

"Did you hear that?" demanded Tarfait. "We've come out of hyperspace." "I'm sure it's routine," Hondo said with a yawn.

He was almost sorry that his time with his tablemates was ending. He'd spent the third day not fretting about forks, not allowing Pelf's meltdowns to jangle his nerves, nor dissecting Monchan's questions for concealed insults. Instead, he'd strolled the Vista Walk and napped and told Porla the Hutt stories and dined and had many refills of Vasarian, which he decided he liked just fine.

And now it was all ending, he thought, checking his chronometer.

Hmm. In fact, it should have started ending already.

Hondo excused himself and ducked into the refresher, where a doleful attendant in *Mariner* livery was stationed by the sink.

"Is the very concept of privacy extinct?" Hondo demanded. "Shoo!"

"It's my job," the attendant objected.

"Behold the miracle of opposable thumbs! That means I can wash my own hands and get my own Cardellian mint!"

A flung credit chip hastened the attendant's departure and Hondo extracted his comlink—which still bore a disagreeable whiff of swamp dog's stomach.

"Goru? What's taking so long?"

"Mines fired as planned, boss," Goru said. "But the captain ain't allowin' us on board. Think he don't believe us."

"If there's one thing I dislike it's a skeptic. Did you follow the script?"

"Well... some pages got lost, so me an' Gwarm improvised."

"What have I told you about improvising?"

Goru sounded alarmed. "Boss! Sector forces are inbound!"

Hondo sighed. "I'll take the captives out in an escape pod."

"But the diversion—"

"Oh, just blow a hole in the ship."

When the *Mariner* shuddered, Hondo was ready.

"That was a missile impact or I'm a bantha cub," he said, finishing his brandy. "Everyone follow me. Quickly and quietly —let's not cause a panic."

Tarfait was on his feet. Pelf gasped and then clapped a hand over her mouth. Monchan and Haffa exchanged a worried look.

"Nothing to fear, gentles—everybody remain calm while I investigate," he told the rest of the first-class passengers, then lowered his voice. "Make for the escape pods in the starboard companionway."

To Hondo's annoyance, Pelf clamped herself onto his arm, eyes wide with terror. Sensing her distress, Higgs and Twiggs began howling.

Hondo thumbed open the escape pod hatch. In the distance, he heard shouting and footsteps.

"Mr. Tarfait, follow me to freedom!" he said, seizing the startled Gotal and flinging him into the pod. "Monchan! Haffa! Make haste!"

"Eject into a combat zone?" Monchan asked. "Are you mad? I'm heading for the safe room at Junction Besh."

"As am I," Haffa said.

"No time to argue!" Hondo said.

"Agreed," Monchan said. "So long, Rosada."

"You're right—take Miss Pachoola with you," Hondo said.

"That screeching lunatic?" Monchan said over his shoulder. "She's your problem."

"I want off this ship!" Pelf wailed. "Women and children first!"

"Pelf, my sapphire treasure—" Hondo began, but Pelf had already scrambled into the pod.

Higgs and Twiggs began to bark. Turning, Hondo spotted Turk and Piit hustling down the passageway, pistols raised. Before Hondo could call out to them, they dodged around Monchan and Haffa.

"No! Stop those two!" Hondo yelled.

"No time, boss!" Turk yelled. "The captain's handed out weapons! And Sector Patrol just came out of hyperspace. Run for it!"

Turk and Piit pushed past him into the now-crowded pod. Scowling, Hondo followed them. Fume, eyes wild, remained in the corridor with Higgs and Twiggs.

"Pelf!" Hondo yelled. "Stay with your father!"

"NO! DADDY! DON'T LEAVE ME!"

"Let me out!" complained Tarfait.

"Turk!" Hondo yelled. "Hit eject!"

A frantic Fume shoved his way into the pod. Hondo tried to push him back out into the corridor, only to be knocked flat by Higgs and Twiggs, who pinned him down and began to lick his face.

"Turk, hit eject," Hondo said with a sigh, activating his comlink.

The pod rocketed away from the *Salin Mariner*, then began to tumble.

"We made it!" Pelf screeched. "I hope Higgsie and Twiggsie don't get space-sick!"

"Oh no," Hondo said.

Hondo and Turk watched as the freighter disappeared into the sky above Florrum. The captain who'd delivered the Vasarian brandy had protested mightily when ordered to take Fume, Pelf and two swamp dogs in addition to Tarfait, but an impressive number of guns aimed in his direction had halted his complaints.

"How many credits did we pay and how much time did we waste in exchange for eight cases of grog?" asked Turk disgustedly.

"Bah—math is for schoolboys and accountants, not dashing pirates like us," Hondo said.

The girl's fiancé said we could keep her. The old man said he'd rather die here than pay us. The swamp dogs ate ten kilos a day. And the Gotal lied about having money.

"Hey, he was rich enough to fetch eight cases of grog," Hondo said. "Plus Mr. Pachoola was persuaded to leave behind this excellent overcoat."

"I forgot about yer fancy garment," Turk snorted. "Guess that makes this a triumph, then."

"The difference between you and me, Turk, is that I am a boundless optimist," Hondo said. "Today, Florrum —and this coat, and this grog. Tomorrow, the stars!"

"Yer an optimist because yeh didn't have to work Sanitation. Or clean up swamp-dog sick."

"Try not to live in the past, Turk," Hondo said. "It can be very bad for your disposition."

SPEAKING SILENTLY

WRITTEN BY **JASON FRY**
ART BY **TOM HODGES**

Captain Rex knew his brisk strides made his annoyance obvious to anyone watching. He didn't care. An entire squad captured, Separatists preparing to collapse his left flank, generals hollering at him from Sector Command, and now someone from local militia was insisting on taking up time he didn't have?

Rex came to a halt in the middle of the forward operating base, scowling at the idea that a jumble of prefab shelters and camo-netting merited so lofty a name. His troopers in Torrent Company saw him coming and found other places to be. From their reactions, Rex knew what the expression on his face must look like. He didn't care about that either.

The militiaman waiting for him gave no sign of noticing the barely contained anger on Rex's face. He was a tall human, slim and nut-brown, with a strong chin and dark, darting eyes. Another militiaman stood behind him.

"Captain Rex?" the man asked languidly. "Lieutenant Sollaw ap-Orwien, Ereesus Planetary Security Forces. And this is Corporal Dafyd."

Technically, Rex supposed, he outranked the militiamen. But this was Ereesus, and locals on many worlds resented taking orders from clones, even when those orders saved their lives. So he kept his voice carefully controlled – brisk but not impolite.

"What's this about, soldier?" he asked.

"The holo of the squad of militiamen captured last night," ap-Orwien said. "I need to see it."

Rex cocked an eyebrow. "And why is that?"

"It was Sergeant Palola's squad, wasn't it?" ap-Orwien asked. "Palola's a miltiaman, about my height and build. The Separatists paraded him on the holo, showing off their captive. That's correct, isn't it, Captain?"

"It might be," Rex growled, thinking of chronos ticking down in the logic units of Separatist tactical droids out beyond the ridge. "If it were, why would it matter?"

"Because Palo's a Lorrdian like me," ap-Orwien said. "Is the holo's visual feed good quality? I need to know what Palo said."

Rex brought one hand down on a console with a bang, no longer caring about being polite or the possibility of complaints from local militia to Sector Command. He couldn't afford to spend even a small part of his precious time answering stupid questions based on misconceived notions.

"He didn't say *anything*," Rex said. "They wouldn't let him, of course. These are tacs we're dealing with, Lieutenant, not those idiot B1s."

A corner of ap-Orwien's mouth jerked upward.

"If the visual's good quality, I guarantee you he said plenty," ap-Orwien said. "Only the tac would never know it, Captain—and neither would you."

"What are you talking about?"

"Only another Lorrdian would understand," ap-Orwien said.

Rex hesitated. What would General Skywalker say? Not that General Skywalker was any guide to running a by-the-book military operation. Still, the Jedi certainly got results.

I'm going to regret this, Rex thought, giving ap-Orwien a curt wave. "You two come with me. You can explain on the way."

"I'll give you the short version," ap-Orwien said as he hurried after Rex, boots slipping and sliding in the thick greenish mud of a late spring afternoon on Ereesus. "You've heard of the Kanz Disorders, Captain?"

"Only just," Rex said. "Ancient Republic, localized conflict."

Ap-Orwien and Dafyd exchanged a quick look. When he turned back, ap-Orwien's eyes had turned cold and flinty.

"You're right about the ancient Republic part – the Kanz Disorders were nearly four millennia ago," ap-Orwien said. "Nearly six billion beings died, many of them my fellow Lorrdians."

"No offense meant, Lieutenant," Rex

said. "I'm afraid these days I don't have time to hit the history books. So. The short version, if you please."

"Very well, Captain," ap-Orwien said as they ducked into the operations room. "During the Kanz Disorders Argazdan fanatics enslaved the Lorrdians. For three centuries we were forbidden to speak to each other."

Rex returned a salute from troopers Jesse and Ringo, then gave ap-Orwien a nod.

"I'm sorry to hear it," Rex said. "Jesse, activate the holotable and play the Separatist transmission we received last night."

Jesse nodded, fingers flying over the holotable's keypad. A moment later a hologram shimmered to life. The captured Lorrdian sergeant stood glumly beside Oz, the Torrent Company trooper serving as a liaison between the Grand Army of the Republic and the militia.

The trooper's face—identical to that of Rex and Jesse—was blank, betraying no emotion. He'd been trained to reveal nothing if captured. They all had.

Battle droids surrounded the two men. A tactical droid turned the Lorrdian to face the holocamera, its mechanical face seeming somehow infuriatingly smug.

The gunships had been modified for stealth—fitted with engine shields and baffles and sprayed with a quick-dry black polymer that reduced its electomagnetic emissions to a whisper.

As Rex had told ap-Orwien, neither Palola nor Oz said a word as the tactical droid made threats, followed by demands it knew the Republic wouldn't meet. In fact, Rex barely saw the Lorrdian move for the two-minute length of the holorecording.

Ap-Orwien glanced at Dafyd, nodded, and looked back at Rex.

"We'll need a gunship," ap-Orwien said. "But the extraction team can be minimal—four or five troopers at most."

"Just a moment," Rex said. "I deploy gunships and extraction teams around here, not you. Now, what are you talking about?"

"My apologies—I sometimes forget not everyone's a Lorrdian," ap-Orwien said. "Your trooper, Palo and the rest of the squad are being held in the basement of a depot at the top of the Hidaci Ridge. Seven captives total. Only way out is up a narrow flight of stairs, so guards are minimal. The tactical droid's base of operations is an old granary halfway down the hill. The Separatists have stockpiled artillery and fuel at points along the road—Dafyd and I can pinpoint them for you on a satellite map."

Ringo looked incredulously at Rex.

"And you learned this how exactly?" asked Rex.

"Palo told us, of course!" ap-Orwien replied. "Well, he didn't tell *us*. But he told any Lorrdian who happened to be watching. Good thing the tacs don't care about culture or history any more than you do, Captain, or they'd never have put him on-camera."

"I still don't understand—"

"We call it kinetic communication, Captain," ap-Orwien said. "With speech forbidden, we learned to talk to each other through the tiniest movements, the smallest gestures."

"And you can use that to discuss granaries and basements and artillery dumps?" Rex asked.

"Perhaps you'd like to test us," ap-Orwien said. "I'll leave the room. You tell your trooper here something, with Dafyd listening. I'll come back in and Dafyd will give me the message."

"Fair enough," Rex said.

Ap-Orwien nodded and left the operations room. Rex stepped over to Jesse and Ringo, then hesitated. Jesse raised his eyebrows.

"I'm, uh, not in the habit of making up tactical information," Rex explained, slightly embarrassed. "Um... send three squads to the ridge line. Squad on left takes point. Squad on the right will deploy with droid poppers. You know what droid poppers are, Corporal?"

"Electromagnetic pulse grenades," Dafyd said in thickly accented Basic. "Very good against the clankers."

Jesse grinned.

"Right," Rex said. He poked his head out to summon ap-Orwien, then turned to watch Dafyd. Now that he was looking closely, he could see the other Lorrdian moving in small, subtle ways—shifting his feet, blinking his eyes, twitching the corners of his mouth. But it was nothing that you'd register as out of the ordinary.

"Three squads to the ridge," ap-Orwien said. "Left taking point, right carrying EMP grenades."

Ringo whistled. "Got it dead to rights, Captain."

"It's not exceptional hearing, or transmitters or something like that?" Rex asked.

"Just the Lorrdian art, Captain, one we've never given up.
Do you need another test?"

"That won't be necessary," Rex said. "Jesse, prep a gunship for liftoff at sundown. You, Ringo, Kix and Dogma. Plus the three of us. Have Kix bring field medi-kits, and... no, wait a minute."

He turned back to the two Lorrdians.

"You're sure about the fuel and artillery dumps?" Rex asked. "You can pinpoint the location?"

Ap-Orwien nodded.

Rex paused. How much would General Skywalker risk on a chance like this—an opportunity based on something he could barely detect and had no hope of understanding?

Rex realized he already knew the answer to that one.

"Don't send that order yet, Jesse — get me Sector Command first," he said.

The gunship had been modified for stealth—fitted with engine shields and baffles and sprayed with a quick-dry black polymer that reduced its electromagnetic emissions to a whisper and its heat signature to a faint smudge. It was also unarmed, its missile launchers, ball turrets and laser cannons sacrificed to eliminate drag and noise.

The modifications made the main hold so quiet that the clones and the two Lorrdians could converse in normal voices—yet Rex still found himself glaring at his troopers whenever they raised their voices above a low husk. The lights were out, but they could see easily enough in the moonlight. It fell through the slats in the gunship's retractable side doors, silvery and accusingly bright.

Stop it, Rex told himself. *You can't turn off the moon.*

"So the Y-wings will come in from the southeast?" ap-Orwien asked, wanting to go over the plan again.

Rex nodded. Better that the Lorrdians ask one time too many than one time too few.

"Right, while we circle and come in from the north," Rex said. "The Y-wings will hit the fuel and artillery dumps. Meanwhile, our units will be making a big show, as if they're planning to advance. That should draw the clankers south, leaving us time to slip in and free our people."

"And their tactical droid, he will not figure it out?" asked Dafyd.

"We'll know soon enough, won't we?"

"Don't worry, boss," said Jesse with a grin. "Sending that fuel dump sky-high will definitely get their attention."

"What makes you think I'm worried?" Rex asked, checking his DC-17s to make sure the power packs were seated properly.

Jesse grinned. "Maybe it's that you've got that look on your face that you get when you're worried."

"And what look is that?" Rex asked—but it was ap-Orwien who answered him.

"I think it is this one," he said, and then his lips pressed into a line, his eyes widened and looked straight ahead, his shoulders and back went rigid, and his hands began moving swiftly and precisely, field-stripping an imaginary firearm.

The clones gaped at the Lorrdian. Ringo was the first to laugh, followed by Jesse and then the others. Rex forced himself to smile. He had recognized himself instantly, though ap-Orwien looked nothing like him.

"Do Jesse next," Ringo urged.

"What's the point?" Rex asked. "We're the same person."

"You're not," ap-Orwien said. "You all move, act, and react differently."

Rex shook his head. "We're clones."

"Which matters until birth," ap-Orwien said. "After that, life makes you different —as it does with all of us."

"Maybe," Rex said. "The mimicry—it's part of your kinetic communication?"

"Related," ap-Orwien said. "With a language of small gestures, you learn to notice things. We're excellent actors, imitators, interpreters."

"And observers," Rex said. "But how does it work? How do you separate the gestures that communicate something from the ones that are just gestures?"

"That's something we don't share," he said. "We have had many enemies over the years. Today we are working with your Republic, but tomorrow things may be different."

Rex started to object, but one of the clone pilots broke in over the comm.

"Captain, fighters are beginning their attack run," the pilot said. "Expect to have you on the ground in eight minutes."

Rex looked around the hold, saw his troopers' faces harden. He knew they were reviewing mission objectives in their heads. That was what he was starting to do, as he'd done in thousands of drills on Kamino, and then on battlefields—so many that he had no chance of remembering them all.

"Buckets," he said, raising his helmet and settling it over his head, reorienting it so faceplate was forward. Jesse, Kix, Ringo and Dogma were doing the same. Ap-Orwien and Dafyd sat rigid.

Rex leapt through the hole in the door, its edges a brilliant green in his night vision. Two battle droids were down on the floor, birdlike heads blown off.

"Check your heads-up displays and comlinks," Rex said, the words automatic by now.

A bright orange flash on the ground somewhere behind them lit up the main hold, followed almost instantly by another. A moment later the gunship shuddered and they heard the roar of the impacts.

"Fighters report ordnance delivered," one of the pilots said calmly. "We are locked in on objective."

The gunship banked to the right, beginning its descent towards the rectangles and squares of fields below, stripped of color by the moonlight.

It wasn't until the gunship doors began to retract that Rex realized he'd forgotten to ask the militiamen something very important.

"It's ten meters down—do you know how to fast-rope?" he asked, even as the doors opened all the way and Jesse and Ringo flung the ends of the heavy cables down into the darkness.

To his relief, ap-Orwien nodded and smiled, pantomiming a hand-over-hand descent.

"Let's go then," Rex ordered, and a moment later the two clones were descending the rope into the compound below. The two Lorrdians went next, then Rex and Kix.

Rex let go of the rope a meter above the ground, slipped in a slick of mud on the permacrete and wound up on his hands and knees. Cursing, he got to his feet, pistols drawn. They were in a small walled area, with a gate at one end and a platform at the other—a loading dock for speeder trucks. His helmet's night-vision filter showed him Jesse and Ringo, scanning the yard with blasters raised. The Lorrdians were standing back to back in the center of the yard beside Kix, night-vision goggles over their eyes.

Dogma landed beside Rex and he heard the faint shush of the gunship's engines as it accelerated, already climbing skyward.

"Yard's clear, sir," Jesse said.

"Into the depot, then," Rex said. "Lieutenant—is there any way we can make use of your communications skills in a combat situation?"

Ap-Orwien shook his head, but Dafyd patted his blaster.

"Good shots," he said.

"Glad to hear it," Rex said. "We go in fast, get our people, get out fast. Leave only footprints and scrapped clankers."

"Roger, roger," Jesse said, a hint of merriment in his voice. He and Ringo hoisted themselves onto the loading dock and attached charges to the broad door leading into the depot, the other clones and Lorrdians arranging themselves on either side. The door blew and the two clones ducked through the ragged hole they'd made, blasters howling in the space beyond.

Rex leapt through the hole in the door, its edges a brilliant green in his night vision. Two battle droids were down on the floor, birdlike heads blown off. Jesse and Ringo were already on the other side of the cargo bay, examining the outer door.

On the other side of that door they'd find a narrow walkway between the loading dock and the depot office—*if* the instructions silently transmitted by the Lorrdian captive could be trusted.

Rex decided not to think about that *if*.

The door's indicator showed it was unlocked. Ringo nodded at Jesse and the two thumbed it open and dashed through, moving low with their guns raised. The walkway was just as the Lorrdians had said. The door on the other side led to a cramped space around an unlovely, squat

office. The clones cleared the yard, moving in pairs with practiced ease, then moved to cover the door leading inside.

It was locked.

"Our people should be two floors down," Rex said as Jesse and Ringo set charges. "Dogma, give them a droid popper as a wake-up call."

The door exploded outwards and Dogma flung an EMP grenade inside, almost immediately wreathed in a nimbus of blue energy.

This is too easy, Rex thought as he stepped over the smoking door jamb, pausing to put a blaster bolt into the cognitive unit of a battle droid whose legs were still spasming. Too easy made him nervous—it never lasted.

Inside, the lights were on. The troopers switched off their night vision and the Lorrdians lifted their goggles. Their boots clattered on the stairwell—and then Jesse yelled.

"Commandos!"

Descending the stairs, Rex ducked his head to try and spot the droids. That saved his life. Even as Jesse and Ringo fired at the commando droids advancing up the stairs, a third commando detached itself from a jumble of pipes on the ceiling above them, vibrosword slashing through the space where Rex's head had been. The droid landed on the stairs behind Rex and kicked him in the rear, sending him tumbling down after Jesse and Ringo as the whistle of blaster fire filled the stairwell.

Rex landed on his chest, nose smashing into the inside of his helmet. His hands and pistols were trapped beneath him. He tried to regain his feet, only to have something slam him down again and drive the air out of his lungs. Blows hammered at his armor – the commando droid, he realized. He flung himself sideways in an effort to free himself, wondering if he'd hear the sound of the vibrosword as it cut through his body glove and then his flesh. Or perhaps he wouldn't hear anything.

The droid was dead weight, he realized. Above him, ap-Orwien raised his blaster and smiled. Sparks spat from the back of the commando droid's head.

"Nice shot," Rex said, heaving the thing aside.

"You okay, boss?" Jesse asked.

"Never better," Rex said. Blood filled his mouth, ran down his chin.

They were at the bottom of the stairwell, in front of a locked door. Rex stared at it, conscious of his troopers' eyes on him.

If the captives were directly on the other side, blowing it open might injure or kill them. But hot-wiring the door would take time —time any guards might use to execute their hostages.

He looked at the Lorrdians. Ap-Orwien shrugged, his face grim.

Sometimes you have to guess, Rex thought.

"Charges," Rex said. "Watch your targets. Dogma, droid popper."

They retreated half a flight up to clear the blast area then raced back down as the light and noise of the blast diminished. No tangle of bodies awaited them on the other side. After a desperate second Rex saw the prisoners sitting against the far wall, arms behind their backs. Their eyes were looking around them.

Rex was firing his pistols before he saw the commando droid above them. Its humming vibrosword hit the floor point first with a shriek, then pinwheeled across the room, just missing Dafyd's head by millimeters. Then the smoking hulk of the commando droid plummeted after it.

"All seven accounted for," Kix said. "Minimal injuries."

Rex started to activate his comlink and call the gunship, then hesitated. He pulled his helmet off, wiping at his bloody nose.

"You—Sergeant Palola," he said. "The granary—how far is it?"

Palola looked up from embracing ap-Orwien and Dafyd.

"A hundred meters at most," he said.

"And you're sure that tactical droid is using it as headquarters?"

Palola nodded, face grim. "It interrogated us there."

Ap-Orwien cocked his head at Rex.

"And there was I thinking that you were a cautious man, Captain," he said.

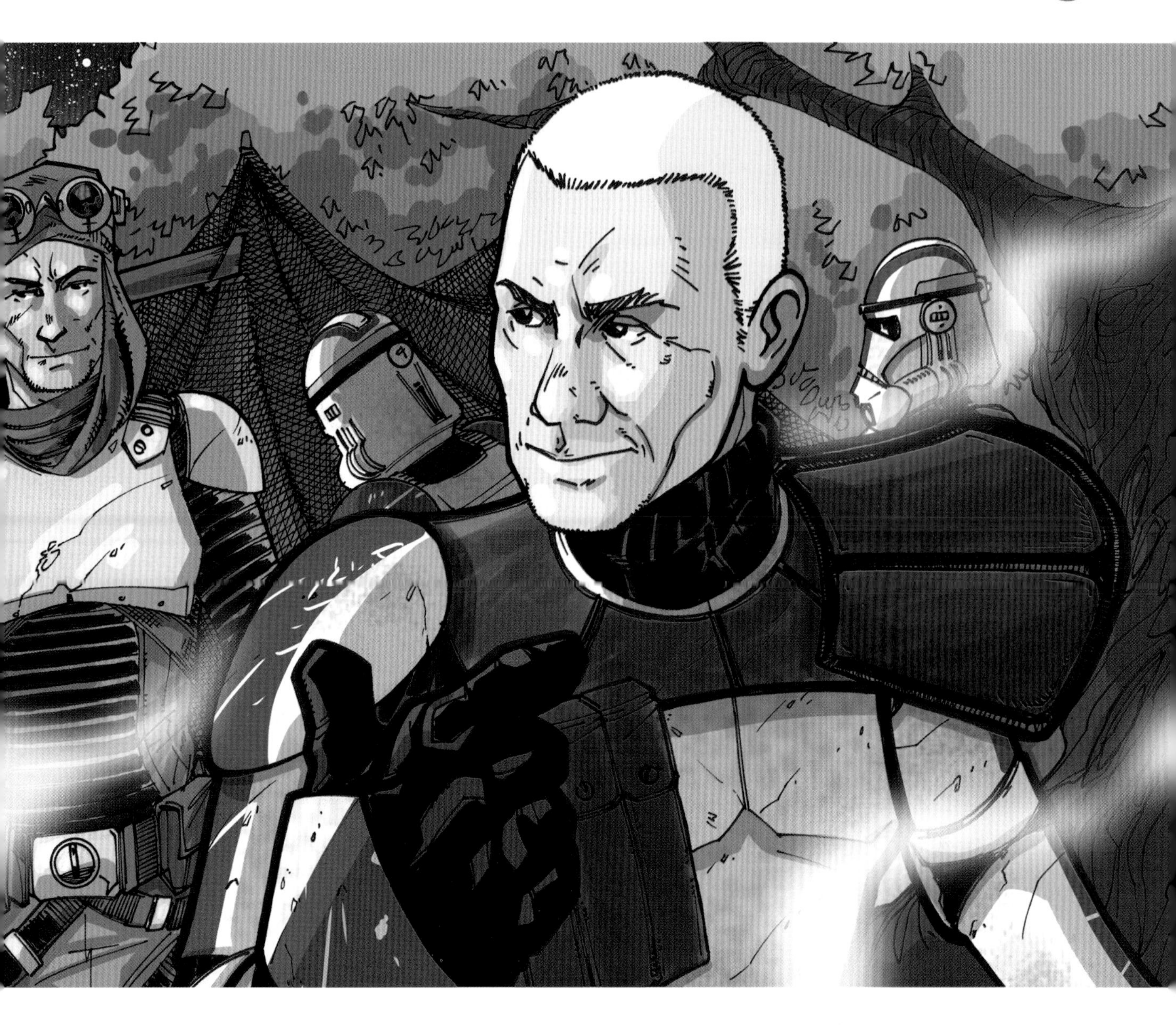

"One day I'd like to be," Rex said. "For now, I want a word with that tac. In person."

This time, there was no need for fast-roping—the gunship settled onto the muddy plain outside Torrent Company's forward operating base and the clones hopped down from the deck, the Lorrdians right behind them.

Rex held up the tactical droid's severed head. He acknowledged the waiting clones' whoops with a brief nod, then turned to the grinning ap-Orwien.

"Impressive work, Lieutenant," Rex said. "Everything was as you said it would be."

"Exactly as *Palo* said it would be," ap-Orwien corrected him. "I was just the translator."

Rex glanced at Palola, who offered a tired smile.

"Well, I wish we had a few more like you," Rex said. "That kinetic communication's a very nice piece of work, but you can shoot, as well."

"I wish there were more of us too," ap-Orwien said. "Despite tonight's victory, we are highly outnumbered. The Separatists can always make more droids, but, alas, we cannot make men."

His voice trailed off and he looked away, embarrassed.

"No offense meant, Captain," ap-Orwien said quietly.

"None taken," Rex said. "We were made to be soldiers, it's true, but we're not machines. At least, the Jedi don't regard us that way."

"May that always be so," ap-Orwien said, then looked around. "It's too late for us to get back to our headquarters tonight. Is there somewhere we can sleep for tonight?"

"We'd be honored to have you bunk with us, Lieutenant," Rex said.

"Much appreciated," ap-Orwien said, then hesitated. "And perhaps you'd like to join us for a few hands of sabacc before we turn in?"

Rex looked from ap-Orwien to Palola. Their faces were blank. *Carefully* blank, he thought.

Rex shook his head and smiled.

"A game of Sabacc with masters of nonverbal communication?" he said. "I may be a product of accelerated aging, Lieutenant, but I wasn't born yesterday."

HEIST

WRITTEN BY **TIMOTHY ZAHN**
ART BY **BRIAN ROOD**

The world of larceny, like every other field of endeavor, had its collection of conventional wisdoms. Near the top of that list was the warning that pulling off a heist aboard a starliner was a stupid thing to do. With a limited roster of suspects, and with nowhere to run until the ship made port, the odds were dangerously high that a thief would be caught.

Bink Kitik had heard that bit of conventional wisdom many times throughout her career. But she'd never much worried about the odds.

"You'll be seeing him again tonight?" Bink's sister Tavia asked.

"Unless you think he'll come rushing into my arms with all those pretty jewels if I stand him up," Bink said as she gave herself a final look in their stateroom's mirror.

"I suppose that's unlikely," Tavia conceded, coming up behind Bink and adjusting a stray lock of her hair.

Bink gazed fondly at their side-by-side images, playing her usual game of pretending to be a stranger trying to pick out which of the identical twins was which. Even knowing all the hidden subtleties that distinguished them from each other it was still a challenge. To the best of her knowledge, no one else had ever figured out how to do it.

It was a happy accident of nature that had come in handy any number of times throughout Bink's career. And would do so again tomorrow.

"At least you didn't have to—you know—in order to get into his stateroom," Tavia continued, her reflection wincing. "I appreciate you at least drawing the line there."

"I know how much that sort of thing bothers you," Bink said soothingly. In actual fact, given the right circumstances, she would probably have been willing to let herself be lured to Cristoff's bedroom. It would have been much easier to break into his stateroom's private safe if she were already on that side of the door.

But while Cristoff had repeatedly angled for an invitation to Bink's stateroom, he'd never offered to bring her to his. Even people with more wealth than they could spend in five lifetimes were wary of being robbed, and apparently he didn't buy into the conventional wisdom any more than Bink did.

"How does the mesh feel?" Tavia asked as she finished with Bink's hair and shifted her hands to the sleek dress wrapped snuggly around her sister's modest curves.

"It's great," Bink assured her. Actually, the sensor mesh Tavia had designed, built, and layered into the dress material was a little scratchy. It was also likely to get unpleasantly warm as the evening wore on, especially given that Bink's neck, shoulders, head, and hands were the only parts of her body the dress didn't cover. But the thing was such a marvel of electronic engineering that Bink couldn't bring herself to get picky. "Wish me luck," she added as she turned from the mirror and headed toward the stateroom door.

Behind her, she heard Tavia's sigh.

More than anything else, Bink knew, her sister longed for a quiet, peaceful, *legal* life. Someday, Bink promised herself. Someday, when the big score finally came. Until then, life would continue to be a struggle to keep their heads above water and daily bread on their table.

With luck, Cristoff would soon be making his own contribution to that goal.

Cristoff was one of those men who exuded a carefully tailored mix of gallant, charming, and predatory. Bink had studied it, and him, from a prudent distance before finally making her approach three days earlier. It was a compelling combination, one that had probably worked on most women.

But Bink wasn't most women. She'd also dealt with more than her share of such men since her teenage years, and she knew exactly what they wanted and how they liked to get it. More importantly, she knew that the chase was more to them than the actual conquest, and that an elusive quarry was guaranteed to pique both interest and a heightened level of pursuit.

Most important of all was that fact that, while she knew his agenda, he had no idea of hers.

And so, once again she sat beside him at dinner, this time among the elite at the Captain's table, playing the prey as adroitly

as he played the hunter. She laughed at his jokes, occasionally reached out to touch his arm or let him touch hers, sometimes subtly pulled back. After dinner came a couple of drinks, then dancing to the surprisingly entertaining rhythm-skee of the liner's comedy caller, then a couple more drinks.

Finally, pleading fatigue and the upcoming busyness of the cruise's final day looming ahead, she let him escort her to her stateroom door. Once again, he tried to finesse an invitation to come inside. Once again, she begged off on the grounds that the falpas sauce he'd ordered for their appetizer glaze had left her stomach a little queasy. Hinting that she would make it up to him after tomorrow's final evening, she offered a down payment in the form of a long, close hug and an even longer and more lingering kiss.

Tavia, as usual, was waiting anxiously for her return. "How did it go?" she asked as she led Bink to the couch and helped her sister out of the tight-fitting dress.

"About as expected," Bink said, resisting the urge to give each freshly released patch of skin a vigorous scratch. She'd been able to ignore the mesh while she was playing her coy temptress role, but now that she was back in the safety and privacy of their stateroom, the itching had come roaring back. "It took a bit of skip-dancing to get him to order the falpas sauce, but I'm pretty sure he remembers it as being his idea." She pulled on the soft and delightfully non-itchy robe Tavia had laid out for her and nodded to the dress now draped over her sister's knees. "The big question is whether it was all worth it."

"We'll know in a minute," Tavia said, moving a small sensor slowly and methodically over the mesh. "Probably depends on whether you hugged him the way you said you were going to," she added, her voice carrying a hint of disapproval.

"*Someone* has to do it," Bink murmured, suppressing a grin.

"Here we go," Tavia said, easing the sensor closer to the dress. "Right hip pocket." She shot Bink a stern look. "I'm not even going to ask how you got in range of *that* part of his anatomy."

Bink shrugged. "Hey, if he would be a proper gentleman and always carry his keycard in the same place, I wouldn't have to resort to such underhanded tricks."

"Underhanded," Tavia repeated, making a face. "Cute."

"Thanks," Bink said modestly. "The point is that we got it. Which means—"

"Hold it," Tavia interrupted, peering at the sensor's display. "What in the...? Oh. Oh, very nice."

"What is it?" Bink asked, sitting down beside her. The data streaming across the sensor's display was way too fast for her to read. "What's nice?"

"Your friend isn't as stupid as he looks," Tavia said. "He's actually *expecting* to have his pocket picked. Hence, this keycard."

"I thought it was hence, he moves it randomly from one pocket to another," Bink said, frowning.

"No, that part is because he doesn't want to be obvious about it," Tavia corrected. "See, this keycard will open his stateroom door just fine. It'll also send a simultaneous alert to ship's security."

"Unless he punches in a code somewhere?" Bink asked hopefully.

"No code," Tavia said. Tapping the reset on the sensor, she started moving it down the dress again. "No, this one's a hundred percent booby trap. *However...*"

She paused. "However?" Bink prompted.

"Wait for it," Tavia said, moving the sensor down toward the dress's lower hem. "However... ah. The other keycard—the real one—is down here in a sock holster. No way anyone could get *that* one out without him noticing."

Bink smiled. "Good thing we don't need the card itself."

"A very good thing," Tavia agreed, studying the display. "I'm also glad I insisted the dress be formal-length."

"Me, too," Bink said. Keycards were shielded against sensor scans beyond a few millimeters precisely to prevent this kind of surreptitious scan-and-copy, which was why she'd had to snuggle up so close to him. "But then, it *was* the Captain's table. They expect a certain elegance there anyway."

"I'll take your word for it." Tavia eyed her sister. "So it's on?"

Bink nodded. "It's on."

Tavia was a lovely woman, Bink had always thought, far lovelier than Bink herself despite the fact they shared the same face. Unlike Bink, Tavia had an inner poise and a plain, simple likability.

It was the last night of the cruise, the last few hours before the starliner docked at the Kailor V transfer station in the small hours of the morning and the passengers prepared for the mass morning departure. Everyone was decked out in full-bore finery, their outfits designed to attract and impress and, possibly, to finalize unspoken hopes and promises that had been made earlier in the voyage.

And for once, it was Tavia, not Bink, who was dressed to the full limit of elegance and style.

But then, Tavia wasn't really herself tonight. Tavia was, rather, Bink.

"Now, you remember all my catchphrases?" Bink asked as she looked her sister over. Tavia was a lovely woman, Bink had always thought, far lovelier than Bink herself, despite the fact they shared the same face. Unlike Bink, Tavia had an inner poise and a plain, simple likeability that Bink herself always had to work hard to counterfeit.

"All of yours, and all of his," Tavia said, her smile showing just a hint of the tension she was obviously feeling. "I also remember his tastes in music, food, and drink, and all the life stories he told you. Don't worry, I can handle this."

"I know," Bink assured her, trying to put aside her own tension. Tavia had long since resigned herself to the necessity of playing these roles on occasion, and despite her ethical resistance she really was quite good at it. But that didn't mean Bink ever felt comfortable throwing her to the wolves this way. "I'll signal as soon as I'm back."

"Don't cut corners on my account," Tavia said. "I'll be fine."

"I know," Bink said again.

Ten minutes later, Cristoff came by to collect his date for the evening. Hidden inside the 'fresher, Bink pressed her ear to the door and listened closely to the small talk as Tavia collected her purse and wrap and the two of them left the stateroom. Everything sounded all right, but Bink knew that could change in a heartbeat.

She wouldn't cut corners, because that was how a job blew up in your face. But she definitely wouldn't be lingering.

She waited another ten minutes before leaving the stateroom herself, dressed more modestly than most of the preening travelers, and with just enough actor's putty layered across strategic parts of her face that she no longer looked like the woman currently hanging on Cristoff's arm. Cristoff's suite was on the liner's

upper-elite deck, behind a locked corridor door which required one of those same elite stateroom keycards to open. The copy Tavia had created from the sensor mesh data passed this first test, opening the door without fuss and letting Bink inside.

As she'd expected, the corridor was deserted, with all the occupants down in the public areas. Bink walked through the silence, watching and listening for any hint that her unauthorized entry had been detected and tagged. But no security officers or inquisitive droids had shown up by the time she reached Cristoff's door.

Once again, the keycard did its job. Bink went inside, wondering briefly if Cristoff might have pulled some kind of double-reverse that would leave this keycard as the one that would trigger the alarm. But Tavia hadn't seen any hidden coding, and anyway Bink's own reading of Cristoff hadn't indicated that kind of overdeveloped subtlety. Whatever creativity the man possessed would more likely manifest itself in the combination he'd arranged for the stateroom's private safe.

Fortunately, creativity was one of Bink's own specialties.

The safe was exactly as the stateroom floor plans showed it: built into the right-hand side of the computer desk, molecularly bonded to the deck, and constructed of hull-metal slabs thick

enough to require a plasma torch, a couple of tanks of fuel, and several perfectly good hours of a thief's life. The electronic keypad was built into the door and surrounded by enough sensor blocks and scramblers to keep anyone from brute-force slicing the combination. Once the pattern was set, only the stateroom's current occupant could get it open.

And Cristoff had recently done just that, Bink saw as she held Tavia's sensor over the keypad. Earlier this evening, probably when he pulled out his rings and the absurdly expensive wristband he liked to show off.

She smiled as she peered at the sensor's display. One of the best things about falpas sauce, aside from its delicious taste, was that the warm, tingling glow it sent through the bloodstream ultimately emerged a few hours later as a slight alteration in sweat composition. Last night's dinner had left traces of distinctive chemicals on the buttons Cristoff had touched, chemicals that could be scanned for.

Which was only half the battle, of course. No one with any brains used a code that utilized any given button only once, and whatever else he might or might not have, Cristoff did have brains.

But Bink had both brains and an experienced eye. The falpas-laden sweat left marks that were distinct enough that she could see the faint double edges where he'd keyed a given button twice, or even three times.

Unfortunately, none of that could tell her the order in which the various numbers had been keyed. For that, she would have to rely on Cristoff's history, his current life, three long days spent hanging onto his every word, and the extensive data-search profile Tavia had worked up while Bink was enjoying the liner's upper-end amenities.

Entering the keystroke data into her datapad, she punched for all the possible combinations. There were, not surprisingly, a lot of them. Calling up Tavia's list of the significant times, dates, and events of Cristoff's life, she ran her eyes down the parallel columns, searching for a match.

And there it was: the date and CTE market number of his first successful corporate takeover, the triumph that had launched him on his path to his current level of wealth and power. Smiling triumphantly, she keyed in the combination.

With a quiet, genteel snick, the safe popped open.

The jewel cases, she knew, would have integrated tracers. So would some of the bigger gems. But Bink hadn't planned to be overly greedy. She dumped out the cases into the safe, spreading the contents around just to confuse the issue a bit, then selected a half dozen of the more modest-sized stones. She put them in an anti-sensor pouch, just to be on the safe side, and slid the pouch behind her belt.

And with that, she was almost done. Almost. Because the minute Cristoff opened the safe and saw the mess she'd left behind there would be hell to pay from one end of the liner to the other.

Which simply meant making sure he never again opened the safe.

A dead energy cell on this kind of sequentially shared public safe typically triggered one of two default modes. The first was for the door to simply unlock, which would allow the current owner to retrieve his or her valuables. The downside there was that it would likewise allow anyone else to do so if he or she got there first. The second, more common approach, was for the safe to lock down completely, requiring a visit from the ship's purser and a specialized power/code pulse to reopen it.

The first step was to make sure the default setting was for a complete safe lockdown. The second was to drain the energy cell. The third was to reset the purser's master code.

Just for fun, she set it to the date and CTE market number of Cristoff's *second* successful corporate takeover.

She'd given Tavia the all-clear and had been waiting anxiously in their stateroom for nearly an hour when her sister finally returned.

"You all right?" Bink asked anxiously once she'd made sure Tavia was alone. "I was starting to get worried."

"I'm fine," Tavia said, kicking off her shoes and dropping tiredly onto the couch. "Your Cristoff has a great deal of stamina."

Bink felt her eyes widen. "*Stamina?*"

"On the dance circle," Tavia assured her hastily. "He also drinks way more than he should."

"And tried to get you to match him drink for drink, no doubt," Bink said sourly.

"He tried." Tavia cocked her head. "How about you?"

"No problems," Bink said. "Everyone will assume the safe's malfunctioned, and they'll be hours cutting it open. By the time they realize what really happened we'll be long gone."

"I hope so. How much did we get?"

Bink shrugged. "We're set for the next month. No more than that, I'm afraid."

"A month works," Tavia said, nodding. "There are some good-sized electronics firms on Kailor V. Maybe I can finally get a job that meets with your approval."

"Maybe," Bink said diplomatically. "I'm sure there are jobs like that somewhere out there."

Only there weren't, she knew. Not the kind of job Tavia was looking for.

But they had a month's worth of breathing space. By then, Bink would have something else lined up. Probably something small, but maybe something big.

Maybe even that big score that would finally let them be free of this life forever.

She could always hope.

GOOD HUNTING

WRITTEN BY **CHRISTIE GOLDEN**
ART BY **JOE CORRONEY & HI-FI**

Jedi Master Jaina Solo shivered as the cold humidity of the mist-shrouded forest bit through her flight suit.

"I needed this," she said to Tenel Ka Djo. "I've gotten too comfortable on Shedu Maad, I think."

"*You've* been too comfortable?" the Hapan Queen Mother snorted, also shivering slightly. "Try living in a palace. It's hard *not* to get soft. I'm so glad you suggested this, Jaina."

Tenel Ka had brought her daughter, Allana—who was also Jaina's niece—to visit the Jedi temple on Shedu Maad. When Tenel Ka had lamented that it had been too long since she and Jaina had spent time together, Jaina promptly proposed that the three of them take a short trip—without the royal guards who typically accompanied Tenel Ka almost everywhere. Allana, sitting cuddled up with her pet nexu, Anji, suggested a camping trip where they could observe wildlife. Jaina thought of her late twin, Jacen, of how, as a boy, he'd had such a great love of animals. Allana was, in this respect at least, truly her father's daughter.

"Sounds wonderful. Where would you like to go, honey?" Jaina had asked fondly.

The reply really shouldn't have surprised her. "I want to go somewhere where I can teach Anji how to hunt."

Allana was, obviously, her mother's daughter as well.

They had decided on Luuhar, one of the many little-explored planets in the vast Hapes Cluster. With their love of beauty and nature, the Hapans had set aside Luuhar as a preserve where visitors could truly "get away from it all." Allana declared it the perfect choice when she learned that, with its ancient forests, misty rains, and rushing rivers, Luuhar's northern continent was similar to the nexu's native habitat.

As she and Anji descended the ramp onto the spongy soil of Luuhar, Allana piped up. "Don't worry, Mother. Camping will keep us from getting soft!"

Even though they had planned camping all along, Jaina found herself battling a twinge of annoyance at the thought of sleeping out in this weather. Instantly she was disappointed at the petty thought. She was... well, annoyed with her annoyance. Anji was now peering toward the dimness of the forest's edge. Her head lifted and bobbed slightly as she sniffed what was no doubt a potpourri of new scents.

"Allana, are you sure you want to?" asked Tenel Ka. "Remember, predator species are active at night."

"We have more than enough weapons to protect ourselves," Allana pointed out. "We can make sure someone is always keeping watch."

"Tell you what," Jaina said, mentally squaring herself against her uncharacteristic resistance. "There's still plenty of daylight left before we have to set up camp. In the meantime, Anji is raring to go. So let's see what's out there."

Allana made a series of quick hand signals. Anji emitted a blood-curdling yowl of pleased approval and bounded off into the forest to lead the way. Allana followed, breaking into a jog to keep up.

Anji had had her bite restraint removed for the trip. Jaina had never seen the nexu open her mouth so wide before, and she was suddenly uneasily aware of just how many teeth the animal had... and how, when fully opened, those jaws could engulf Allana's entire head.

What am I thinking? Anji would never harm Allana! She adores that girl, and has fought to protect her before.

Irritated again at her jumpiness, she shouldered her small backpack of day-hike rations and first aid items, wondering if this trip really had been such a good idea after all.

Anji ran eagerly, her claws scoring the mossy, humus-covered soil with deep gouges, her head up and four sharp eyes bright. Allana called her back when she wandered too far, and she, Tenel Ka, and Jaina kept up a comfortable yet brisk pace that took them deeper into the woods. The huge trees towered over them, their trunks as wide as Allana was tall. The day remained overcast, and the canopy of the forest seemed

reluctant to permit even that feeble light through.

Jaina found her hand dropping to the hilt of her lightsaber. Like Anji, she was highly attuned to her environment. More so than was reasonably warranted. As Tenel Ka had said, no predators on Luuhar stirred until dusk. The relative safety of the place was one of the main reasons Tenel Ka had selected it. There was, of course, always the threat of pirates in this system, the Hapes Cluster had been colonized by them, and the "tradition" hadn't been entirely stamped out.

And the Queen Mother and Chume'da—her heir—lived under the constant shadow of possible assassination attempts.

But Jaina was realizing her earlier jumpiness hadn't stemmed from a dislike of cold, rainy weather. This came from the Force. Something bad was afoot, though danger wasn't imminent. Not yet.

She decided to speak with Tenel Ka. If the other woman sensed the same thing, they'd have to turn their grand hunting adventure into something much duller, but safer. Allana would be disappointed, but she'd understand.

Watching Anji revel in her freedom, however, Jaina wondered if the nexu would.

They stopped for a rest and a bite to eat in a small clearing next to a stream. The water was icy, and again Jaina shivered. The cold and damp of the place clung to her like a clammy hand. She caught Tenel Ka's eye. The Hapan queen rose from where she and Allana had been watching Anji stare at the fish darting through the water and came to sit next to Jaina.

Jaina offered her a ration bar, leaning in and saying quietly, "There's something not right here."

"I know," Tenel Ka said, and sighed. "I feel it, too. Allana and Anji are having such a wonderful time. It's been hard on her at the palace, after living such an active life with your parents for so long. I hate to cut this short, but..."

"It's not worth the risk," Jaina finished, and with the words, knew she was right.

Tenel Ka nodded sadly. "Allana?" She reached out an arm to her daughter. "Come here, sweetheart. We have something to tell you."

Allana didn't answer. Her attention was focused on Anji. Just as Allana started to reply, Anji stiffened and jumped into the stream. For a moment, Jaina thought the nexu was simply going after the fish, but Anji plunged through the stream with a purpose. So confusing was her behavior that Jaina didn't realize what was going on

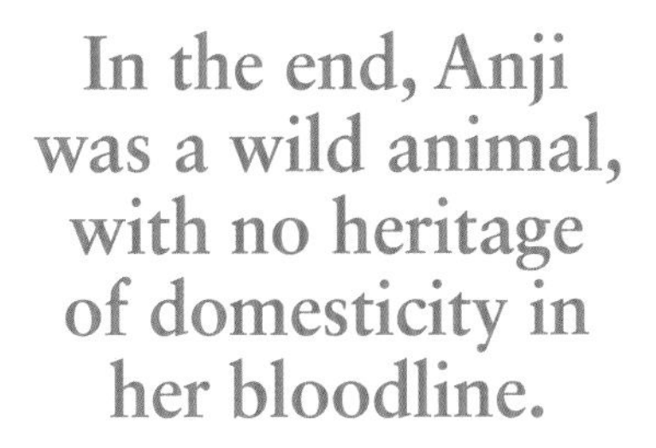

until Allana shouted in a heartbroken voice, "Anji! Don't run away!"

Anji twitched in reaction to Allana's voice, willfully disobeying the command. Jaina leaped to her feet, furious with herself for her slow reaction, and reached out in the Force to Anji to try and halt her flight. Too late. Anji was on the other side of the stream and up a tree in two bounds, leaping to the branches of a second tree several meters away.

She moved like she was born to do this, which, of course, she had been. In the end, Anji was a wild animal, with no heritage of domesticity in her bloodline. Maybe it was inevitable that she would forsake Allana one day. But she had known nothing of wilderness in her own lifetime, she didn't even know how to hunt for herself.

Almost as one, the three set off after the escaped nexu, splashing through the frigid water with less grace than Anji had shown. They easily picked up her trail on the far bank. They would find her, it was just a question of how long the nexu would lead them on the chase.

Deeper into the murky woods they went, following the trail of churned-up, leafy soil and the occasional patch of fur caught on rough tree bark. The nexu had a good lead on them, and night wasn't far away. They had glowrods against the encroaching darkness, but Jaina worried about losing the trail. Her fears were confirmed a few short minutes later.

"We must have missed something," she said after going a few yards with no more signs. Tenel Ka and Allana had spread out a little, but they looked more than a little puzzled.

"It just... ends," Tenel Ka murmured, a frown creasing her forehead.

"Aunt Jaina," came Allana's voice, "I can't sense Anji in the Force anymore. I... there's some blood here."

Jaina hastened to where Allana stood. Allana turned a small, somber face up to her aunt. "Is it... is it Anji's?"

Jaina, fearing the worse but hoping she was wrong, knelt to examine the disturbed earth. "It could be... but even if it is, there's not enough for Anji to have been killed here," she stated. "She might have killed a small animal, but where would she have taken it?"

"Nexu are really good at climbing—"

"—trees," Jaina finished, and all three of them craned their necks to examine the treetops. At that moment, Jaina's danger sense kicked into high gear. She activated her lightsaber, whirling just in time to return blaster fire back toward the man who'd fired it, burning a curiously small but lethal smoking hole in his chest. He crumpled.

Beside her, Tenel Ka uttered a war cry in Dathomiri and drew her own lightsaber, its hilt fashioned from a rancor's tooth. Teal and violet blades moved in a blur, sending streaks of white blaster fire back to target their owners. The cool night air was suddenly filled with the unmistakable hum of lightsabers and the cries of wounded and dying beings. Out of the corner of her eye, Jaina saw Allana drop, making herself a smaller target, and begin firing with her own blaster.

The cool night air was suddenly filled with the unmistakable hum of lightsabers.

Jaina pressed the attack, pausing to hurl one of the three remaining men into the trunk of a nearby tree before leaping and somersaulting in mid-air, striking another full in the chest with her feet. Tenel Ka was more than at home here, fighting to defend herself and her daughter on a world that so resembled that of her mother.

As quickly as it had begun, it was over. Four shapes lay on the ground. They looked to be human males, and they wore camouflaged clothing that enabled them to blend in with the browns and greens of the forest. Jaina frowned. The weapon still clutched in the severed hands of the man she had slain was a sporting rifle, a recent model. The blast was powerful, but narrow, so it wouldn't unduly mar a game animal's pelt. These weren't assassins. They were hunters.

"This one's still alive," Tenel Ka called. Her green eyes blazed as she knelt over the fallen foe. "Why did you attack me and the Chume'da?" she demanded, even as she began to tend to his injuries.

His eyes widened. "Majesty... no idea... forgive me..."

Jaina took in his wounds. Tenel Ka's efforts would be in vain. "Who are you?"

He was struggling for words. "Came... just to hunt. Big game, you know?"

"I'm sure *you* know that's illegal on Luuhar," Jaina said. "You're poaching. Did you think we'd turn you in? Is that why you attacked us?"

His gaze was confused. "I... he told us to." He grew increasingly agitated and struggled to sit up. "Our guide set the ambush... I'm not a murderer! I don't know why..."

"I believe him," Tenel Ka said quietly, and so did Jaina. "Do not fear. Your queen and your Chume'da are unharmed. We forgive you. Rest, now." She lifted her hand and made a gesture. His contorted features eased, and he smiled. His chest rose and fell in a deep sigh, and did not rise again.

Jaina checked the other two. The one she'd Force-hurled had collided too hard with the tree trunk; the one she'd kicked was unconscious.

"We have to get him back to the ship," Jaina said, and Tenel Ka nodded. Allana looked from her aunt to her mother.

"We're leaving, aren't we?" Allana said softly.

Tenel Ka stroked her daughter's hair sadly. "I'm afraid so, sweetheart."

"But—but Anji doesn't know how to hunt!"

"It looked like she might have caught herself something to eat, back where you—" Tenel Ka stopped abruptly.

"Where I stopped being able to sense her in the Force," Allana said, her voice thick. The dim light caught the glitter of tears in her eyes, but she blinked them back and straightened her small shoulders. "It's okay. As long as she's able to take care of herself, she should have the right to be free, if she wants to. All beings should."

"We can come back to check on her," Jaina said, "after we take care of this fellow. Just to make sure she's all right. Let's get going."

Allana brightened, just a little. Jaina levitated the unconscious poacher while Tenel Ka calculated their whereabouts. Though they'd wandered a lot, there was a particularly dense swatch of woods nearby. Something about the thicket unnerved Jaina, but according to Tenel's calculations, if they took this shortcut they would emerge closer to the ship than Jaina had thought. They set off as quickly as they could.

As they wound their way through the thicket, the trees seemed even larger, more ancient, and they pressed in so tightly their branches intertwined. Jaina felt as though the temperature had suddenly plunged. *Stang*, she was mad. Filled with righteous fury. Poachers were the lowest of the low. She wasn't big on hunting in the first place, but to do so illegally and in such a cowardly way and to drag her niece, her friend, and Anji into this—

"Stop!" came Allana's voice. Jaina halted, peering at the churned-up forest floor she had missed and Allana hadn't. The area was muddy, and the moist, cool air carried the scent of blood. Tenel Ka knelt and plucked a small, crimson-stained scrap of fabric from the ground.

Came... just to hunt... the dying poacher had gasped. *Our guide set the ambush... I'm not a murderer! I don't know why...*

Oh, now Jaina knew why. And she knew why she had been feeling so uncharacteristically out-of-sorts the entire

trip—and maybe even why Anji had turned feral.

"The poachers' guide was a Force user," Tenel Ka said, figuring it out almost as quickly as Jaina.

"The poachers thought they were doing all the work, meeting a sporting challenge, and in reality, the sleemo was using the Force to coerce animals to come to them for slaughter. There was no real hunting involved at all!"

She and Tenel Ka drew their lightsabers, and Jaina extended her senses in the Force. "It's not just him. He's using this *place*." This part of the forest was crawling with dark-side energy, pressing in on them hungrily. "It intensifies his abilities," Tenel Ka said. "That's why he takes hunters here."

The area was muddy, and the moist, cool air carried the scent of blood.

"Let's get the poacher to the ship, and then we'll try to find this kriffing scum. We defend *only*. Do not initiate the attack." Jaina was fine with anger and fear, in the right places. They could be very useful. But she was not about to let this man use them against her. It took a great effort, but she opened herself to a feeling of serenity and devotion to her duty from the Force. Centered now, she began to search for their enemy.

Now that she knew what to look for, the nebulous anxiety she'd been only vaguely aware of earlier formed into a specific cold, slithery chunk of arrogance and greed... and apprehension. Jaina focused her mind on her resolve and the certainty of his capture, and was rewarded with a sudden frisson of fear.

The dark side energy enveloping them still dulled her clarity. She could sense him now, but couldn't tell if he was nearby or far away. The answer came abruptly—Jaina felt an intangible pressure on her chest and went flying. Immediately, she

regained control and turned the fall into a tumble, landing smoothly on her feet. Tenel Ka had engaged him, and her blade's aqua glow sizzled against the white bolts of blaster fire, illuminating the battle. Calmer now that she knew what was going on, Tenel Ka was attempting to disarm the Force-user rather than kill him.

While Tenel Ka distracted him, Jaina reached out with the Force, attempting to snatch the blaster out of his hand. She did, but just barely, and her own hand wavered as if someone had attempted to shove it aside. She caught a glimpse of his face—so young to have such an expression of cruelty on it. He was injured and outnumbered, and had realized by this point that there would be no victory against either Tenel Ka or Jaina—certainly not both. He had nothing to lose.

He leaped over them and ran for Allana.

A heart-stopping screech rent the night air and a nightmare of teeth, claws, and barbed quills descended from the tree branches. For a second that lasted an eternity, the man's scream matched that of the beast, then all was abruptly silent.

Anji lifted her head, licking her bloody jaws. Her four eyes sought Allana.

"Anji!" Allana rushed toward the nexu. Jaina's heart leapt into her mouth as Anji sprang, knocking the Chume'da off her feet.

Allana went down giggling.

Anji's massive jaws were parted in a happy grin as she butted her head against Allana's. Jaina let the relief wash through her, and she felt almost physically warmed by Tenel Ka's pleasure, which had bathed her through the Force. Anji had been summoned and controlled by an unusually powerful will. But instead of turning against her mistress, or even staying out of the fight, the nexu had fought to defend and protect Allana.

She shouldn't have been able to. Jaina knew it.

But Anji hadn't known that. Her simple love had been stronger than the dark side's will. She hadn't abandoned Allana, and, Jaina now realized, she never would.

"Good girl, Anji," she murmured, sending love in the Force to the nexu. "Very, *very* good girl."

CONSTANT SPIRIT

WRITTEN BY **JENNIFER HEDDLE**
ART BY **MAGALI VILLENEUVE**

"We really must leave, Your Highness." The dance music being played by the distractingly attractive Zeltron band in the cantina nearly drowned out Gorhan's words, but even if Leia hadn't been able to hear him, the solemn expression on his tanned and weathered face would have gotten the message across.

The young Senator Organa checked the time yet again, the gnawing feeling in her stomach worsening. "Rafe Ballon is one of our most reliable agents." *And a friend of Father's*, she added silently. Not that it could afford him special treatment. "If he isn't here, it has to mean something happened to him. Can't we give him a few more minutes?"

Gorhan appeared uncomfortable about his answer, but resolute nonetheless. His determination to give her bad news even when he knew she wouldn't like it was one reason she kept him around. That and the fact that he was practically the size of a Wookiee. "I'm afraid not, Princess," he said. "We've already stayed too long. If anyone were to find you here..."

"I know, I know." Leia shook her head. She wasn't supposed to be in this sector at all; her ship's official flightplan listed only a diplomatic visit to Duro, keeping this side trip to the nearby planet Quellor a secret. They had landed here under false names with a forged manifest. She was still new to solo missions, and the plan was to be planetside just long enough to rendezvous with Rafe and retrieve the tactical information he had for her. Anything longer than that was dangerous, especially for a still-inexperienced operative. Gorhan was right.

But that didn't mean she had to like it.

"Fine," she said, trying not to sound like a sulky teenager—even if she was one. She pulled the hood attached to her pale blue gown back up over her head. "Let's go."

They left the cantina and made their way through the twisting streets of Quellor City in the direction of the spaceport, an alert Gorhan leading the way, looking from side to side with small, precise movements that contrasted with his hulking build. It was minutes past dusk, the dark of night just beginning to settle on the city's ornately spired buildings, and the temperate air smelled sweetly of the katella flowers that were famous in this region. Despite the Imperial presence that hung over the place like an oppressive fog, it was a lovely setting, and for a moment Leia wished she could simply appreciate her surroundings.

But only for a moment. She wasn't one for wishes.

Her senses twinged and she whirled around just as a hand reached out and grabbed her upper arm. Gorhan's blaster was already in the other man's face when they both realized it was Rafe, huddled in the doorway of what appeared to be a residential building, the collar of his jacket pulled up to hide his features as much as possible.

Gorhan muttered a curse and lowered his sidearm.

"Rafe!" Leia said. "What –"

"Princess." Rafe's gray eyes darted from side to side; the short, slim man was as nervous as Leia had ever seen him. "Moff Toggan is onto me. Somehow he found out that I'm the one who's been slicing into his systems." He held out a datacube in a shaking palm. "Everything I've collected to date is on here. Troop movement schedules, security protocols, everything you need from this sector. Take it and go."

"But what about you?" Leia protested. "If they catch you, they'll kill you." *Or worse*, she thought queasily.

"I'm already dead." Rafe said it with a shrug, but Leia could see that his effort at nonchalance was failing. "Leia," he said more seriously, and she had a sudden flashback to him discussing strategy in her father's study, his expression increasingly somber with each new glass of brandy. "I've always known this was a possibility. Take the cube and don't worry about me."

Leia's mind reeled, refusing to accept what he was saying. "Don't be ridiculous. You're coming with us."

"Whoever you are, you're in league with the Rebellion," Task said. Leia felt a pang of relief that he at least didn't know her identity. Their aliases must have held up under inspection.

"Your Highness—" both Rafe and Gorhan began at once. Gorhan glared at the small, wiry Rafe, who subsided. "We can't take him onboard," Gorhan continued. "If they know he's with the Rebellion, and he gets connected to you. It's too much of a risk."

Leia knew, at least intellectually, that her escort was right again. But she couldn't bring herself to agree this time, while Rafe looked at her with death in his eyes. "I know all about the risks," she said, summoning her best tone of royal command. "My entire *life* is a risk. And I'm not going to let anyone die who doesn't need to." She looked at her father's friend reassuringly and repeated, "You're coming with us."

Out of the corner of her eye she could see Gorhan shaking his head, she ignored him, keeping her gaze on Rafe.

The spy swallowed hard, then sighed. "Thank you," he whispered. "But if there's even a hint this is going to go wrong…"

"How about we quit talking about it and move," she said. The three rebels took off in the direction of the *Constant Spirit*, none of them noticing the smell of katella blossoms or the stars beginning to appear in the night sky.

Despite the collective nervousness of everyone onboard, the *Constant Spirit* left Quellor's airspace without difficulty. Seated in the cockpit of the compact light freighter with her pilot and navigator, Leia allowed herself a glimmer of hope that they would leave the planet as unobtrusively as they had arrived.

But shortly after they left atmo behind for the vacuum of space, emergency klaxons started blaring. *Should have known we wouldn't get off so easy*, Leia thought.

"A single Imperial Customs corvette approaching," reported the pilot, Minna. "They're hailing us."

At least the Moff hadn't had time to send more ships after them. Yet. "Let's hear what they have to say," Leia said.

Minna nodded, and a moment later a clipped male voice filled the cabin.

"Attention *Constant Spirit*, this is Captain Task aboard the *Gatekeeper*. You are transporting a known spy. Surrender him and we will spare your vessel."

Right. She was young, but she wasn't stupid. "I'm afraid we don't know what you're talking about, Captain," Leia said, keeping her voice as even as possible. Her heart pounded in her chest. "We're shimmersilk merchants who were delivering a shipment to a loyal client in the capital."

"Whoever you are, you're in league with the Rebellion," Task said. Leia felt a pang of relief that he at least didn't know her identity. Their aliases must have held up under inspection. "Turn over Rafe Ballon or we will fire on your ship. I will give you one minute to respond." The communication ended.

Rafe appeared in the opening to the cockpit. "Let me turn myself in," he said. "You can't allow one person to jeopardize the mission—not to mention the danger this puts you in."

"Minna, begin evasive maneuvers," Leia said, not looking back at him. "Youk, how soon until we can jump to lightspeed?"

The Mon Calamari navigator consulted his screen. "Six minutes, Your Highness."

That was at least five minutes longer than she'd like. "Gorhan?" she said into the comm.

"Already in place, Princess."

Good. The *Constant Spirit* only had one gun, the better to make it appear a peaceful merchant vessel, but Gorhan would make the best of it. "Fire at will. And everybody hold on."

"I never should have come onboard," Rafe said. He slammed his palm against a bulkhead in frustration.

"You might want to sit down," Leia told him. No sooner were the words out of her mouth than her stomach lurched as the ship went into a steep climb. Rafe stumbled and put his hands out to keep from slamming head-first into the cockpit's opposing bulkhead.

"Like I was saying..." Leia murmured. The ship rocked again, this time from a laser blast, snapping her head back. Rafe threw himself into the chair beside her and strapped himself in.

"How are we doing?" Leia asked Minna.

"Hanging in for the moment, but I don't know how long our deflector shields are going to hold up under their attack." As if on cue, the ship shuddered ominously. Minna blew a black curl of hair out of her face as she checked her console. "Just what I was afraid of: shields are fading fast," she said grimly. "Down fifty percent already."

"Gorhan?" Leia asked.

"Doing what I can," he responded. "*Their* shields seem to be holding better than expected."

"Naturally," Leia said under her breath. "Youk, how are those calculations going?"

"It'll still be a few more minutes, Your

High—" He ended with a yelp as another blast rocked the ship. "My apologies."

"It's all right, Youk," Leia said, trying to sound calm. "I know you're doing what you can." Despite her tone, her mind was racing. If this mission failed, it would reflect badly not only on her, but on her father. She was determined not to let that happen.

Then again, if she wound up dead, it probably wouldn't matter much to her either way.

"Just got in a good hit!" Gorhan shouted. "We'll have them on the run yet!"

Leia grimaced. They must *really* be in trouble if Gorhan was pretending to be optimistic.

With the next impact against the hull, Minna spat a curse. "Shields are gone," she barked. "I'm doing what I can, but if something good doesn't happen fast..." The ship banked hard again as the pilot tried her best to continue to evade the larger craft.

Leia looked over at Rafe to solicit his advice, but the man was breathing loud and fast, almost as if he were having a panic attack. He looked back at her, and his gray eyes revealed his agony. "I can't do this anymore," he said. He pulled off his safety harness and ran out of the cockpit.

"Where are you going? Rafe!" Leia considered going after him, but the ship shuddered again and she stayed put. She'd have to deal with him later.

Another hit, and alarms started blaring. "That last blast took out the hyperdrive," Youk said in dismay. "And disabled the alluvial dampers."

A pit opened in Leia's stomach. "I think we're in trouble." She bit her lip, wondering

what her father would do in this situation. Not get himself into it in the first place, most likely. "For now just keep trying your best to outfly them, Minna. And Gorhan, keep barraging them with gunfire." *And I'll try to come up with something brilliant.*

"Guess now we find out if my best is good enough," Minna said. She was gripping the yoke so tightly that the brown skin on her knuckles was turning white. Leia reached over to squeeze the other woman's shoulder.

"Senator, something's happening... We've lost our escape pod," Minna said in confusion. "It just launched by itself. Youk, check to see if it's a malfunction."

The Mon Calamari pressed a few keys. "It doesn't appear to be, no."

"Rafe," Leia said with a gasp. "It has to be. But what is he doing? Turning himself in?"

A moment later, the pod came into view, headed directly for the Imperial ship—more specifically, the *Gatekeeper*'s bridge—and as they waited, the pod made no indication of changing course.

"I don't believe it. He's going to ram them," Minna said breathlessly.

"Can you open up a comm channel to the pod?" Leia asked.

"I'm trying, but he isn't responding," Youk informed her.

Leia moaned. How would she ever explain this to her father?

"It's as crazy a plan as I've ever seen, but if it works, he just might save our skins," she heard Gorhan say.

Everyone in the cockpit seemed to be holding their breath as they watched the pod make its way toward the larger ship. The *Gatekeeper*, presumably intent on finishing off its more important quarry, didn't take action against the pod until it was too late. The ship began to turn and fired its main gun, but both last-ditch

A pit opened in Leia's stomach. "I think we're in trouble." She bit her lip, wondering what her father would do in this situation.

efforts failed. Rafe's pod found its target well enough, ramming into the bridge in a spectacular conflagration.

A death bier, Leia thought.

Completely disabled, the *Gatekeeper* listed to one side aimlessly, looking almost pitiful as it floated in space like a ghost ship. But there was only one lost soul for which Leia grieved.

Gorhan appeared in the cockpit opening, his bulk blocking out all light behind him. "Whoever's left onboard is going to have bigger problems than us to deal with now. We owe Rafe a debt."

"Yes," Leia said, her voice rough. She closed her eyes, willing herself not to cry. She couldn't let her crew see her that way, like a lost little girl.

After a long moment, Minna cleared her throat. "What are your orders, Senator?"

"Take us to the closest non-occupied planet," Leia said wearily. "We'll arrange for either repairs or transport."

"Yes, Your Highness."

The crew of the *Constant Spirit* was quiet for the remainder of the trip.

Leia told her father about it when she returned to Alderaan, wanting to deliver the news in person. She sat in his plush, expansive office, where she had spent so many hours while she was growing up, and haltingly explained what had happened. She expected Bail Organa to be angry, or frustrated, but instead he was just sad.

"I'm so sorry," she said, not for the first time since she'd sat down. "I can't help but feel that this is my fault."

"Rafe knew the risks of his mission," her father said. He stood in front of the picture window, his back to her as he stared out at rolling green hills and a bright blue lake that twinkled in the sunlight. "He was prepared to die for the Alliance, and he did. As a hero. There are worse ways for a man to die."

"But he didn't *have* to," Leia said stubbornly, wincing at how young she sounded even to her own ears.

"He didn't?" He turned to look at her. "What could have gone differently?" he asked, more gently than she expected. "What would have saved both the intelligence we needed and the rest of your crew?"

"I don't know," she said, bowing her head. "But there must have been something. I didn't think fast enough..."

"You can't save everyone, Leia," Bail said. He sat down next to her on the couch and took her hand in his. "Your feelings do you credit, but war requires sacrifice. A sacrifice we all must be willing to make." He squeezed her hand. "You can't save everyone," he repeated.

She squeezed back, glad he was there, taking comfort in the familiar warmth of his skin. But his words nagged at her. "Maybe I can't always save everyone," she conceded. "That doesn't mean I shouldn't try." She raised her chin defiantly.

His dark eyes showed his doubts, but he smiled at her anyway. "You wouldn't be you if you didn't," he said.

They sat together until a servant called them to dinner, heralding the end of another day. There was always tomorrow.

THE SYROX REDEMPTION

WRITTEN BY **JOE SCHREIBER**
ART BY **JOHN VAN FLEET**

There's an inmate like me in every prison across the galaxy, I suppose. I'm the one who can get it for you: Glitterstim, juri juice, or maybe just flimsiplast from the Core Worlds, if you;re partial to that. Since my arrival here, I've smuggled in everything from shimmersilk slippers to spiced mynock wing for a Cyblocian assassin from the Meridian sector, who wanted to celebrate his birthday in style. With the exception of weapons and hard drugs, I can get my hands on just about any kind of contraband you might want. So when a new con named Waleed Nagma came up to me in the mess hall and asked if I could find him a bulb of Anzati snot garlic, I told him it would be no problem. And it wasn't.

"You're Zero, aren't you?"

I glanced up from my tray, taking my time, and favored him with an easy smile.

"Depends," I said. "Who's asking?"

He examined my outstretched hand for a moment before reaching out to give it a quick, uneasy shake. His eight-fingered grip was cold and clammy. Like most new arrivals on the Hive, he was trying his hardest to come off tough, cool, and imposing all at once, and it wasn't going well. I could already see droplets of sweat around his hairline and upper lip, and his eyes twitched too fast, showing too much white around the edges.

"I heard you can get certain things," he said.

"Well." I blinked at him, still smiling, the picture of serene innocence. "I'm not sure where you might have heard such a rumor. I'm just another happy face here at the Hive."

"One of the guards told me about you," Nagma said. "I need to place an order." He was so jumpy that he could barely stand still, and I guess I should've recognized trouble, but something about him intrigued me. "I can pay whatever it costs."

"Take it easy," I said, nodding at the empty place across the table. "Just have yourself a seat. We've got nothing but time."

After another hesitant beat, Nagma bent down and folded his lanky torso into the bench opposite mine. There was a lot of him to fold. At full height he stood almost two meters tall, gangling and narrow-shouldered and so skinny that the orange prison-issue uniform hung off his frame like the flag of some defeated principality. The pale dome of his elongated bald head was threaded with fine blue veins, and when he leaned across to whisper in my ear, I could smell the fear coming off of his skin in waves—at least I thought it was fear. Looking back, I had no idea how sick he was.

"How does this sort of thing usually work?" he asked, rummaging down into his uniform. "Do I pay you first, or—"

"Relax, friend." I locked my eyes onto his. "We hardly know each other. Tell me your story. Where you're from. That sort of thing."

He squinted at me. "What's that got to do with anything?"

"I like to be properly introduced to anybody that I do business with," I said. "It insures that I'm dealing only with clients of the highest moral fiber."

"The highest...?" He glanced at me for a second, bewildered, then let out a snort. The joke was that every convict here in Cog Hive Seven, all five hundred twenty-two of us, represented the scum of the galaxy—murderers, mercenaries, and psychopaths of every stripe and species, walking genetic disasters that wouldn't hesitate to slash your throat for half a credit, or no reason at all. Our one unifying trait was that no one would miss us. Which was why our esteemed warden, Sadiki Blirr, could run the Hive like she did, pitting us against one another in daily gladiatorial matches that had already become one of the galaxy's most lucrative gambling operations.

It didn't help that every inmate had a microscopic electrostatic charge injected directly into their heart upon arrival. A tiny explosive which could be triggered by any of the guards at any moment, for any reason. Walking around with an undetonated bomb in your chest had a peculiar effect on your general outlook—gives life here a certain transitory quality, you might say.

Nagma didn't seem to care about that now, and it didn't look like he was one for idle small talk. So I gave up trying to make conversation and sighed. "What are you looking for?" I asked.

"You know what Anzati snot garlic is?" he asked.

"What, you mean the cooking ingredient?" I frowned. "I think I had it in a shaak pot roast once. Why?"

"I need an entire bulb of it. As soon as possible." He laced his fingers together and cracked his knuckles, a nervous habit.

"How long will it take to smuggle in?"

"If you don't mind my asking," I said, "what's the big emergency? Are the Bone Kings planning a banquet I'm not aware of?"

"It's this place," Nagma said. "You know that as well as I do, Zero. Everything's an emergency."

I didn't reply, but I understood what he meant. We were all well aware that the Hive's algorithm could select any of us at any time. When the prison walls began to pivot and twist and reassemble themselves around us, one cell would be paired with another, the occupants forced into a match where there could only be one survivor. In short, you never knew when your number was up.

"What do you need it for?" I asked.

"That's personal," Nagma said, but when he looked back up at me, I could see that his whole body was trembling, the sweat-stains already soaking through his uniform, forming darkened half-moons beneath his arms.

Nerves, I thought.

I was wrong.

Nagma's snot garlic arrived a week later, smuggled in alongside a shipment of replacement droid components and medical supplies. By the time he came to pick it up, I realized that whatever was ailing him had gotten significantly worse.

Since the last time we'd spoken, his eyes had sunken into his head, giving his entire face a gaunt and haunted look, like a skull with the thinnest veneer of skin stretched across it. He somehow seemed to have become even more skeletal, except for his belly, which bulged grotesquely outward from his uniform. He held it when he sat down, clutching it and wincing in pain as if he were in the throes of some terrible misbegotten pregnancy.

"You all right?" I asked.

He shook his head, waving the question away. His voice was thin, reedy with pain. "Did you get it?"

"Yes, and I'm happy to be rid of it," I said, reaching down into the hidden pocket I'd stitched inside my pantleg, and passing the bulb of snot garlic under the table. "This stuff reeks worse than a wet tauntaun."

"Here." Grabbing the garlic, he thrust a wad of crumpled credits notes into my palm, already rising up to leave. He didn't make it far. Three meters away, there was a sharp scream of pain, and we both looked up as one of the other cons—a sociopathic Rodian named Skagway—went flying across the next table over, blood geysering from the hole in his throat, splashing down to soak the front of his uniform. The moment that he hit the floor, Bone Kings, three of them, leapt on top of him, and I saw Nagma's expression sicken.

"What are they doing?" he asked.

"Deboning," I said, and reached for his arm. "Best not to watch." The one in charge was a mass murderer named Vas Nailhead, known especially for making weapons from the sharpened femurs and ribs of his kills.

For an instant Nagma stood paralyzed, unable to look away. After a second, Vas straightened up, his hands slathered with fresh blood. "What are you looking at, maggot?" Before Nagma could answer, Nailhead's hand shot out and grabbed him, yanking him forward so fast that his long skinny legs tangled underneath him. I saw Nagma's jaw drop open, hopeless, eyes goggling in panic.

"Easy, Vas." I held up one hand. "He's nothing to you."

Nailhead glared at me and his lips wrinkled back. "Zero? You're standing up for this puke?"

"He's a customer," I said with a shrug. "I have to protect my income stream, don't I?"

We locked eyes for a second, and I lifted my right foot off the ground. My prison-issue boots were lined with plexisteel, and Nailhead knew what it would do if I decided to put one through his face.

He let out a snarl and released his grip and shoved Nagma back to his spot at the table. For a moment neither of us spoke. After what felt like a very long time, Nagma gazed up at me.

"You stood up for me."

"It's nothing," I said. "Forget it."

He shook his head. "I won't."

I sighed. "Listen. Everything here is a test. It's just a matter of choosing your moment, and not hesitating when it comes."

Nagma let out a low, slow breath, and his bony shoulders trembled. The cloyingly sweet smell that I'd initially attributed to fear had become irrefutably stronger, and I realized now what it was—some form of fever, an illness that was only getting worse. In his sickened state, the attack seemed to have drained whatever strength he'd had, leaving him visibly depleted.

Nagma let out a low, slow breath, and his bony shoulder trembled. The cloyingly sweet smell I'd initially attributed to fear had become irrefutably stronger...

"You asked for my story." Something passed over his face, a grim tightness at the corners of the lips that could've been a smile—except the emotional component had been stripped away from it, leaving a kind of unplugged hopelessness. "I'm from Monsolar. Little backwater dirt-clod tucked into the Alzoc system."

"Never heard of it."

"You're not missing much." He shook his head. "It's a pit. Heavy canopy, primitive tribes, most of them at war with each other... not many get out."

"You did."

He gave me a wry look. "Only to end up here," he said. "It's my own fault. I got caught with a stolen load of thermal detonators in a spaceport on Urdur. That's an automatic life sentence in any system."

"Tough luck," I said.

Nagma shrugged. "The gangster who hired me said he could help me. I was desperate. I guess I still am."

I looked at him again, saw the sweat pouring down his emaciated face, the bulging stomach.

"You're sick," I said.

"It's worse than that," he said. "It's the worm."

"The what?"

He stared down at his trembling hands for a moment, as if the rest of the story might magically materialize in front of him, preventing him from having to tell it out loud. When it didn't, he drew a deep breath and pressed on. "Ever hear of the Syrox? The Wolf Worm of Monsolar?"

"Can't say that I have."

"It's an alpha species, native to my home planet." He let the breath out slowly. "An ectomorphic life-form, evolved in some way but not in others—a highly efficient, brainless predator. Feeds on blood. Imagine a blind river parasite half the size of this mess hall, with a mouth ringed in rows of teeth, and you'll start to get the idea."

I said nothing, just waited for him to continue.

"Back home," Nagma said, "most of the local tribes either worshiped it, feared it, or both. Over the generations, we built our culture around it, our stories and myths and rites of passage." He gave me a queasy smile, and glanced down at the swollen bulge of his belly. "Every season the Syrox lays its eggs in the streams of the river. They start out small—microscopic. That's why we never drink unfiltered water on Monsolar. But say a kid gets lost in the jungle... and gets thirsty enough..."

I stared at him, seeing how it could have happened. Nagma nodded again and gave me that terrible, meaningless smile.

"Incubation time is slow. It can remain in the gut of the host for years, feeding and growing stronger." He looked down at his swollen stomach, and a terrible hopelessness flashed over his face. "But eventually it always finds its way out."

"And the gangster who hired you to transport those detonators—"

Nagma nodded again. "He said he could get it removed for me, that he could set me up with tricky surgery in a clinic back in the Core Worlds. But the authorities caught up with me first. Not that it matters now." He patted his stomach tenderly. "It's getting larger each day. I can feel it getting bigger, pushing my organs aside. Sometimes at night..." He swallowed hard. "I can feel it moving around inside me. And I have to get it out."

He took the bulb of garlic out of his pocket and placed it on the table, and for a moment we both looked at it. "So what's with the garlic?"

"Back on Monsolar, we had an old folk remedy for those who've been infected. Go to sleep with a bulb of snot garlic on your pillow. They say the Syrox is attracted to the smell. It comes crawling out on its own."

"Respectfully..." I stood up, reached across the table and tapped my finger over his chest. "You've got a bomb implanted in your heart. And at any given moment you could be matched against another inmate who will in all likelihood kill you." I waved my hand, gesturing to the inmates lined up at the mess hall tables. "Any one of us could be dead tomorrow. Why do you care so much about getting this parasite out of your system?"

Nagma gazed back at me, and for just a second I thought I saw a flash of the young tribesman that he'd once been, steadfast and unafraid with his whole future ahead of him. Before the worm had gotten into him. Before he'd been brought here. When he spoke again his voice was low and calm, but there was deep steel in it.

"My tribe is founded in the traditions of justice and honor," he said. "I can accept my sentence, because I chose to smuggle those detonators. It was my mistake, and I'll pay for it—with my life, if I have to." His eyes narrowed, growing cold. "But I want to go my way, Zero. Clean." He grimaced. "Without this godforsaken thing crawling around inside me."

He opened his mouth to say something else, and the clarion bell went off. In the Hive, that meant only one thing. The matching was about to begin. When the alarm sounded, you had five minutes till lockdown, and I knew what Nagma was thinking—what would happen if the algorithm, in its infinite wisdom, selected him, and when the countless moving parts of Cog Hive Seven finished their reconfiguration, the wall of his cell opened up to expose the inmate that would almost certainly be the death of him.

When I looked up again, he was gone.

Waleed Nagma wasn't matched to fight that day, or the day after that, or the weeks to come. Every so often, I saw him lingering around the mess hall or the central pavilion where the halls of the Hive came together like spokes in a great wheel, where the cons milled around listlessly throughout the day, serving out their sentences and waiting to get matched. He never approached me or tried to make contact, but I could tell from looking at him that the thing he'd told me about—the Syrox, the thing he called the Wolf Worm—was still incubating inside him. His belly looked enormous, as if it were about to burst.

Then one day I was heading back to my cell for the night when a guard named Voystock came up behind me and tapped me on the shoulder.

"Zero?"

I stopped and looked around, and he waved me forward, back down the way I'd come. "Got a message for you. This way."

"Where are we going?"

He didn't answer, and I didn't really expect him to. We weren't heading for any of the cell blocks, but lower, following a narrow stairway to the abandoned manufacturing area that the cons called Nightside. Rounding a corner, Voystock swung open the broken hatchway and nodded me into the flat, darkened space beyond it. After a moment of standing there, letting my eyes adjust, I sensed

something curled in the corner, fifteen meters away, moving in the shadows.

"Zero," a voice croaked.

The voice froze me. It was a raspy, almost incoherent whisper, so heavy with pain that I almost couldn't recognize it. "Nagma?"

"Don't come any closer," the voice said, and there was something clotted about the words, as if they were forcing their way through a thick obstruction. "It's coming up now. It's almost—"

The words broke off. I tried to step back, but my feet felt nailed to the spot. When the thing in the corner shifted slightly into a rectangle of light from the hatchway, I saw what I hadn't been able to make out before—or as much of it as I could stand to see, anyway. Enough to last me for the rest of my life.

Waleed Nagma was sprawled on his side, curled into a desperate, fetal clutch, with his cheek pressed against the durasteel floor. He was convulsing wildly. His eyes were pinched shut, but his mouth was stretched open so wide that I thought his jaw had dislocated.

Something was coming out of his mouth.

At first I thought it was his tongue. Except it was white. And huge. Ropey. And then I saw it plainly, slithering into view, slow and pale and thick and I knew what it was.

The worm.

Its slimy, pale length was emerging from between Nagma's lips with a hideous laziness, slithering forward as its broad flat head quested after the withered bulb of snot garlic he'd placed in front of it.

I couldn't breathe. Could only watch in something that wasn't just revulsion, but went beyond that.

As the worm came. And came. And just kept on coming.

At the sight of it—the sheer repulsive length of the thing, several meters long at least—I heard myself curse aloud. I felt my own stomach give an uneasy lurch, and heard Nagma scream.

By now the worm had pulled itself completely out, whipped its tail free, then reared back, twisting its blind head in my direction, as if only now realizing that I was here. For an instant, time seemed to freeze. As the Syrox faced me, the entire front of its head peeled back to reveal a perfectly round mouth, perhaps half a meter across, lined with rows of inward facing teeth. It lunged.

"Kill it!" Nagma shrieked. *"Kill it, Zero!"*

He said something else, but I didn't hear it. Springing forward, I lifted my foot, encased in the heavy prison-issue boot, and brought my heel down as hard as I could on the worm's head. There was a horrible scrunching squelch as whatever was inside of it collapsed and burst open. And I watched as its narrow hooked teeth scattered sideways in a skittering profusion across the floor.

The body of the thing fell still, deflated.

For what felt like a long time, neither of us moved. Then Nagma reached up and wiped his mouth and spat, and with great effort, started to stand up. I reached out and helped him rise to his full height. He nodded his thanks.

"I suppose... this means..." He hitched in a breath and glanced over where the bulb of snot garlic still sat, "...I owe you again...?"

"Forget it." I wiped off the bottom of my boot, scraping it against a pile of discarded droid parts that had been left in the corner. "Just so I don't ever have to look at that thing again."

Nagma stood there in the corner for a long time without speaking. Looking at the way he stood now, with his back and shoulders held straight, I thought I understood something about him now, the connection that I hadn't grasped earlier. And I saw why he'd asked for the snot garlic, and why it was so important to him. Why, in the midst of this living hell, it *did* matter.

True, we inmates of Cog Hive Seven walked around with bombs implanted in our chests, and we couldn't know when the algorithm might send us into a bout... but there were still some things that we had control over. A part of us that the guards and the warden and the fights couldn't touch. And I guess I knew what the word for that was. It was a strange word to use in a place like this, but it fit.

Freedom.

"Zero?"

I looked at him. "Yeah?"

"I can't help but wonder..." He stared at me, hollow-eyed and haunted. "What if I didn't get it all? What if part of it broke off inside of me? What if...?"

He didn't finish, and in the end, he just went back to his cell, alone.

When the thing in the corner shifted slightly into a rectangle of light from the hatchway, I saw what I hadn't been able to make out before.

All of this was a long time ago, several years at least, although time has a funny way of passing differently here. Sometimes when I'm lying in my cell waiting to go to sleep, I wonder why Nagma sent for me that night. It might've been because I was the only one he'd told about the worm, or maybe I was the closest he had to a friend in this place... or he'd just wanted to make sure that someone was around to finish the thing off. Someone who wouldn't hesitate in the moment when it mattered the most.

Two weeks after those hideous few minutes in Nightside, his number was matched by the algorithm, and he went up against another inmate. It wasn't much of a fight. Nagma's opponent killed him within just a few minutes. I never had another opportunity to find out what happened with the worm, whether there was any left inside.

But at night sometimes, when the hours draw out and I can't find sleep, I do wonder.

I think about the holovid of Nagma's Match—I've watched it several times—and what happened at the very end, when his slack face hit the floor. I think about the thing that might not have been his tongue that came out from the corner of his slackened lips. The detail and resolution on the holovid isn't great, and no matter how many times I watch it, I can't quite be sure.

But it makes me think about that thing, the worm that came all the way from Monsolar inside of his belly, and how it got here and discovered something that the rest of us only think about in the abstract, something that under the circumstances might not have been good for the rest of us at all.

And sometimes I think about the last comment that he made to me, before going back to his cell that night. Not a statement but a question, one that I couldn't answer—not that he seemed to expect one.

I just wonder... What if I didn't get it all? What if part of it broke off inside of me?

And that's when I think about the Worm inside the dark recesses of the Hive, the ductwork and the walls, moving in silence and growing fat on the blood of the cons that die in the fights.

What it might find here, in the dark.

And I think about that word again. That terrible word.

Freedom.

HAMMER

WRITTEN BY **EDWARD M. ERDELAC**
ART BY **JOE CORRONEY AND BRIAN MILLER**

The hilt of the lightsaber hummed in Telloti Cillmam'n's hand as the blade hissed to life and cast the wall of inscrutable carvings in a green glow.It wasn't Telloti's lightsaber. He would never build one of his own. And yet here was Master Ryelli, content to use his own lightsaber as a light source.

"Hold it steady," Master Ryelli directed, muffled by his breath-mask, wrinkling his balding brow as he stooped and ran a three-fingered hand across the ancient stone. Master Ryelli had lost those fingers in the Petranaki Arena on Geonosis three years ago, just as he had lost his Padawan, Lumas Etima. Telloti had known Lumas. They had been initiates together in Boma Clan as younglings at the Jedi Temple.

Although Telloti had dueled and bested Lumas and most of the other Initiates during the Apprentice Trials—before finally succumbing to Wollwi Enan, a girl from Berchest—Master Ryelli had selected Lumas as his Padawan learner. No Master had claimed Telloti. He had been transferred by the Council of Reassignment to the Explorer Corps. For seven years he had been a Pathfinder pilot in the Corps. What else could he do? He had never known any other home but the Jedi, had been taken too young to remember his parents or his home on Taanab. He had nowhere else to go. From infancy, he had been told he was special, that the Force had chosen him. But the Force had apparently changed its mind.

The war was in its fourth year. A war against a real Sith Lord, the kind Masters Piell and Nu had told him stories of as a boy. Telloti ached to join the fight. He thought maybe if he could prove himself a warrior, the Council would reconsider its decision not to train him. It wasn't unheard of. Master Kenobi had languished in the AgriCorps on Bandomeer before Qui-Gon Jinn had finally seen in him what others had missed and taken him on as his apprentice. Look at Kenobi now.

But there was little chance of that under Ekim Ryelli. After being wounded at Geonosis, after Lumas' death, Ryelli had requested this duty. He was an archaeologist, and wanted to be as far from the war as possible, digging in the dirt and scrutinizing pottery shards.

The war was close. Closer to Telloti than it had ever been. Ord Radama, where they had departed for their latest expedition, had belonged to the Separatists only last year. But he knew it was winding down. Soon his chance to prove himself would be lost. He had always thrilled to Master Piell's stories of the Jedi Knights and their clashes with the Sith. It seemed unfair to him that he should be sidestepped by history, even as it was unfolding only parsecs away.

"I don't recognize these letters," Ryelli admitted.

"Really?"

That was a surprise to Telloti. If it was old and forgotten, surely Ryelli was familiar with it.

"Can't you read them?"

"Given time," Ryelli said. He captured images of the wall with his datapad, then reached for his lightsaber. Reluctantly, Telloti handed it over. It receded into the hilt, bathing them in darkness.

"Check your light now," Ryelli suggested.

Telloti pursed his lips. He had forgotten to charge the portable torches before they'd left the ship, and had recharged his own battery with his datapad rather than turn back.He flicked the torch on, and a cone of light spilled across the floor.

"Good," said Ryelli, keying his comm. "Staguu, do you read?"

Their Givin astrogator's voice crackled over the comlink. He had remained aboard their ship on a flat area outside the structure.

"Everything all right, Master?"

Staguu Itincoovar had failed his Apprentice Trial as well, but Ryelli had requested him for the Explorer Corps. His race had a gift for astrogational computation which his latent Force ability enhanced. It was an exceptional talent, but the only one the bony, awkward humanoid possessed.

Ryelli called Staguu his best kept secret. He had plotted the course here to the remote world of Nicht Ka almost without the aid of the navicomputer. Ryelli joked that the Navy would snatch him away for service on some cruiser if they weren't careful. That kind of talk rankled Telloti. What if Ryelli was thinking of training him? Telloti's heart shriveled to think he might be passed over again. He had a

destiny. He knew he did. They had told him so, ingrained it in him. Why had the Jedi, why had the Force itself, abandoned him?

"Yes. I'm going to upload some images to the ship's computer. Can you run them through the philology database and transmit me any results?"

Telloti shined the light across the dais. The broad shoulders of the figure were adorned with wicked spikes, its head an upswept, sinister great helm.

"Certainly."

Ryelli hunkered down on a broken column and Telloti watched his face in the glow of his datapad. His eyes went to the scarred, three-fingered hand holding it. A droideka had done that on Geonosis, blown the lightsaber from his grasp. Ryelli could have had the fingers replaced with cybernetics, but he refused. Once Ryelli had told him it was a reminder, but of what, Telloti hadn't asked. Lumas, maybe? Weren't the Jedi supposed to forgo past attachments? How had a man like Ryelli ever become a Jedi Master? And why hadn't Ryelli chosen him as an apprentice that day? He had never asked. After a moment, Ryelli looked up.

"This may take some time, if you want to look around."

Telloti nodded and turned away from the older man.He wandered the corridors of the ancient structure, his torch-light sliding along the stone. Nicht Ka was a world lost to memory along the old Nache Belfia loop that had marked the frontier of the ancient Sith Empire. Ryelli, excited by the prospect of re-surveying it, had jumped at the chance now that it was once again within Republic space, ostensibly inside the 11th Army's expanding lines. It was no Korriban scattered with forbiddingtombs and ancient statues, however. It was a cold, barren rock, lashed by ammonia rains and uninhabitable. Yet Telloti's sensors had detected this hexagonal stone structure set into the broken foothills of the southern mountain range upon entering the atmosphere.

Why anyone would bother to engineer a shelter on this desolate rock was anybody's guess. No one had been here in ages.

Telloti followed the dark corridors aimlessly, hearing the voice of Ryelli and the squelches of Staguu echo behind him. The light of his torch caught a reflective glint from a dark chamber. Telloti tensed and touched his sporting blaster, but remembered the sensors had detected no lifeforms.

He passed into the room cautiously. The air was cooler here. There was a dais and alcove set into the back wall. A stone block chair stood atop the dais, and seated on that was a colossal figure forged in reflective black metal. Strange, that metal. He had made tracks across millennia worth of dust on the chamber floor, but the surface of that giant figure shone undimmed, as though nothing would settle on it.

Telloti shined the light across the dais. The broad shoulders of the figure were adorned with wicked spikes, its head an upswept, sinister great helm. A skirt of plated steel encircled its upper legs. It had apparently been vandalized at some point. There was a crooked molten scar across the neck, and the right arm was missing entirely from the elbow down, the stump hollow. It was no statue, he realized, but an archaic suit of battle armor.

He came closer, fogging his breath-mask in excitement. Ryelli would be ecstatic at this discovery. Telloti started to call him, when his eyes fell upon a long object lying on the dais between the metal-shod feet of the figure.

It was an archaic, two-handed lightsaber. Telloti hesitated. He could take the weapon, slip it into his pack before Ryelli came. It probably didn't work, but he could tinker with it, get it working again, maybe. Ryelli would never know.

He knelt down and reached out to take it.

As soon as his fingertips touched it, a wave of cold air blew over him, through his clothes, his skin, through his very soul. He shivered.

The emerald sabers flashed and buzzed as they clashed and were batted aside.

The right-hand gauntlet fell from the bent knee of the seated figure and clamped down over his hand, the whole suit lurching forward, suddenly animate.

No, just shifted, that's all.

He pulled away, skin rippling, but the metal fingers groaned and closed tightly around his wrist.

He put his foot on the dais and pulled. The suit fell forward with a clatter, the great helmet tumbled from the shoulders, and a fine white cloud of bone dust roiled from the neck. Telloti clenched his eyes against the stinging chalk even as it filled his nostrils, choking him. Behind his eyelids, he saw things. A shimmering shadow towering, legions of red skinned warriors spread out to the horizon of an alien world, chanting. "Adas! Adas!" He saw enormous alien warships cast their shadows across the multitude, which raised their pikes in defiance. He saw a gleaming axe cutting down gray amphibian warriors seven at a time, wielded by his own red hand. He saw fire rain down, decimating cities, smashing towers flat. He saw strange stars and the darkness in-between, and a thick book of strange writing, like what they had found on the wall. The axe became a hammer, ringing blows on sheets of glowing metal in a dim workshop, bending it into the form of the ebon armor. He heard a voice.

"Do not worry, my disciple. You will have your place in the history of the galaxy. You will go where I cannot and help restore the glory of the Sith, Warb Null."

He felt pain, searing, his flesh pressed against superheated iron. Was it real? No, more images. Roaring beast riders. Jedi. The clash of battle, just as Master Piell had described it. Exultation. Blood. Then, a single Jedi (*Ulic Qel-Droma!* his brain screamed) fighting ferociously towards him, cutting away his hand, passing his green blade through his neck.

He shrieked.

Died.

When Telloti opened his eyes again, the helmet was in his hands, poised over his head, its dark iron hood casting a shadow over his blinking eyes. Inside, secret glyphs glowed with orange light, waiting to brand his cheeks, imbue him with their power.

He had shed his clothes. He was wearing the armor. Only the brown skin of his right hand and face were uncovered.

"Stop!"

He whirled.

Master Ryelli stood in the door in his brown robes. His lightsaber hummed in his malformed hand."Take that off, Telloti," Ryelli urged, a tremor of something in his voice. Fear? It excited him to think a Jedi Master was afraid of him.

"It's of the Sith. This place... it's a tomb of some kind. That armor... it's *infested* with the dark side of the Force."

The dark side? With this kind of power, he could be a hammer to *crush* the dark side. What did Ryelli know? He had no insight at all. Why shouldn't he take this armor for himself? It had power in it. Real power. He could feel the Force like never before. With it, he could be a warrior. He could join the war, cut his way through legions of battle droids and take the Count of Serenno's head, be the hero the Republic needed.

"Why did you choose Lumas over me that day, Master Ryelli? What did you see in him that you didn't see in me?"

"We can talk about that later," Ryelli said, advancing into the room.

"Maybe you were afraid I'd be a greater Jedi than you. Is that what you thought?"

"You're not thinking clearly."

"You're afraid now, aren't you? Were you afraid on Geonosis? Is that why Lumas died?"

Ryelli shook his head, grimacing. He would not let Telloti leave with the armor. That was plain. He would send it off to EduCorps to sit in some corner of the Archives.

"You have your lightsaber out, Master. Do you want to fight? I have a lightsaber here..."

"Telloti, it's the armor..."

"No. You're wrong. You've always been wrong. If I'd been at your side on Geonosis, there'd be no war now. I would've killed Dooku. I would've crushed the Confederacy in its cradle. As a matter of fact, you've only been right about one thing, Master," he grinned as he slid the helmet over his face and felt the runes inside burn his flesh. He did not cry out. It was no more than a fervent kiss. He ignited the long green blade of the ancient lightsaber. "This *is* a tomb."

Ryelli charged.

The armor was like a web of conduits. It drew the Force into him. Telloti felt it surging through his blood vessels, contracting muscles, swinging his arms up to defend the downward stroke of Ryelli's lightsaber almost before Telloti could even think it. He was fast. So fast. And *strong*.

He drove Ryelli back with shuddering blows. The emerald sabers flashed and buzzed as they clashed and were batted aside, inadvertently hewing chunks of glowing stone from the walls. Telloti grinned ecstatically behind his grim metal face. His heart thundered.

Ryelli seemed so small now. Was he himself larger? He felt immense. Ryelli's blade skimmed his shoulder, sending sparks cascading into the air. He laughed. He hadn't even felt it. He forced Ryelli out into the corridor, and there locked blades with the Jedi Master. *Master.* What right did he have to that title? This squinting bookworm? This ditch digger? He looked for greatness in small, broken things, and failed to recognize it when it towered over him. The blades squealed and sizzled. Something strange happened. Ryelli forced him back. The Jedi Master with the mangled hand was winning. His expression grew serene. Why was he so calm? It was infuriating, like the face of that girl Enan during the Trials all those years ago, when she'd made a fool of him. Ryelli's blade angled ever closer, forcing the great two-handed lightsaber of Warb Null down. Telloti's left knee buckled and clanged against the stone floor.

The archaeologist *was* stronger. How could that be?

Stronger... perhaps, but not smarter.

Telloti knew the weapon in his hands. Somehow, he knew it. He had fashioned it, millennia ago. Or rather, the man in his vision, Shas Dovos, the man who became Warb Null, had, inspired by the dark teachings of Freedon Nadd and dread King Adas before him. He knew these things. He had their memories, their wisdom, the cunning of the Sith.

His bare thumb felt along the length of the two-handed hilt to a small toggle, and as Ryelli forced his superior position, bearing down with all his strength, Telloti triggered it and sidestepped.

The extra-long green blade of the ancient lightsaber retracted into the hilt. In the same instant, the butt sprang open like the maw of a sarlacc, revealing a hidden, secondary emitter. A blade of red energy erupted from it, the ingenious mechanism within realigning and refocusing the power in a nanosecond.

He grinned as he slid the helmet over his face and felt the runes inside burn his flesh. He did not cry out. It was no more than a feverent kiss.

Without the resistance of the green blade, Ryelli stumbled forward, dangerously off balance. Telloti shifted his grip and flipped the new red blade over, slicing neatly through the nape of Ryelli's neck. The Jedi Master tumbled to the floor. Telloti straightened, listening to the sound of his own breathing, feeling his heart pounding deep behind the black shell of his breastplate.

Ryelli's comlink began to beep.

He stooped and picked it up with his bare hand. He would need to fashion a new gauntlet to replace the one Qel-Droma had destroyed.

He triggered the comm.

"Master," said Staguu. "I'm getting an urgent message from Coruscant. It's from the Jedi Temple beacon and it's repeating. It says the war is over!"

The comlink slipped from Telloti's fingers, clattering beside his steel boot.

"Did you hear that, you two? It's over! We've won!"

The glee in the Givin's voice. He laughed. He was actually *happy*.

Telloti raised his foot and crushed the comlink beneath his heavy heel. He roared unintelligibly behind the metal helm, ignited the red-bladed lightsaber once more, and chopped at the stone walls and floor in his fury, carving deep gouges, like the marks of some caged beast.

This couldn't be—not when he finally had the power to seize his destiny.

It had to be a lie.

He stalked down the hallway toward the exit.

Telloti wrenched the body of Staguu from the chair at the communications console, and replayed the message himself. *"Calling all Jedi. This is Supreme Chancellor Palpatine. The war is over. I repeat, the war is over. All Jedi are ordered to return to the Jedi Temple immediately. You will receive further instructions when you arrive."*

He drove his mailed fist into the speaker, silencing the wizened voice in an explosion of sparks.

He stood then, alone in the cramped cabin of the Pathfinder, over the broken body of the astrogator, listening to the rain pattering the hull, watching the acrid-smelling ammonia streak from his shining metal hide as though repelled by its power, thinking furiously, feeling his heart slide into the deepest pit of his stomach. The old man's words played and replayed in his fevered brain.

Calling all Jedi. The war is over. All Jedi are ordered to return... The answer was there.

That message was not for him. He was no Jedi. He went to the controls and fired up the converters, chuckling to himself.

Maybe this war really was over. But it was a big galaxy. There was always war somewhere. There were voices in his ears, whispering of glories and triumphs past and yet to come. Dark, hissing voices that promised him secrets, and bade him use those secrets to great and terrible ends.

But not in the name of Telloti Cillmam'n. That was not even a Jedi's name, and he was now something more.

He was Malleus. The Hammer of the Dark Side.

SILVER AND SCARLET

WRITTEN BY **JAMES S. A. COREY**
ART BY **JOE CORRONEY AND BRIAN MILLER**

"Seddia Chaan," the guard said, repeating the name on my identification papers.

"Yes," I lied.

He handed the papers back, nodded his massive green-grey head, and stepped aside. I tried for the cool, polite smile I imagined a high-level arms manufacturer would spare to a doorman and walked into the club. After the heat and humidity, stepping into the cool, dry air was like arriving on another world. Oolan was a barge city on an open sea, its buildings linked by bridges and separated by canals in a constantly shifting architecture. This month, the currents had taken it north, almost to the planetary equator. Next, it might drift south until blue-green ice pounded against the buildings' foundations and frost covered the bridges' handrails. By then, I planned to be back with the rebel fleet, deliveries made and my latest false-self a fading memory. If I was still in Oolan tomorrow, it would mean something unexpected had happened.

Given my track record, it could go either way.

The private club was built as a single wide circular room with windows three meters high at the outer edge. At the center, a hub of black made up the private meeting rooms and lifts to the upper levels. A recording of Bith harp music filled the air, the reproduction so clean the notes felt like they had edges. Outside the great windows, the city curved up, shifted, fell away, then curved up again, carried by the ocean swell. A dozen brightly colored skimmers buzzed along the canal, the human and Quarren drivers seemingly in competition to see who could be the most reckless. I tugged down on the hem of my jacket and looked around casually at the dozen or so club members lounging at tables and couches. The man I was looking for was human, older, and I'd only seen pictures and holograms of him. Trying to seem nonchalant, I touched my comlink.

"Elfour?"

"Ma'am," the droid's deep, gravelly voice came.

"How sure are we that he's here?"

"Ninety-six percent certainty."

"Okay, so run down that last four percent for me."

"The general might have been discovered, and the individual who rode his flyer down from the orbital base might have been an impostor," my lookout droid said. "Trouble inside, ma'am?"

"Just trying to find him. Let me take another pass," I said, and dropped the connection. Seddia Chaan, security engineer for the Salantech Cooperative, would have marched around the room with the crisp, studied movement and impassive expression of the ex-military operative that she was. Since I was playing her, I faked it. A serving droid floated over to me and asked in a carefully designed voice whether it could bring me anything to drink. Seddia Chaan didn't use intoxicants, so I asked for tea. The people at the tables and couches glanced at me and then away, polite and distant in a way that would have told me I was at the heart of the Empire even if I'd woken up there with my mind blanked.

I'd started the operation months before, following a rumor that the warden of an Imperial political prison might have been growing sympathetic to some of his prisoners. It had taken weeks to run down, since it wasn't an Imperial warden, there wasn't a prison involved, and General Cascaan didn't actually have much sympathy for the rebellion. But apart from every single bit of information being wrong, things had gone pretty well. I'd tracked Cascaan to the Entiia system, found his clandestine lover in Oolan, and opened negotiations. The whole process had been about as safe and certain as balancing a Verdorian fire rat on my nose, but I'd managed it, all except the last part. The actual meeting and exchange.

I was on my third pass around the room and almost done with my cup of tea when I recognized him. He was sitting alone at a small, high table almost against

the window. His hand was pressed to his mouth, his gaze fixed on the glittering crystal-and-silver of the complex across the canal from us. Once I spotted him, I could forgive myself for not recognizing him at once. All the pictures I'd seen had been of a straight-backed, high-chinned man with bright black eyes and a challenging glare. The man at the table was slumped over. His dark skin had an ashen tone, and his eyes were wet and rheumy. When he shifted in his seat, I could see the physical power in his body, but when he was still, he looked like someone's grandpa.

I felt my heart drop into my belly. Last-minute changes were always a hazard in this kind of operation.

In my work, I'd seen the whole spectrum of betrayers, from the ones who were afraid of getting caught to those who were excited by being naughty to others for whom it was just business. The man at the table looked sickened by it. That was bad. I put on Seddia Chaan's smile and started over.

"Ma'am?" L4-3PO said.

"It's all right, I found him."

"We have another problem. A flyer has landed on the tower's upper pad. Registration identifies it as the private craft of Nuuian Sulannis."

"Maybe he's a club member," I said.

"The chances of the Imperial interrogator who has been investigating the general arriving at the meeting by coincidence are—"

"I was joking, sweetie. Thank you for the warning. Talk to the club's computer system if you can, and try to slow him down. I'll be quick."

"Yes, ma'am."

I slid into the chair across from Cascaan. He looked up, and for a moment surprise registered in his eyes. Then a slow, rueful smile. "You're Hark, then?"

"Yes, sir," I said.

"I was expecting a man."

"That's a common prejudice," I said. "I won't take it personally."

I plucked the credit chit out of my jacket pocket and placed it on the table. The black tabletop made the silver chit seem brighter than it was. The general scowled at it and took a red-enameled memory crystal from his pocket. I waited, forcing my body to stay relaxed and calm while the sense of the chief interrogator landing his ship five levels above me crawled up my spine.

"I take it those are the plans we discussed?" I said, trying to make it sound casual and still keep the ball rolling.

The general scowled and nodded at the same time. The grip of his finger and thumb on the memory crystal didn't relax. I had the sense that if I'd reached out for it, he'd pluck it away from me. When he spoke, his voice was low and precise.

"Have you ever betrayed something?"

I felt my heart drop into my belly. Last-minute changes of heart were always a hazard in this kind of operation. Usually, I could budget a few hours to get the target drunk and maudlin, sing a few songs about glory and lost love, and pretty

much provide whatever handholding and consolation they needed to make the exchange. This was not one of those times. If he decided to turn me down, the plans for the next-generation Star Destroyers would fade away from me like smoke in a fist. Also, I'd probably get killed. Not the outcomes I was aiming for.

"I have, but not lightly," I said. "I always had my reasons."

"Do you regret them? Your betrayals?"

"No."

He dropped the memory crystal into his palm and closed his fist around it. There were tears in his eyes. In other circumstances, I would have found the gesture less frustrating. "I have been a loyal subject of the Emperor. I have followed the orders of my commanders. I told myself we were bringing order to the galaxy because that was what they told us. Who was I to disagree?"

I leaned forward and put my hand gently on his wrist. "I understand," I said.

"If we do this thing," Cascaan said, "I will be responsible for the deaths of thousands of soldiers."

"And if we don't? How many people will die if we call the whole thing off? And will they be soldiers, or innocent people who happen to live on worlds the Emperor has decided don't pay him enough respect?"

"No one else has access to these. When they get out, it will be known that I have turned against them. They will slaughter me for this."

His fingers didn't loosen their grip. I switched tack, taking my hand off his and tapping the silver chit. "There is enough money on this to make you safe. You'll be able to fade into the Rim, find a quiet spot, a new name. A new face. You'll be all right."

"Will I, Hark? Does my conscience count for nothing?"

Don't rush him, I told myself. *He's already halfway to spooked, and if you hurry him, he's just going to freeze up.* I took a deep breath, let it out slowly, made my shoulders relax and my expression soften. The serving droid hissed up to my left with a fresh cup of tea. The city outside the windows rose and fell.

I had maybe two minutes.

"Of course it counts," I said. "I'm getting the sense, sir, that there's something you want to tell me."

"You know I commanded the assault on Buruunin."

I wondered, if I lunged for him, if I'd be able to get the plans and run out the door before anyone tackled me. It didn't seem likely.

"I do," I said. "I lost people I cared about in that attack."

"The cities were undefended," he said. "As soon as we received the order for the bombardment, I knew I would have to betray my Emperor. My Empire. Those deaths brought no order. Only fear. They were wrong."

"Didn't call off the attack, though," I said, more sharply than I should have. He didn't flinch or tighten his grip on the plans.

"It would have made no difference. I would have been executed, and my second in command would have given the order. Insubordination is a fool's way to die. I have my honor, but I am not a fool."

I had maybe a minute and a half. This wasn't going well.

"Afterward," General Cascaan said, "there were any number of collaborators. They came to every outpost we made, telling us that they had information for sale. Where the rebels were hiding, who had aided them, where their caches of weapons were. For a few credits, they would have informed on their mothers."

"They were desperate," I said. "They were afraid."

He turned to look at me straight on. I hadn't realized until now that he'd been avoiding my eyes. There was a pain in his expression that took my breath away. I'd been working underground for a long time, and somewhere along the way, I'd let Cascaan and men like him turn into a kind of faceless enemy to me. Well, here was his face, and the foursquare leader of soldiers wasn't in him.

"*I* am desperate," he said softly. "*I* am afraid. Those people I despised—and I *despised* them, Hark—I have now become. I am selling the trust I have been given for money. For safety. For the beautiful lie that I can be a better man by making this devil's bargain."

"They were refugees of a planet-wide military attack. You're one of the most powerful men in the Empire," I said. "Seems to me, you're in a kind of a different position."

"And does that speak better of me? Or worse?"

"Better," I said, mostly because it seemed like the answer most likely to get him to open his fingers. I wondered, if I lunged for him, if I'd be able to get the plans and run out the door before anyone tackled me. It didn't seem likely. And if I told him we were both about to get arrested by the Empire, I didn't like my chances for moving the process any further forward.

"I disagree," the general said. "This trade is ignoble. It leaves me no better than them. I cannot take your money."

He was backing out. My comlink chimed. Grimacing, I touched it. "Bad time, Elfour. Kind of in the middle of something."

"Ma'am, I have done all that I could. That... *situation* will require your attention."

Cascaan had opened his grip. The red enamel caught the light from the window, shining in his palm like he was cupping a handful of blood. I looked over to the dark wall of private rooms and lifts at the club's center.

Time for plan C.

"Can you hold that thought?" I said, holding up a finger. "I'll be right back."

I walked toward the lifts, thinking through all the ways this could go and how I could affect which one actually happened. The serving droid swooped in to see if I wanted something for my tea, and I waved it away. I couldn't tell if my unsteadiness was the adrenaline or if the city had hit some bigger waves than usual.

The difference between safe and too late was going to be seconds. The doors shuddered and slid open.

"Elfour," I said to my comlink. "Do we know where he is?"

"Interrogator Sulannis is in the lift, coming toward the main floor, ma'am."

"Can we shut down the lift?"

"I have already done so once, ma'am. He is using his security override. I am locked out."

A whole host of solutions crumbled and died. On the one hand, less to think about. On the other, they were the ones I liked best. I was over halfway to the center. "Which lift is he in?"

To my right, a lift door slid open and an older Quarren woman stepped out. Not Sulannis.

"Elfour, which lift is he in?"

"Querying, ma'am."

"Sooner's better."

"Six."

I angled off to my left, not running but walking faster. My choices were getting thin quickly. The coppery taste of panic filled my mouth, and I ignored it.

The lift doors were black enamel and smooth as a mirror. I made my reflection look calm, prim, maybe a little bored. The difference between safe and too late was going be seconds. The doors shuddered and slid open. Nuuian Sulannis stood in the lift car, the light seeming to fall into his black uniform like it was woven out of black holes. He started to step out, and I faked my way in front of him, then corrected when he did, making it into a little dance of awkwardness and social misstep. His scowl could have peeled the shell off a Keeb beetle.

"Sorry," I said. And then, "Aren't you Interrogator Sulannis?"

He had time to register surprise and I planted a straight kick just above his pelvis. The blow was designed to stagger him back, and it worked. The lift doors slid closed and I slipped between them as he regained his balance. I pushed the controls for the landing pad.

Close quarters fighting, especially when the opponent was so much bigger than me, meant grappling techniques. I started

with an elbow lock, but he shrugged it off through equal part luck and brute strength. He hit me twice in the ribs, but the cramped lift car made it hard to get much power behind the blows, giving me the opportunity for a leg sweep that took him down. Once I got my arm around his neck, it was over, but the choke took long, terrible seconds to take effect. When he finally went limp under me, we were already at the landing pad. I hit the controls to take me back down before anyone could see a disheveled weapons engineer straddling the unconscious body of an Imperial interrogator.

I had one dose of sedative left in my shoe. I used it on him, stopped the car on the third level, dragged Sulannis to the women's room and propped him in a stall. All in all, it took less than five minutes.

On the way back down, I tugged my costume back into place, smoothing out the wrinkles while I tried to think how to coax the general back into making the trade. As soon as the lift doors opened, I knew it was over. The little table we'd been sitting at was empty. Cascaan was nowhere I could see. Little wisps of steam wafted from my cup of tea as I came close. The sinking in my gut was disappointment and anger and frustration, but there was something else, too. Some part of my mind that told me I was missing something. This wasn't what it looked like.

"Ma'am?" L4-3PO said on my comlink. "Is all well?"

On the black table, the silver chit with Cascaan's payment glowed. Beside it, the bright red of the memory crystal. He'd left the plans and the payment too. He was going to get caught, and he knew it, and there was nothing I could do to stop it. When I looked up, he was there. Outside the window, walking across the canal bridge and away from me. His back was straight and proud, his head high. It was the first time he'd seemed like the man from the holograms. A warrior, ready to fight. Ready to die.

I scooped up silver and red and put them in my pocket before I touched my comlink. "Time to go. Get the skimmer warmed up, and let's get back to the ship. We need to be out of here before Sulannis wakes up."

"Yes, ma'am," the droid said. "May I ask whether you got what you came for?"

"I did," I said.

"And the general?"

Cascaan reached the other side of the bridge, turned right, and stepped out of my line of sight.

"He did too."

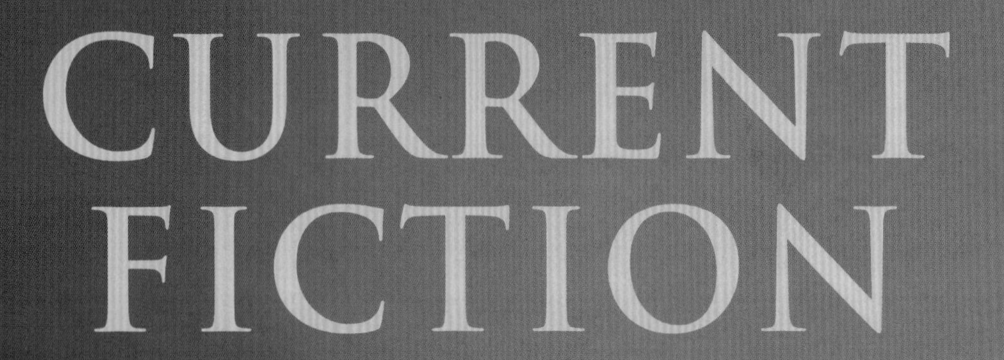

The following stories represent tales from current continuity, that ran from 2014 to 2017.

LAST CALL AT THE ZERO ANGLE

WRITTEN BY **JOE SCHREIBER**
ART BY **JOHN VAN FLEET**

Tana Chellaine knew trouble was coming for the TIE fighter pilots of Nashtah Squadron when Huck Trompo started to sing.

The problem wasn't that Trompo was singing a ground-hog anthem in the bar—the Zero Angle was no stranger to pilots bellowing beloved unit anthems over the thump of its jukebox. It was that Trompo was singing that anthem while staring challengingly at a table a meter away, one occupied by a quartet of angry-looking vac-heads.

"Trompo, you better end transmission," Chellaine warned. "Florn's giving you the evil eye."

Sax Hastur, Nashtah's squad leader, turned in his chair to regard Florn, the tough old cyborg bartender who ran the Angle with a literal iron fist. Florn was washing a glass with his usual grim precision, but the red pinpoints of his cybernetic eyes were locked on Trompo.

"Better do something, Sax," muttered Artur Essada. "Before Sully starts singing too."

Essada's prediction was right, as was true annoyingly often. Sully Olvar shoved his chair back and rose unsteadily to his feet to join his wingmate and partner-in-crime in song. Trompo grinned and raised his glass, but found Hastur's hand locked on his forearm.

"Throttle down, Huck," Hastur warned. "It's too early to start a furball between ground-hogs and vac-heads."

"C'mon, boss," Trompo complained. "Been a long day."

"I know it," Hastur said. "But I'm not signing you out of the brig again. Hey, Flornie? Couple more Eblas?"

Chellaine shook her head as Trompo and Olvar reluctantly planted their rears back in their chairs. The Nashtahs were ground-hogs—TIE fighter pilots who flew in planetary atmospheres on missions for the Imperial Army. Maneuvering a TIE through goo was more difficult than flying through the emptiness of space—that was the domain of the vac-heads who flew for the Imperial Navy. Yet it was the vac-heads who wound up on the recruiting posters, and whose victories over rebels, pirates, and slavers dominated the HoloNet.

No ground-hog thought that was fair. But resenting it was one thing—trying to goad vac-heads into fistfights while off duty was something else.

With the threat of a brawl momentarily averted, Chellaine let her gaze wander around the bar. As usual, the Angle was packed with Imperial pilots—crashing glasses together, arguing loudly about tactics, or just sitting quietly. Nearly all of the pilots were human, and Chellaine could judge how long they'd been at the bar by the state of their olive-green uniform tunics. Some were perfectly crisp, suggesting their owners were new arrivals. Others were wrinkled and/or stained, adorning pilots who should have left some time ago. And a few had been removed and discarded on the backs of chairs, a sure sign of a debacle in progress.

Chellaine's own tunic was immaculate, but then she never drank anything stronger than water—and distilled water at that.

The Angle was famous for a number of things: its implacable bartender, its policy of serving ground-hogs and vac-heads alike, and its long-standing tradition that anyone above the rank of squad leader stayed out. That made it a sanctuary for the pilots of Bright Jewel Oversector Flight Base, which dominated the drab surface of the moon Axxila III. Within the confines of the Angle, a pilot was free to get sloppy, angry, or maudlin without risking a black mark on his or her service record.

Trompo drained his Ebla and gazed at the ceiling for a long moment. Chellaine waited for his eyes to close and his head to flop backwards in his chair. If that happened, should she grab his chair, or let him crash to the floor? She wasn't sure.

But then Trompo leaned forward, eyes bright above his flushed cheeks.

"Those vac-heads were going to *love* my song," he insisted, bringing his fist down on the table hard enough to make the glasses jump.

"They *absolutely* were," Olvar said, backing up his wingmate as always.

Chellaine shook her head, deciding that if it came to it this time she'd let Trompo risk a cracked skull. Perhaps it would knock some sense into him. Trompo was a brilliant pilot with an instinctive grasp of

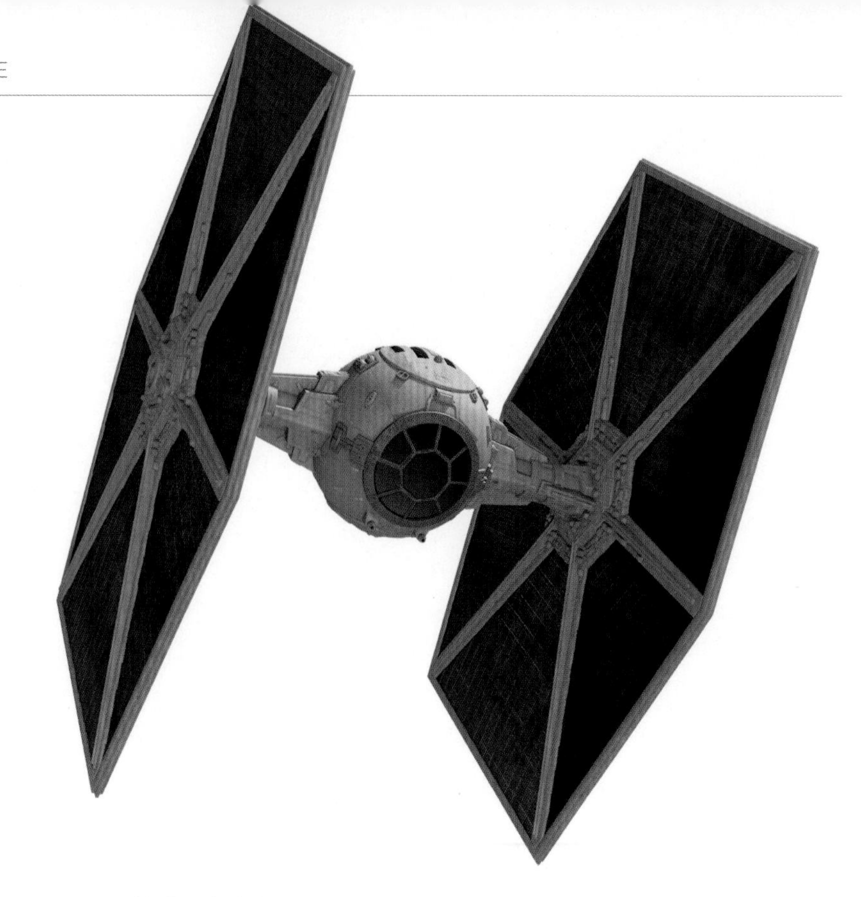

tactics, but he had the impulse control of a sand-panther in heat.

"We should talk about what happened at Portocari," Essada said quietly.

The other Nashtahs' eyes all turned to Essada, who was gazing down at the scarred surface of the wooden table.

"There's nothing to talk about," Hastur said, seeking refuge in his glass of vosh. "We accomplished the mission. That will happen again. We lost people. That will happen again, too."

"But the intel—" began Essada.

"The mission's *over*," Trompo said angrily, slashing at the air for emphasis. The gesture knocked over Essada's glass of lum, sending the other Nashtahs backpedaling from the table to avoid the rapidly forming lake. "The mission's over and I feel like a song. A song that all these laser-brained vac-heads better enjoy."

Thrusting his Ebla into the air, Trompo roared out the opening line of the ground-hogs' anthem:

"Oh who flies so high in the skies so blue?"

Which prompted Olvar to shout the traditional response:

"WE DO! WE DO!"

"Brace for impact," Chellaine muttered to Hastur as other tables of ground-hogs joined in the singing.

"It's been a bad day, Tana," Hastur said quietly. "Blowing out a few bad ions keeps them sane."

Chellaine scowled behind the cup she'd rescued from the flooded table. The vac-heads at the next table exchanged glances and got to their feet, nodding at each other. When Trompo stopped to breathe, they were ready with the beginning of their own song:

"Who's on the attack in space so black?"

Which was followed by shouts from at least four tables of vac-heads:

"WE ARE! WE ARE!"

Essada sighed and sipped what he'd been able to salvage of his lum. "I wouldn't mind all the commotion if even one of these idiots could carry a tune."

For a minute or so, disaster remained hypothetical. Trompo and Olvar circulated through the Angle trying to rally their fellow ground-hogs to drown out the vac-heads, the vac-heads redoubled their efforts, and Florn confined himself to a slow, annoyed shake of his head. But then a drink got spilled, or perhaps thrown, and words were exchanged, and soon enough glass was breaking and fists were flying.

"Let me know when Lightning shows up," Hastur said wearily.

Hastur stepped back as Olvar and a wiry vac-head began grappling. A moment later, Essada dodged as Trompo hurled a burly pilot onto their table. The fallen pilot sprang up and bull-rushed the Nashtah, the two coming together with an impact of flesh punctuated by grunts and curses.

A vac-head who'd been on the wrong end of a punch stumbled into Chellaine, sending a ribbon of water out of her cup and up into the air. She moved smoothly to one side to catch the water as it fell and then booted the vac-head in the rear, propelling him back into the melee. Trompo tried to get behind the vac-head he was fighting, but was too slow and took a hard left on the point of his chin. He staggered and crashed down on the corner of the table, which let out a groan of overstressed wood and tipped, depositing Trompo on the floor surrounded by glasses and puddles. Then the table fell on him.

"Incoming," Chellaine warned Hastur as a glossy black astromech adorned with jagged yellow stripes rolled out from behind the bar. A sphere on a metal stalk rose from a hatch in its dome. Florn followed a step behind the droid, tucking his rag into his apron.

The Nashtahs clapped their hands over their ears, as did all the pilots who weren't too busy fighting to notice the droid's arrival.

"Five seconds ought to do it, Lightning," Florn said.

A shriek from Lightning's sonic emitter filled the Angle. The brawling pilots crumpled to the floor, hands fumbling to protect their ears.

"That one started it," Florn said, pointing at Trompo, who was trying to crawl away. Lightning tootled cheerfully, and a panel opened on his front. He extended a prod and jabbed it into Trompo's side, enveloping the pilot in brilliant sparks. Trompo yelped and rolled into the fetal position, kicking feebly at his tormentor.

"Really, Flornie?" he complained. "The shrieker wasn't enough so you had to try and stun me?"

"You were doing a capital job stunning yourself," Florn said. "Now get up, all of you. Get up and shake hands."

The ground-hogs and vac-heads

GLOSSARY: SELECTED PILOT SLANG

Dupe: a TIE bomber
Fangs out: eager for a dogfight
Furball: a hectic dogfight
Goo: a planet's atmosphere
Hop: a mission
Impstar: an Imperial Star Destroyer
In the black: operating in space
In the blue: operating in a planetary atmosphere
Sitrep: situation report
Skull: a Z-95 Headhunter fighter
Splash: shoot down
Stitched: hit by enemy fire
Suicide sled: a starfighter with weak or no shields
Zero angle: the position behind an enemy's stern

muttered mutinously, but Lightning rolled forward with an electronic chuckle, prod crackling with energy. The pilots shook hands mulishly, then began righting fallen chairs and retrieving tumbled glasses.

"Most flight bases have one bar for ground-hogs and another for vac-heads," Florn said. "You know why the Angle's different? Because all your little feuds are a bunch of poodoo. Doesn't matter if you fly in the blue or the black, in goo or vacuum. We all fly suicide sleds—no shields and no defenses. Except for the skill of the hand on the stick."

Florn signaled for Lightning to go back behind the bar, then swept the room with his cybernetic gaze.

"Rack up half the flight hours I had before the crash and you can talk as much trash as you want," he said with cool disapproval. "Or get turned into a fireball—that means you go on the wall and we'll speak well of you. But until you do one or the other, you mind your manners."

The servos in Florn's artificial legs whined as he stalked off. Chellaine wasn't the only pilot who found herself staring up at the wall above the bar, at the shimmering holos of faces and unit designations. Those faces belonged to ground-hogs and vac-heads alike, all of them men and women who'd flown out of Axxila on missions from which they'd never returned.

"There are Suthers and Plix," Chellaine said, pointing at two holos.

"And Ashanto," Hastur added grimly.

"You mean Poul Ashanto?" asked one of the vac-heads, sounding surprised.

"I do," Hastur said. "We were friends."

Chellaine wondered if anyone besides her knew what an understatement that was.

"Poul was at Prefsbelt with my brother Alois," the vac-head said.

"Alois Akrone?" Hastur asked. "The three of us were classmates together. He was your brother? Then you must be Heiwei."

"The same," Heiwei Akrone said, nodding at the three vac-heads with him. "We're Banshee Squadron, attached to the Impstar *Solar Storm*. Just in from Phindar."

"Sax Hastur. We're the Nashtahs. Just finished debriefing after Portocari."

Hastur and Akrone shook hands as the other Nashtahs and Banshees eyed each other uncertainly.

"Since you're all best friends now, you can share a table," Florn called from behind the bar.

"That's not happening," Trompo said as the hulking Banshee standing beside him said, "No way." Both men's faces were puffy and cut.

Florn shrugged. "You broke the table, so it's share or stand."

The Nashtahs and Banshees dragged over the one remaining table, gathered the dispersed chairs, and sat down together amid glances of mutual suspicion. Hastur and Akrone ordered a round of drinks.

The muscled Banshee next to Trompo touched his swollen cheek gingerly.

"They call me Bruiser," he said. "You threw a good punch back there."

Trompo looked surprised. "Really? It didn't even make you blink. And if you hadn't slipped back there, you'd have flattened my nose."

Within the confines of the Angle, a pilot was free to get sloppy, angry, or maudlin without risking a black mark on his or her service record.

Trompo and Bruiser plunged into an animated conversation about the finer points of brawling, while Olvar waited for a chance to join in and the other pilots looked up at the wall, lost in their private thoughts.

"My brother's on the wall, too," Akrone said, pointing.

Hastur located the holo of his old classmate and raised his glass. One by one the others did the same.

"Now we've got three more Nashtahs to add," Essada muttered.

Akrone nodded. "We lost two pilots at Phindar ourselves. I saw Portocari on the sitrep. It was rough, then?"

"It was," Hastur said before Essada could speak. "We were hitting rebel artillery in the hills when we got the call to regroup for a strike on an urban safehouse. The brass said hitting it would prevent house-to-house fighting and civilian casualties."

Akrone nodded, listening.

"The rebs brought down Muller with an anti-air warhead—she's in bacta. Barsay got stitched by a Z-95 inbound to the safehouse —he's dead. We splashed the Skull that killed him, along with its wingmates. Then one of our bombers hit the safehouse. Turned out it was full of munitions—the blast vaporized both our Dupe and her escort."

"Riggs and Chan," Essada said. "They had names too, you know."

"You think I don't remember that?" Hastur snapped, and Essada lowered his eyes.

Hastur shook his head, finger tracing the rings on the table left by generations of previous drinks. "Riggs and Chan. We would have opted for a high-altitude run with burrowing warheads if we'd known."

"They never knew what hit 'em," Trompo said. "That's something at least."

"What are you talking about?" Essada demanded. "It's *nothing*. Three pilots dead, and Muller may never fly again. And for what?"

"So the intel was bad?" Akrone asked quickly, mindful of the two Nashtahs glaring at each other.

Hastur shook his head, but his hand went for his drink. "That's above my pay grade."

"You want to blame someone, Artur?" Trompo growled at Essada. "Start with the rebels for once. They claim they're fighting for the common people, and now thousands in that city are dead because of what they did."

"That's right—if the brass had learned it was a munitions depot, they'd have canceled the strike," Olvar said.

The Nashtahs and Banshees nodded—except for Essada.

"I'm not sure I believe that any more," he said.

"That's rebel talk, Artur," Trompo said. "How many times have I got to tell you I don't like hearing it?"

"And how long are you going to fly blind?" Essada asked heatedly, then pointed an accusing finger at Hastur. "And how long are you going to pretend this isn't happening?"

Chellaine had had enough.

"If you've got something to say, Essada, say it," she said. "What is it you think is happening?"

"We've been flying fangs out for a week, and on half the hops, we've been given intel that's unverified or out of date or both," Essada said. "And it's not just us—I hear it's been like this for squadrons all the way to the galactic rim. Something's happened, and the Empire's responding by pounding every target it can find."

Trompo's face had turned an ominous purple. He started to object, but stopped when he saw the look on Bruiser's face.

"It's been the same for us," Akrone said. "Listen to this—four days ago, a whole wing from Celanon was diverted to sweep duty, looking for a high-value target in the Gordian Reach. And I hear the Empire's sending a task force to the Jovan system."

"Jovan?" Hastur asked. "There's nothing out there but grain barges."

Akrone shrugged. "I know. The point is, something big's gone down, and it's got the brass scared. I hear Weller himself just came back from Ord Mantell."

"Look, maybe something big *is* going on," Chellaine said. "But what does it matter? We'll never find out what it was."

"It matters because it's our lives," Essada said. "Or at least it does to me."

Chellaine heard the doors to the Angle open behind her, as they did dozens of times an hour. But then the eyes of the pilots looking that way widened, and chairs began to scrape on the floor. She turned and was getting to her feet even before her brain had processed the astonishing fact that Commander Weller himself was standing in the Angle.

"At ease," Weller said. "Haven't been in here since I made wing commander. I've missed it."

He walked over to the bar, where Florn stood waiting.

"Corellian brandy," Weller said. "The good stuff."

Florn placed a glass on the bar, then set another one beside it. He filled them with deep, golden-brown liquor. He and Weller raised their glasses and drank them down, returning them empty to the top of the bar at the same moment. Weller put his hand on Florn's flesh-and-blood shoulder, and the bartender did the same.

Then Weller turned to the assembled pilots.

"I apologize for invading sacred territory, but these are not normal times," he said. "There's something you all need to know—because pretty soon the whole galaxy will have heard the news."

Chellaine glanced at her fellow Nashtahs. Hastur was waiting grimly, while Trompo chewed his lip in anxious silence, next to a wide-eyed Olvar. Essada was leaning forward expectantly, eyes locked on Weller.

"The DS-1 platform," Weller said. "It's been destroyed."

Chellaine and Akrone exchanged a stunned glance. The DS-1? The so-called Death Star? Chellaine had assumed that was a codename for some kind of coordinated fire-control technology among fleet units, while Essada had dismissed it as a black-budget item created for propaganda purposes. But here was their wing commander, telling them it was real. Or *had* been real.

"Destroyed, sir?" someone asked from the back of the bar. "How?"

"By the Rebellion," Weller said. "Along with its entire complement."

There was a moment of shocked silence

"I hear it's been like this for squadrons all the way to the Galactic Rim. Something's happened, and the Empire's responding by pounding every target it can find."

and then everyone began talking at once. A bark from Weller stilled the tumult.

"Your current Army and Navy affiliations are rescinded effective immediately," he said.

The Nashtahs and Banshees gaped at one another.

"You heard me," Weller said. "All elements of the Imperial starfleet have been placed on full alert. Return to quarters for assignment to new squadrons. Ladies and gentlemen, the Empire's enemies are on the move, and we must meet them on the battlefield—whether that battlefield is in the sky, or in space."

Weller nodded at the pilots, then at Florn, then turned and strode through the doors. As the pilots hurriedly gathered their gear, Chellaine found herself next to the bar, staring up at the wall of holos.

"There'll be a lot more faces up there before this is over," she said to Florn.

"Yes, there will be," the bartender replied, beginning to wash the glasses. "Some of them will be ones you know."

Chellaine nodded.

"Only one thing to do about it," Florn said.

"What's that?"

"The rebs have their own watering holes and their own walls," he said. "All pilots do. Make sure you put two of theirs up for every one of ours. Then you can come back here with your head held high, and raise a glass to the ones who didn't."

REBEL BLUFF

WRITTEN BY MICHAEL KOGGE

Lando Calrissian couldn't believe his bad luck. Another round of sabacc had dealt him yet another awful hand. To win the main pot and clear his debts, he needed his cards to total a positive or negative twenty-three. Right now he had a negative five—and things weren't looking like they were about to improve any time soon. It had been ten lousy deals in a row and he was down to his last credits.

He took stock of how his competition fared around the table. Old Jho, the cantina's Ithorian proprietor, remained quiet and still, except for a vein twitching along the trunk of his neck, betraying his distress. On the other hand, the young woman seated next to him, a brunette in an expeditionary jacket and baggy trousers, didn't seem at all bothered by her cards. She took sips from her beverage and looked absently around the cantina.

Lando wagered she came from Capital City, as her face had none of the wind-cut lines of growing up on Lothal's plains, and her hands, delicate and uncalloused, spoke of office work, probably in a data center. Her eyes revealed the most, as they always did with humans. There was a roguish glint to them, a sparkle of intelligence that belied her naïve appearance. No matter how hard she tried to affect a casual indifference, she couldn't hide from Lando that her gaze kept drifting to the cantina entrance. This woman was anticipating that someone might storm in, perhaps a crazy ex-lover or bill collector. This was a woman on the run.

The final player, a Devaronian with a broken horn, showed no hint of anxiety. Nor should he have. Cikatro Vizago was the big winner so far, having collected most of the hand pots from the individual rounds. Still, it was obvious he wanted more. His nails clicked on the table's surface, fingers encroaching on the sabacc pot that, unlike the hand pots, grew in credits with every round.

"Claws off, Vizago," Lando said, "unless you're calling sabacc."

The gangster gave Lando a sharp-toothed smile that could've made him a star in a horror holo. "I might just be," he said in his thick accent. "Ready to fold?"

"You should know I don't fold. I only win," Lando said. He might have the lousiest hand of the bunch, but he'd never show it. He'd won with less.

"Then let me make this worth your while." Vizago dumped a handful of credit chits to the sabacc pot, raising the bet by a thousand.

"I'm out," groaned Jho through the translator covering his mouths. He dropped his cards into the table's suspension field which locked their face values to a total of negative nine.

"Me too," said the woman, to Lando's surprise. She didn't seem to realize that she'd folded on a strong hand. The positive eighteen she put into the suspension field might have won if she'd continued to play.

Vizago spread his fingers out on the table, stretching them. Few would have thought anything of it, but for Lando the action exposed the gangster's bluff. The Devaronian had been rapping his nails against the table throughout the game, and this brief moment of respite demonstrated a change in his mood. Mostly likely he was relieved that the woman had folded, which meant he possessed a card total lower than the woman's eighteen.

Lando touched the chits in his pocket. He had nowhere near the thousand needed to stay in the game. What he did have was a keycard to his Ubrikkian 9000. He'd recently bought the landspeeder for scouting potential mining sites on farmland he'd purchased from Vizago—and for which he still owed a chunk of credits.

He sized up the sabacc pot, significantly fattened by Vizago's contribution. The pile would more than pay his debt. And with two players out of the game, Lando liked the odds. Years on the casino circuit had taught him when to double down. In the right situation, luck could be as reliable as a trusty blaster.

Lando tossed in his keycard. "All I got."

Vizago snarled. "Oh no. Don't try to pawn off your junker on me, Calrissian."

"An Ubrikkian 9000? That's not junk."

The woman's roving eyes fixed on the keycard. "Even as parts, it's worth more than the pot. Miners are clamoring for them."

Lando gave her an appreciative nod. "The lady knows."

"Those Ubriks are a sight for sore eyes if you ask me. More like an escape pod than a speeder," Old Jho said.

"I agree." Vizago's pupils narrowed to needlepoints. "But I'll let you slide this time, Calrissian—though I pray you'll have something left to pay me after our fun is done."

"How about the pot?" Lando said, smirking.

The sabacc table beeped, indicating commencement of the shifting phase. This was Lando's favorite part of the game, when the table's randomizer took control of the cards and transmitted signals to the receptors embedded in each. His cards began to blur and cycle through the various suits of Staves, Coins, Flasks, and Sabres, presenting brand new totals, new ways to win—and lose. Like a cosmic tease, an Idiot's Array flashed before his eyes, only to be replaced moments later by a pair of Evil Ones. Those cards themselves vanished to become something different, then something different again, offering up a cosmos of possibilities.

Lando's heart pounded. His mind speculated. While the cards kept changing, the shifting phase could end at any moment, its duration as random as its shuffle. Not knowing was the thrill. It was why he gambled. It was why he played. This was life, lived right on the edge, where one's future and fate could be determined by nothing other than pure chance.

Everyone was watching him. They would see nothing unusual. Unlike them, he'd perfected his sabacc face. Though his heart might hammer and his mind might race, on the surface Lando remained calm and collected.

When the phase ended and the cards resolved into their final ranks, his instincts proved him right again. He put his cards into the suspension field, showing an Eleven, Three, and Nine, all positive, all of Sabres. "Sabacc," he said, smoothly, as if it was to be expected.

Vizago roared, pounding the table. He chucked his cards into the field. "Cheater!"

"Nope. Just my luck."

Lando reached for the pot when a loud clunk distracted him. He turned to see an IG-RM enforcer droid stationed outside the cantina's rear doorway.

"I thought we agreed your buddies weren't permitted," Lando said.

"Inside, we did," Vizago said. "And I promise, it won't come in."

It didn't need to. One of the droid's arms had been rigged into a blaster cannon.

A well-placed shot could end Lando's sabacc career for good.

But Lando should have known not to underestimate Old Jho. "You bet it won't," the Ithorian said. Old Jho pressed a button on his belt, and a blast door whisked shut in front of the droid. "I can't stand those droids. Now get out," he told Vizago.

"Jho, come on, I just wanted to make sure everything was fair. Why don't we forget about it and keep playing, so everyone has a chance to win back their credits," Vizago said. "You'd be up for another game, wouldn't you, Calrissian?"

"Sorry, Vizago. Gotta get home. My puffer pig gets huffy if she isn't walked."

Vizago rose from the table. "How about I take *you* for a walk?"

Lando ignored him, noticing the chair next to Jho was unoccupied. "Where'd our friend go?"

Jho swiveled his head. "I didn't even see her leave."

Lando scanned the cantina. A group of freighter bums made merry at the bar, while two Snivvians snuggled in a dark booth. There was no sign of the young woman.

"The sabacc pot," Vizago said. "She stole it!"

A glance at the table confirmed it was missing. "*Karabast*," Lando swore, using a word he'd only recently learned. He should've been paying more attention. In all the commotion with Vizago, she must have grabbed the pot and slipped away.

The sudden arrival of an Imperial troop transport set those concerns aside. The gray-hulled repulsorcraft parked outside the entrance, its forward and aft gun turrets pointing menacingly at the cantina. Three stormtroopers debarked from its cab.

All merry-making at the bar ended, as did cuddling in the booth. Vizago slunk back into the shadows. The cantina became so quiet Lando could hear the clacking of the stormtroopers' armor plates as they marched inside, rifles ready.

"Can I get you all some refreshments?" Jho asked.

The squad leader, his rank indicated by the orange pauldron on his shoulder, snorted. "I should arrest you for attempting to poison an officer of the Empire. Humans don't drink alien swill."

"Sir, I've served some of the best TIE pilots on Lothal—"

"Shut your mouths, leatherneck." The squad leader gestured and the trooper behind him activated a holopad. It projected a blue hologram of the now absent young woman, except instead of the jacket and trousers she wore the garb of a government bureaucrat.

"We have reports this traitor was in the vicinity. Has she come in here?"

Old Jho hesitated, his vein bulging like a tree root. Despite the fact that the woman had robbed them, Lando knew Jho would never risk his reputation and hand someone over to the Empire.

Lando stepped forward to study the hologram. "Who is she?" All blasters immediately turned on him. "Gentlemen, please," he said, using his best placating tone. "I want to help you."

"Identify yourself," ordered the squad leader.

"Name's Lando Calrissian. Recent transplant to Lothal and loyal patriot of the Galactic Empire. You can check my record."

There was a pause as a trooper did just that. For a few seconds, all Lando heard was garbled comm traffic echoing inside the trooper's helmet. He wasn't nervous. His past might not be squeaky clean, but his datafile in the Imperial Security Bureau's computers was. Before he'd come to Lothal, he paid a slicer a princely sum to polish his ISB record to make him seem like a shining paragon of Imperial citizenry.

"He's clear, sir," said the trooper.

The blasters lowered, but only a degree or two. "Her name is Ria Clarr," the squad leader said. "Previously an analyst at the Imperial Mining Institute, until her treasonous activity."

"What'd she do? Steal some files? Embarrass a lieutenant?"

"She deleted the databases for Lothal's geological surveys." The squad leader's blaster lifted again, and the others followed suit. "Where is she?"

"All right, all right, no need to get testy," Lando said, backing away. "Your hologram does resemble a woman I saw in here a few minutes ago. She had a quick drink, then made an exit out the way you entered."

"In what direction did she head?"

"No clue. Wasn't paying that much attention. But if I'd known she was wanted by the Empire, I would've done something. We all would've." Lando prompted Old Jho with a glance.

"Yes, yes," the Ithorian said. "I always report any treasonous activity I see."

The squad leader gave Jho a faceless stare, causing the Ithorian's vein to throb even more. Then the leader turned and walked out of the cantina, his troopers following.

"You're welcome," Lando said to the troopers. They did not respond.

Once the transport sped off, Vizago

emerged from the shadows. "I hadn't realized you were so devoted to the Empire, Calrissian."

"I came to Lothal to make my fortune as a miner, not a trouble-maker," Lando said. "But I also want my winnings. If she'd gone out the way I mentioned, she would've run smack into those stormtroopers before they got here."

Vizago glanced at the rear door, which remained shut. "Then how'd she leave?"

Lando looked to Jho for the answer. "In the kitchen, there's a door to the back lot," the Ithorian said.

Lando scowled. That was where he'd parked his Ubrikkian. And if she'd stolen the pot, she had his keycard.

He hurried through the kitchen, ignoring squeals from the Ugnaught cooks. But by the time he made it to the back lot, the spherical shape of his landspeeder was vanishing into the grasslands.

"Shouldn't have let you slide, Calrissian," Vizago said, coming up behind him.

Lando checked his chrono. It was linked to his speeder's navigation systems, allowing him to scroll through all pertinent information, from velocity to altitude to surrounding traffic and potential destinations. That final bit of data made him shudder.

"Game's not over yet. Warm up your speeder."

Vizago leaned over his shoulder. "You know where she's going?"

Lando looked up from his chrono. The plains dominated the horizon in all but one dark spot.

All merry-making at the bar ended, as did cuddling at the booth. Vizago slunk back into the shadows.

Though Tarkintown had received no official Imperial designation other than "Lothal re-settlement camp 43," everyone, even stormtroopers, identified it by its colloquial name. It had come into being when its namesake, Grand Moff Tarkin, had exercised the Empire's right of eminent domain on Lothal and ordered that all land rich in resources be seized for Imperial use. Those dispossessed of their land were forcibly resettled in a place so barren no crops could be cultivated, where even Lothal's ubiquitous grass grew sparse. This made it difficult to find a place to conceal Vizago's speeder. They had to park it a half klick away from the camp and leave the IG-RM droid behind as a guard.

Approaching Tarkintown on foot, Lando observed that it wasn't even a town, per se, but rather a collection of huts and hovels fashioned out of old shipping containers that were all huddled around the spire of a weather-beaten moisture vaporator. Rust had bored huge holes through the vaporator's shell and probably contaminated the drinking water it supplied. It also clearly didn't double as a communal refresher or pump a sanitation system. Coming to the outskirts of the camp, Lando sloshed through sludge he knew wasn't mud. He had to hold his nose—and breath—at times. Tarkintown reeked of filth and trash and all things gone to rot. The stench of extreme poverty.

"Lovely, eh?" Vizago said.

Lando said nothing. His mind was on his farm, only a few klicks away and yet a paradise compared to this. If his puffer pig ever sniffed out ore and his mining venture proved successful enough to hire a crew, he'd make sure he and his people all lived in comfort and peace. He would never be a Tarkintowner.

Lando's chrono directed them to the town's eastern edge, where they spotted the Ubrikkian hovering in standby mode behind a shanty. A man wearing a steel headband stood beside it, pressing Lando's keycard to the circular ports that ringed the capsule. When a hatch opened, the man jumped for joy and crawled inside.

"Hey—"

The noise of the Ubrikkian's micro-thrusters drowned out Lando's protests. Before he could get to the speeder, the man zoomed off into the prairie.

Vizago, meanwhile, went in the opposite direction, hurrying down an alley. Lando glanced one last time at his Ubrikkian, then followed.

In the center of the camp, Ria Clarr stood on the ledge of the moisture vaporator, besieged on all sides by refugees. Rodians, Gran, and humans alike reached and grabbed for the credit chits she doled out from her pocket like confetti.

"That infernal witch—how dare she!" Vizago drew his blaster and fired high into the air. Refugees scattered like Loth-rats, likely fearing an Imperial attack. TIE pilots were known to use the resettlement camps as target practice during patrols.

With the crowd disbanded, Vizago aimed his pistol at Clarr. "What in Malachor are you doing?"

Clarr dropped the few chits she still had and raised her hands in surrender. "Making amends."

"With my credits? I should burn a hole through your heart."

"Your memory is failing, Vizago." Lando strode forward. "I won those credits, so I decide who gets burned and who doesn't. Put the gun down."

"Calrissian, I'm done with your tricks."

Lando walked into the path of Vizago's blaster. "Shoot me or get paid. What'll it be?"

Sneering, the Devaronian lowered his pistol. Lando then faced the woman and studied her for the second time. The strange glint in her eyes he should've recognized. He'd seen it in a number of acquaintances he'd recently made.

He bent down and picked up a credit chit. "Amends for what?"

"For Tarkintown," she said. "I'm the reason this exists."

"That's ridiculous," Vizago said. "Everyone knows Tarkin ordered this camp built."

"Based on my reports," Clarr said. "My research for the Mining Institute concluded that a rich vein of ore lay below these people's farms. I personally convinced the Grand Moff that mining would be worth the effort. At the time, I believed the Empire was a force for good, and would help lift Lothal out of poverty and obscurity."

"What changed your mind?" Lando asked.

"Discovering the lies behind Imperial propaganda. Like most, I was aware this was a poor area, but only when I flew out here for a follow-up survey did I realize how bad conditions had become. For the longest time, I agonized over what to do, knowing I had been complicit in what was happening here. But I was afraid of doing anything myself—I was afraid of what the Empire would do to *me*—until I heard the Holonet broadcast by that boy, calling everyone to stand up against Imperial tyranny. I thought, if a kid wasn't afraid of defying the Empire, I shouldn't be either."

She was referring to Ezra Bridger, the youngest of those same acquaintances who had helped Lando acquire his puffer pig. Not soon after, the group had hacked into the Imperial communications network and spread a message of resistance to anyone with a Holonet receiver.

It was an inspiring message, Lando had to admit. But he preferred to stay out of galactic politics. Dealing with black

The stormtrooper squad leader leaned out of the hatch of the Imperial troop transport as it emerged from the smoke. He leapt down to the ground, joined by two troopers. All aimed their blaster rifles at Lando and Vizago.

market gangsters like Vizago caused him enough headaches.

"So you wiped all your research and fled Capital City," Lando said. "But why stop at Old Jho's? There are better places to hide in than in a sabacc game."

"She wanted the credits!" Vizago said.

Clarr shook her head. "The sabacc pot was an opportunity I couldn't pass up. But I came to Old Jho's searching for someone like you," she said, looking at Lando.

"You need the services of a gambler?" Vizago asked.

"A rebel."

Lando chuckled and gave her the same generous smile he'd given a thousand ladies whom he'd refused for one reason or another. "I'm humbled by your request, truly. But revolution is the one game I don't play."

"That's what I once thought," Clarr said, "but if you don't get involved, it's a game you're going to lose."

Lando's chrono beeped. He glanced at his wrist. The tracker showed his Ubrikkian had turned around and was traveling toward Tarkintown at high velocity. A second icon blinked behind it in pursuit and was gaining so fast, Lando didn't need to enlarge it to know what it was.

"I recommend hiding your true colors at the moment. We're about to have company," Lando said, "of the Imperial kind."

The pinging of lasers punctuated his warning. Speeding toward them from the west was Lando's Ubrikkian, with its aft section on fire. The man with the steel headband sat in the cockpit, turned upside down as the craft spun and arrowed right toward the camp.

Lando dove to the ground for cover. Seconds later, the man's joyride ended in a ground-shaking crash.

A scorching wave of heat passed over Lando, singeing his clothes and his back. He held his breath until he couldn't any longer, waiting for the smoke to clear. Finally he stood, coughing. Other than some minor burns, he'd suffered no injuries. His Ubrikkian, however, had experienced a horrible mechanical death. It lay twisted around the moisture vaporator, pieces of its fuselage strewn about. The figure in the cockpit did not move.

"You again," said a familiar, filtered voice.

The stormtrooper squad leader leaned out of the hatch of the Imperial troop transport as it emerged from the smoke. He leapt down to the ground, joined by two troopers. All aimed their blaster rifles at Lando and Vizago, and were backed up by the transport's forward laser turrets.

"Why, hello," Lando said, regaining his breath. "We should get a drink sometime, seeing as we run in the same circles."

"Where is she?" the squad leader barked.

The question carried with it a certain implication, one Lando was unable to fully confirm. When he didn't answer, Vizago stepped forward. "Has the smoke fogged your visors? She's on the vaporator."

Two of the troopers marched past them to inspect the crash site. Only then did Lando get his confirmation. Neither Clarr nor anything that resembled her remains lay among the wreckage.

Vizago flexed his gloved hands. "I swear she was there. I just saw her."

Lando saw her, too—darting through the smoke on the other side of the troopers. He exchanged a momentary glance with her before she slipped behind the transport.

The two troopers returned to their commander, pressing their rifle barrels into Vizago and Lando's sides. "If you don't tell us the truth we will tear this town apart," the squad leader said, "after we reduce you to ash."

The Devaronian hissed at Lando, as if ready to bite. "Tell him—tell him that was the truth!"

Lando stared at the squad leader, focusing on the helmet's curved lenses, which concealed the trooper's real eyes. Though Lando couldn't get a read on those eyes, he reminded himself that they were there, that beneath the white plastoid armor there was a person, regardless of how faceless and robotic he or she seemed. And people could be bluffed.

"Order your troopers to lower their rifles and I'll tell you where she is."

The squad leader leaned close to Lando. "We don't bargain with scum. This is your last chance."

Lando couldn't see Clarr, but he had to trust to luck that she knew what she was doing. All he had to do was keep the troopers' attention off the transport for a couple more moments. "That wouldn't be smart, sir. My partner and I are worth more alive than dead." He put on his most serious sabacc face. "You see, we're rebels."

Rebels. That single word proved incendiary. They ignited the squad leader's eyes under the lenses, widening their pupils, making them at last visible. Lando had never seen such hate.

"*What*? I'm not a rebel," Vizago said. "He's lying, I tell you, he's lying!"

"Stuncuff them," the squad leader said. "We will bring them to Agent Kallus for—"

A laser blast cut short the squad leader's order. He was pitched forward into Lando, and both smacked the ground. Lando rolled to his knees, but the squad leader remained face down, a gaping hole in his back.

The two other troopers whirled and opened fire on the transport. The body of the transport pilot dangled out the hatch, yet the transport's forward turrets continued to move. Clarr must have

infiltrated the vehicle and taken control of its weaponry.

But managing two targets proved difficult for someone unskilled in military tech. Her next rounds missed. The stormtroopers didn't. They concentrated their fire through the transport's open hatch. Within seconds, its turrets stopped rotating.

The troopers re-trained their rifles on Lando and Vizago. "You'll pay for this, rebel scum," both said.

Lando waited for the inevitable blaster bolt to come. There was no way to bluff out of this one.

A rock struck one of the troopers' helmets. Surprised, the trooper and his comrade wheeled around—into a hailstorm. Refugees came out of their hovels and threw whatever objects they had to hand, from bent hydrospanners to shattered glowrods. While almost everything bounced harmlessly off the stormtroopers' armor, the impact was enough to take them off their feet. Once down, they never got back up. The refugees descended upon the troopers, their initial fear replaced by a seething fury. The crackle of nerf-prods silenced the troopers' screams, but the refugees continued their attack. They would have their revenge.

Lando hastened away from the mob, heading toward the Imperial transport. He dreaded what he would find in there, but he had to go. Clarr had risked her life to save his, so he owed it to her to see if there was any chance he could save hers.

The stormtroopers' shots had turned the interior of the transport into a smoldering ruin. Cockpit consoles sizzled. Live conduits sparked. The piloting yoke hung from a rope of melted wire, while the gunnery controls were nothing but a blackened mess.

On the floor in the middle of all this lay Ria Clarr.

Lando stepped over to her and bent down to inspect her wounds. She'd been hit in the hip and abdomen, painful for sure, but not necessarily lethal. His dread edged to hope.

"Ria?"

When she opened her eyes and looked up at him, he offered her his most rakish grin. "Not bad for a geologist."

The glint in her eyes shone even brighter than before. "Not bad for a rebel," she said to him.

On the boarding ramp of the *Broken Horn*, Lando looked back one last time at Tarkintown. The place was nothing like the desolate camp of his arrival. Refugees hurried about between the hovels, arming themselves with blasters from the troop transport or fashioning crude weapons of their own. Directing all this was Ria Clarr, confined to a repulsor sled because of her injuries, but no less deterred in her fight against the Empire.

Lando sighed. He had pleaded with them—he'd *begged* Clarr—to board Vizago's freighter and leave Lothal, explaining that the Empire would be back in full force and wouldn't take prisoners. But no one would be swayed, least of all Clarr. Her act of resistance and the resulting victory over the stormtroopers had shaken these people out of their doldrums, given them a purpose, inspired them. Yes, Tarkintown might be a wretched, miserable place to live, but it was their home. And they would defend it, to the death if need be.

Clarr drove her sled near the ramp. She gave him a look and a smile. "Thank you. For everything."

"Sure," Lando said, unable to muster a smile of his own. "Good luck."

Entering the freighter, he almost felt guilty he wasn't staying behind. But the truth was, Tarkintown wasn't his home, and the Empire wasn't his enemy. Not yet, at least. And if that day did come to pass, one thing was certain: Lando Calrissian wouldn't count on his luck. Wise gamblers knew when to double-down, and when *not* to, particularly if the odds were stacked so heavily against them, as they would be with the Empire.

The *Broken Horn* took off, piloted by Vizago's enforcer droids. The plan Lando had hatched with Vizago called for them to be safely off Lothal for a couple weeks, so they wouldn't be swept up in any Imperial investigation.

"Hide my cache of transponders in the shed and remember to walk the puffer-pig," Lando told his protocol droid, W1-LE, over the comm. "I want her sniffing for ore."

He shut off his comlink and stood alone in the main cabin. In the viewport, Tarkintown diminished in size until it was just another light on Lothal's surface. Soon it wasn't even that.

Vizago came up beside him. "You still owe me for that land, Calrissian."

Lando fingered the few credits he had left in his pocket, the ones he hadn't bet. They weren't much, but perhaps they'd be enough, if he was lucky.

"Sabacc?"

THE END OF HISTORY

WRITTEN BY **ALEXANDER FREED**
ART BY **CHRIS SCALF**

Antron didn't know much about starfighters, but he felt strongly that a wing should be attached to its vessel, not scattered in sizzling fragments across the blue scrub plains of a nameless moon. As he beat away clouds of smoke, cursing his age and protruding gut, he decided that the pilot of this particular starfighter—which had fallen blazing past the mesa that Antron called home barely an hour before—was likely to agree.

He hoped it wouldn't be the *only* thing he and the pilot agreed upon, since he doubted he had the charm or the muscle to keep an irate pirate or murderous fugitive in check. But he reassured himself as best he could: "Jedi Master Vonkhel managed to befriend the Sith Lord of Gairm," he muttered. "All *you* have to do is not admit anything stupid."

As Antron approached the starfighter's cockpit, the viewplate jumped, shuddered, then rose steadily. A flight-suited figure coated in soot, grease, and dried blood climbed out from the vessel and staggered onto the ground.

The figure's voice was sharp and strained. "I need to find Antron Bach."

Antron froze a moment, then hurried forward and saw beneath the grime a woman young enough to be his granddaughter. "I *am* Antron Bach," he said, before he noticed her hand was touching the blaster at her hip. So much, he thought, for not admitting anything stupid.

"Miru Nadrinakar," the woman said, "of the Corellian Resistance. We need to run."

Antron started to ask a question, but as he sorted through the half-dozen that came to mind he caught sight of something through the smoke—a trio of lights in the sky, winking and following a jagged path among the stars.

"TIE fighters," Miru explained. She hobbled forward and wrapped one arm around Antron's shoulders for support. She stank of sweat, and he flinched at her unexpected nearness. "Their frigate is on the other side of the system," she added, and smiled grimly. "I took out its engines. Give it three hours to get here."

Antron stumbled as Miru urged him away from the wreckage, then quickly found a rhythm as he led her across the scrub plains toward the mesa. She was limping on her right leg, and though Antron searched for a glib comment to distract her from her pain, he thought better of it when he saw the concentration in her eyes.

The winking lights overhead were growing brighter.

"I've hidden from Imperial patrols before," he said, trying to be encouraging. "We'll batten down the hatches, make them think you're wandering the wilds—"

Miru interrupted, quick and harsh. "No hiding," she said. "I need weapons and transport ASAP."

"You what?" Antron asked.

Miru gripped Antron harder as they walked. "The Empire's planning a purge of resistance cells. I've got a day to get to Corellia and warn them."

Antron's voice dropped an octave. "Let's find shelter," he said.

When they reached the shadow of the mesa and Antron turned at an angle toward the cliffside, they heard the sound of thunder. Antron hadn't seen a storm in all his years on the moon, and when Miru said "They're bombing the crash site," he nodded and searched for courage.

He reminded himself: Jedi Master Va Zhurro had spent six months caring for refugees in a basement during the Clone Wars. Antron could survive a day or two of bombardment.

At the base of the mesa, where the scrawny and twisted bushes of the scrub plains failed to scrabble up the steep sides, Antron guided Miru through a crevice barely wider than his shoulders. The crevice, in turn, led to a great steel door embedded in the stone, nearly camouflaged by dust.

With a groan, Antron climbed atop a boulder. The door's rusting keypad was over two meters above the ground, and he strained to tap in the code. "Geonosians colonized this place centuries ago," he said as the door hummed open, "and left it not much later. The mesa's riddled with warrens. Only problem is, most Geonosians *fly*, and I'm not a tall man."

Miru said nothing as Antron returned to her side. He sighed and led her down a tunnel and into the vault.

In a great cavern supported by bare metal beams stood rack after rack of winking, glowing data cartridges that brought a sparkle to the dusty air. In between the racks were long tables piled with curious artifacts: handwritten parchments and sets of silverware shared equal prominence with delicately etched crystalline cubes and a six-fingered cybernetic hand. Some of the objects had been well-preserved and polished, while others were spotted with rust or stains Antron had failed to prevent.

"What is all this?" Miru asked.

"This," Antron said, with a soft smile and a flick of his hand, "is what's left of the Jedi of the Old Republic."

Miru shook her head, then stepped forward, walking unsteadily around the racks.

Antron went on. "You're looking at generations of history: journals and temple archives and philosophy tracts. Broken lightsabers and thises and thats. Proof of a better world. Everything the Empire wants us to forget."

Miru turned back to Antron, her eyes wide. "Are you..?"

Antron peered back at her, then realized what she was asking and laughed. "I'm not a Jedi, no. I sold *antiques* before the dark times. I made Jedi friends because you get better prices when you drink with your clients... even if you're only drinking tea."

For an instant, Antron remembered the good days, laughing with smugglers or academics or archaeologists in a Coruscant cantina; appraising trinkets or swapping tales with Padawans. He missed drinking. He missed *talking*.

He ran a hand through what was left of his hair. "When it all went south, and Master Uvell asked me to help..." He smiled wryly. "You know he called me a huckster once? Wasn't nice about it, either, but he gave me a ship, loaded up all the artifacts we could find and told me about this place. He must have been desperate."

Miru didn't say anything. Antron found himself compelled to fill the silence. "I've been here ever since. Not a smart call on my part, but I didn't much like the look of the Empire and I didn't have the heart to say 'no' to a war hero like Uvell—"

"Your name and coordinates were in an old resistance file. Your Jedi must have passed them along," Miru said.

She lifted a charred fragment of metal from one table and turned it over in her hands—the last of the Chronicles of Med'eeth, salvaged from the ruins of Ossus before Antron had been born.

"I don't know much about them," she said. "I was a kid when they died."

"That's why I'm here," Antron said, his voice softening. "When the Empire finally falls—a hundred or a thousand years from now—the galaxy will have a lot to relearn. The Jedi were the best of us, and I want their stories preserved."

Miru rubbed her thumb against the charred metal.

"People deserve a history and heroes they can look up to," Antron continued. "That's why I can't help you race off to Corellia. If the Imperials see a ship launch—"

"They'll know there's a base here. The Empire will find you and burn everything."

"Yes," Antron said.

Miru tossed the metal fragment back to the table and the sound rang through the cavern. She straightened, winced at the noise or her injuries, and looked at Antron. "Then I'm sorry," she said. "I'm not here to jeopardize your mission. But the resistance takes priority over—" She waved a hand at the fragment. "—stories."

They stood and watched each other a while.

Then Antron snorted and forced a smile. "Well," he said, "you can head back to your ship if you like. Otherwise, we can work together—for now—to save our own lives."

Breath-masked residents scurried for cover as the gunship raced over glass-littered avenues, past boarded-up storefronts, toppled monuments, and gloomy cantinas.

Miru merely scowled.

Antron added with a shrug: "You're no good to the resistance dead."

"The good news," Antron told Miru as they crept through cramped tunnels leading higher into the mesa, "is that the colony warrens are pretty sturdy. Hard to spot, too. The bombers shouldn't be a problem."

"And the bad news?" Miru asked.

"As soon as that Imperial frigate gets close, even the most dimwitted bridge officer will detect the colony power generator. We need to shut it down, or it won't be long before the vault is discovered and the frigate atomizes this whole mesa. Bad for us, regardless of your *priorities*."

Antron went on. "No generator means no light, no water, and no filtered air. We'll be miserable while we hide, but your pursuers will eventually write you off as lost or dead in the scrub plains. Marooned without allies."

"By then," Miru said flatly, "it'll be too late to save the resistance."

Antron didn't reply to that. The thought made his chest ache, but what could he do? Instead he shrugged and added, "There's more bad news."

The generator was near the top of the mesa, he explained, in the colony's old industrial center, now it only housed a few aging machines and Antron's rickety ship. The tunnels would get them partway there, but circumventing the Geonosians' vertical shafts meant a detour onto the cliffsides. "Unless," he added, "you're hiding wings under that flight suit."

As clouds of dust swirled and the bombs rumbled, Antron and Miru emerged onto a path halfway up the mesa and began to hike a bramble-ridden slope toward their goal. "Give it two hours until the frigate arrives," Miru said softly.

"Time enough," Antron replied, fearing it wasn't.

As they walked, stopping only to lie flat whenever a TIE fighter shrieked into view, Antron found himself humming fragments of an old Bith opera: the story of a Jedi Knight who had returned to save his people after journeying across the stars. Since Antron had come to his moon, his musical options had been limited, yet he'd grown fond of the Song of Lojuun.

Miru had been scowling, limping behind Antron and scanning the horizon for signs of their foe. But the more elaborate Antron's off-key humming became the more she began to smile, until finally she let out a hoarse laugh.

"You're awfully cheerful," she said, as they crested the top of the slope.

"Petrified, too," Antron said. "But the Jedi say fear leads to suffering, so I try to busy my mind."

"When you live under the Empire, you *learn* to fear."

"Maybe that's why so many people—" Antron began, before Miru's hand struck between his shoulders, pushing him to his knees. For an instant, Antron wondered if he'd misjudged her—if she'd decided to get rid of him and take her chances alone.

A second later, Miru lay prone at his side, and Antron felt shame at his doubt.

Together, they looked ahead onto the flat top of the mesa. Less than fifty meters away, four figures—three armored in white, one in a black Imperial officer's uniform—prowled the edge of the cliff carrying rangefinders and macrobinoculars.

Miru spoke in a soft, clipped voice. "Search coordinators. I thought they'd set up at the crash site. They must have wanted altitude. They'll keep watch while more troops search the ground."

"They're practically *standing* on the hatch to the generator," Antron breathed. "It's concealed, but if they find it..."

"We need a new plan," Miru said. "Can you get us offworld?"

Antron shook his head. "I've got a ship, but it's barely lightspeed-capable. That frigate won't have any trouble shooting it down."

Miru squeezed his shoulder. "We'll figure it out. No other choice. Lead on."

But Antron didn't move. "If we run, they'll detect the colony and destroy the vault!" he insisted. "Wait for those four to leave, then get in the hatch and shut that generator down."

"They're not going to *leave*," Miru said. "Where's your ship?"

Instead of replying, Antron rose to his feet and began to run along the mesa's top. His legs shook as he waved his arms frantically at the stormtroopers and shouted, "You're here! Thank the stars you're here!"

You're already an eccentric old fool, Antron thought to himself. Just look the part, and you'll be fine.

The stormtroopers trained their weapons on him. "This is my moon," Antron hastily explained. "I saw the crash—a *pirate* attacked me. She ran off! I'll show you!" He flailed vaguely toward the dry forests beyond the scrub plains.

Two of the stormtroopers turned to speak to the officer. The third kept his weapon leveled at Antron.

Finally, one of the troopers—Antron couldn't tell which—raised his voice. "Get on the ground. This moon is supposed to be unoccupied."

Antron lowered himself to his knees and tried to keep babbling about pirates even as he ran out of fresh things to say. But he could make this work, he thought. He didn't need a Jedi mind trick to direct the search away from the mesa. He only hoped Miru would follow his instructions.

She could turn off the generator. She could hide. And Antron could find her once he convinced the stormtroopers that he was just some crazed hermit and that she'd run off to the forests or been disintegrated by a bomb blast.

Unless, of course, Miru stole his ship and exposed the colony anyway.

Antron heard boots crunch on brittle grass, then the crack and hiss of a plasma bolt. He cried out in instinctive panic and clenched the rocky ground.

Then there was another shot. A third.

He scrabbled backward, scraping his palms on stone chips and keeping his nose to the dirt. By the time he'd crawled behind a boulder that passed for cover, the shooting had stopped.

Raising his head, Antron saw the four Imperials sprawled on the ground, flames licking burnt holes in their outfits.

"Your plan was stupid," a voice called. He turned to see Miru limping toward him, her blaster in her hand. "They would've killed you and stayed right here."

Antron stood and stared, sputtering sounds that didn't quite form words. Miru scowled, moving to Antron's side and leaning on him again.

"They won't need to search anymore," she said, and Antron realized she was correct. The screaming of the TIE fighters had suddenly grown louder.

The closest bomb detonated less than a hundred meters away, deafening and blinding Antron. For those few, terrifying seconds, Miru kept moving, tugging Antron along with a strength she surely should have lost during the crash.

But the TIEs didn't seem to spot them. Antron's dazed mind struggled to understand before it snapped to a conclusion: The Empire assumed Miru had killed the landing party, and was bombing her last known position.

They still didn't know about Antron or the vault.

By the time Antron and Miru descended through a hatch into the colony's industrial tunnels, Antron's skin was caked in a paste formed from sweat and dust. Miru watched him as he leaned against a rock wall riddled with metal pipes and dim yellow lamps. She was sweating worse than he was, and at some point—during the fight or the bombing, if not hours earlier—she'd developed a cut in her left arm. Blood trickled into her palm.

"Thank you," Antron said. "For saving my life. Several times."

Miru shrugged. "Who'll take over this place if you're blown to bits?"

Antron smiled grimly. "If they blow me up, this place is next."

The tunnels quaked and metal wailed in the distance as something came untethered. Miru took Antron's arm and began walking again. "My father was a historian," she said.

Antron shook his head, trying to follow her logic.

Miru kept talking. "He believed in the Jedi. Believed in the Republic. Before the Empire got to him."

She didn't look at Antron. "I don't remember life before the Empire," she said. "I don't know whether your cave full of stories counts for anything. I can't."

They reached a branch in the tunnel, and Miru halted, waiting for Antron to take the lead.

"But you believe in this stuff. You almost died for it. If you say your mission takes priority... we can do it your way."

Antron watched Miru in surprise, as she stood as straight as she could despite her exhaustion and bruises and cuts, waiting for orders without a word of complaint.

He listened to a dim, distant rumble and thought of the Jedi Padawan Nes Ukul, who'd given his life protecting a species whose language he didn't speak on a planet whose name he didn't know.

It was Ukul's Master who'd said,

crates and toolboxes. The generator hummed comfortingly under the floor, and after surveying his surroundings he wiped his brow and set to work.

He thought about Miru, and how in a few moments she'd arrive in the hangar bay and realize he'd lied about the backup generator. He'd have to seal her inside in case she tried to turn back and find him. After that, he could power the bay doors so she could get his heap of a ship out of the mesa and off the moon.

There was also the Imperial frigate. He'd need to distract it to give Miru any chance of escaping the system intact. For this, Antron didn't have a plan so much as a grab-bag of stalling tactics: The "confused old man" routine; maybe a fake message from the search party. Somewhere, the colony even had a few weapons waiting to be turned on, with luck, they might be functional.

Antron tapped a command into the workstation, then fumbled through a crate, looking for the colony schematics.

As he dragged a tool chest over to a third console and sat down with a sigh, he wondered whether Miru would understand what had changed his mind.

He thought of all the Jedi whose stories he'd read, their noble deeds and ends. Miru didn't need their inspiration—she'd learned nobility even under the Empire's boot. And she'd reminded him of the ideals he'd wanted to protect.

Sacrificing the vault would be a tragedy. Sacrificing the resistance—sacrificing tough and courageous men and women who struggled every day—didn't seem like a very Jedi thing to do.

Jedi died for *people* above *things*.

Antron was humming again as he scrubbed dust off a screen with his sleeve and saw that his ship had been powered on. Miru had taken the hint.

The generator room rumbled, metal supports shrieking like TIE fighters, as another bomb struck. He switched to scanners, watched them blink as the Imperial frigate came into orbit around his moon. He cracked his knuckles, tried not to think about the vault. He had a job to do. One way or another, Miru would get away clean.

And maybe if he was fortunate—if the Force was with him—the vault would survive. If the mesa collapsed under a barrage of plasma, some enterprising researcher might dig up the rubble in a century or two. And if Antron somehow *survived* the ordeal, well...

He laughed as he remembered one last story and one last lesson: Jedi might sacrifice themselves, but they never give up hope.

Antron watched Miru in surprise, watched her stand as straight as she could despite her exhaustion and bruises and cuts, waiting for orders without a word of complaint.

"There is no more selfless act than to perish for another's cause."

Antron swallowed, considered praising Miru, thanking her, and decided against it. She didn't seem to need comfort, and he didn't have the dignity to spare.

"You take the left, and I'll take the right," he said. "There's a backup generator you need to shut down while I handle the primary."

Miru frowned. "Can you make it on your own?" she asked.

Antron flapped a hand dismissively. "I'm old and fat, but I can walk down a hallway. Shoo!"

Miru limped into the darkness. Antron turned on his heel and headed down a narrow corridor, emerging into a chamber lined with consoles and cluttered with

KINDRED SPIRITS

WRITTEN BY **CHRISTIE GOLDEN**
ART BY **MAGALI VILLENEUVE**

"This enterprise is doomed to failure," Asajj Ventress muttered. Her hands were securely bound behind her, and she was sweltering beneath the blazing Florrum sun in a long dark robe and heavy cloak.

"Only if you blow it," Lassa Rhayme whispered back. The blue-skinned Pantoran wore Ventress's clothes: black boots with blue protective shin plating, leggings, and a black, high-collared shirt beneath a tunic. There was more plating on the left shoulder and across the hips, and plenty of places to fasten a variety of gear. The pirate captain looked born to it.

Ventress had no intention of "blowing it," but she was definitely having second thoughts about this scheme.

Taking the bounty had seemed like a good idea at the time. The job had appeared on the roster with an impressive number of credits attached to it, and Ventress had recently laid out a sizeable amount for repairs to the *Banshee.*

Seeking half-dozen skilled fighter pilots to serve as escort for the cargo ship Steady On. *No questions asked. Half payment upon agreement, half upon safe delivery of* Steady On*'s cargo.*

"Smugglers plus cargo equals pirates" was an equation Ventress had learned long ago, so the attack on the *Steady On* was not unexpected. What *was* unexpected was getting rescued by a *second* group of pirates, the Blood Bone Order, who had also intended to plunder the freighter.

"We've been planning this for weeks," Lassa Rhayme had told her. "You can imagine my surprise when, upon the *Opportunity*'s arrival at the proper coordinates, the only ships we saw were fighters floating dead in space."

Ventress had been the only survivor. Rhayme had brought the wounded woman to the ship's sickbay and healed her injuries. She had also towed the *Banshee* in for repairs.

"Why?" Ventress had asked, curious.

"When your ship was in such bad shape and you were still alive, I had a hunch. It paid off. We found this." Rhayme had reached behind her back, withdrew Ventress's lightsaber, and tossed it to her. "I can use your help recovering the *Steady On.*"

Ventress welcomed the familiar weight of the weapon in her hand. She had expected to miss her twin red lightsabers, but was glad now that they had been stolen. The old ones reminded her too much of Dooku, and she found she preferred the yellow light of this one. "I might be willing to help you—provided I get to keep a certain piece of cargo."

"What might that be?"

"That might be my business," Ventress had replied.

Rhayme's golden eyes had narrowed as she speculatively regarded the woman she'd rescued. "One item?"

"One item."

She nodded. "Help me get the freighter back, and whatever it is, it's yours."

Rhayme had sent a crew member to go undercover on the *Steady On*. He had reported back that Hondo Ohnaka, the pirate responsible for the theft, was currently not on the Florrum base; only a skeleton crew led by an underling was unloading the *Steady On*. "It's a break for us—Hondo's sharp, and a nasty piece of work, even for a Weequay."

Weequay.

"Now, you have my attention," Ventress said. "I am... not fond of Weequays."

It was an understatement. Ventress despised the species, with their leathery, wrinkled skin and sour dispositions. Weequay raiders had murdered both her slave master and, later, Ky Narec, the Jedi who had taken her on as his Padawan. Her hand had tightened on her lightsaber in anticipation.

"Don't get too free with that," Rhayme warned, nodding at the weapon. "*I'm* not fond of high body counts. We kill when needed, not for sport."

"You sound like a Jedi," Ventress had said scornfully.

"Don't insult me."

Jiro, the pirate put in charge in Hondo's absence, had been intrigued by Lassa's proposition when contacted via hologram, and permitted them to land in the flat, rocky depression in front of Hondo's complex. The area was cluttered with debris. Somebody had ferreted out this hideaway not too long ago, and it was definitely the worse for wear. Ventress had spotted the *Steady On*—noteworthy for being completely intact amid the rubble—being unloaded as they were "escorted" inside what remained of a large, multi-level complex at blasterpoint.

"I'm beginning to think this wasn't such a good idea," Ventress continued as they walked through a triangular door and passed from sunlight into gloom.

"Hey there, no talking!" One of the pirates shoved a blaster into Ventress's midsection. She gritted her teeth to keep from Force-hurling the disgusting creature the length of the enormous and poorly named "grand hall."

A few of the pirates were engaged in activities such as drinking, flirting with the female members of the crew, fighting

about flirting, betting on fighting, and the fine art of sliding off a chair, completely smashed. But there were others—their cold gazes crawling over the newcomers—who speared food with knives as if they were simply practicing carving up flesh. Jiro awaited Ventress and Rhayme at the far end. Seated at a long table on a raised dais, he sprawled comfortably in an ornate chair that commanded the best view.

He was one of the ugliest Weequays Ventress had ever seen, with a row of single locks of hair standing up in spikes on his overlarge head and two longer braids trailing down his back. The pirate who had brought in the two women handed him Ventress's lightsaber. Jiro looked at it carefully, then at Ventress, and finally at Rhayme.

"You must be someone special, to catch a Jedi. How'd you manage it?"

"The magnificent Captain Rhayme," and Lassa spat on the ground, "sends her crew off to scout for news of ships to plunder. That's how I came across her." She gave Ventress a scornful look. "I found her pretty badly injured, from what or whom I don't know, but still alive. I took her back to my ship, healed her up—enough to walk, at least—and contacted you."

Ventress gave Lassa a look that she hoped was both defiant and exhausted. Jiro leaned back in his chair, plunking filthy boots on the table. At the next table over, someone belched.

"I've heard of Lassa Rhayme. Sounds like she's not your best pal."

"Hardly," Rhayme said, with just the proper amount of loathing, her lip curling slightly. *She's good,* Ventress thought. "That witch is brutal. We boarded a Separatist ship once, and she stole its torture droid. Rhayme'd always been harsh to her crew, but now..." the "bounty hunter" shook her lavender head. "I'd do anything to get out from under her thumb."

"Like deserting your captain to join Hondo's Gang, eh? How could we trust a turncoat?"

Rhayme smiled sweetly. "Hondo gave *you* a second chance when you turned on him, didn't he?" Ventress stifled a smile as Jiro's face darkened at the reminder. She and Lassa had done their homework. Rhayme folded her arms.

"Look—I've got everything to lose and nothing to gain by lying. I'm giving you a *Jedi.* The ransom the Order will pay for her safe return will be staggering. Plus..." She placed her hands on the table and brought her face close to his. "I'll tell you everything you need to know about Lassa Rhayme's plans. Hondo will come back to find that in his absence, *you* have defeated a dangerous pirate captain, captured her ship, have a new loyal crewmember, and a Jedi prisoner in the bargain. He just might make you second in command."

Rhayme waved the yellow, humming blade and cut the piece of furniture in half. She laughed with sheer delight. What a glorious weapon! She swung it simply to hear the sound that it made.

Jiro considered this, removing his boots from the table and leaning forward. "Still, why not keep the Jedi yourself and collect the bounty?"

Ventress's patience had worn out. The more the Weequay grilled them, the more likely he was to simply order both her and Rhayme shot and claim all the glory himself. *Time to shake things up a bit.*

The lightsaber sailed from Jiro's hands into Ventress's just as she spun around to catch it. She could not use it to cut her bonds with her hands bound behind her, but she could fight. With a yell, she sprang over Rhayme, turning in mid-air and angling the lightsaber so precisely it singed Rhayme's lavender braid.

"What—" cried Jiro, then dived for cover under the table.

Rhayme gasped and stared at Ventress. Her brilliant gold eyes narrowed and she lunged for the nearest blaster, which happened to belong to the pirate who had brought them in. Ventress was therefore not displeased when Lassa used him as a shield while firing at the "Jedi."

The shots barely missed Ventress. Rhayme looked furious. Her color was up and her white teeth were bared in a grimace of pure hatred.

Oh, no. She thinks I've turned on her.

It was a perfectly reasonable assumption. There had been a time, not long ago, when it would have been the correct one. But not today. Ventress would have to hope that Lassa Rhayme would understand what she was doing—and that Jiro wouldn't.

With her back to Rhayme, Ventress used the Force to sense the bolts coming and bat them away. She heard a yelp behind her, but it was decidedly not feminine. Good. She jumped onto the table, whirling in a circle down its length and catching any stray arms or torsos

unfortunate enough to be in her lightsaber's blazing yellow path.

"Stand down, Jedi!" came Lassa's clear, strong voice.

Has she caught on yet? One way or another, either to continue the plan or end it, Rhayme would have to stop Ventress. Two Weequays charged the table, raising their blasters. Ventress leaped to meet them, kicking out with both feet. The toe of each boot caught a startled pirate under the chin. Their heads snapped back and they crumpled, either unconscious or dead.

As she landed, a powerful kick in the small of her back sent her sprawling. Her lightsaber was snatched from her hands and a second later, pain blossomed in her wrists. Lassa Rhayme, pirate captain, planted a boot on her back—Ventress shifted her head to one side and looked up, still uncertain as to whether Rhayme was friend or foe. Rhayme brought the humming tip of the lightsaber so close to Ventress's face that she was forced to squint against its brightness.

She struggled for breath, and finally gasped, "I... yield."

"I didn't believe you were really able to capture her," Jiro said, somewhat grudgingly, as the "defeated Jedi" was led away. "I am... impressed."

Rhayme's shoulder ached, and she would have several bruises shortly, but she'd had worse. "No question, Jedi are tough to defeat. I'm lucky she's not at her best."

She casually fastened the lightsaber to her belt, as if there was no question that it belonged to her. Jiro noticed the gesture, but let it go, doubtless reasoning that the amount the gang would receive from the Jedi Order would more than compensate him for a lost lightsaber.

"So I take it we're agreed?" Rhayme continued. "You get the bounty on the Jedi and accept me as a crewmember, and I tell you where to find Lassa Rhayme's fleet."

"Well," Jiro hedged, "It's Hondo who has to make the final decision."

She took a seat without being invited, and again, Jiro did not object. "I'm not surprised. It's his gang, after all. I'll wait. When is he expected back?"

That threw Jiro. "He didn't say. But I could put in a few good words for you if you were to tell *me* where to find this fleet. So I could, ah, prep the ships and get them all ready-like."

So you could send off your men now and take all the credit-like, Rhayme thought, amused. *And likely try to kill me in the bargain.* Rhayme pretended not to have come to this obvious conclusion.

"That's a great idea!" she said. Jiro visibly relaxed. "Now... let me start by telling you how many ships Rhayme commands, what kind, and their names." She smiled. "I think a drink might loosen my tongue... if you'll join me."

Jiro gave her a lascivious look, reached for a no-doubt filthy mug, and sloshed a bright green liquid into it.

The lightsaber burns on Ventress's wrists were exquisitely painful, but she didn't care. In taking Ventress down, Lassa had sufficiently damaged the stun cuffs so Ventress could break free—and that meant Lassa believed her. She could take a little pain.

Once the doors to the grand hall closed behind her and her escorts, Ventress wasted no time. She used the Force to shatter the remains of the binders and extended her hands, palms up, to each side. Two of the pirates slammed hard into the walls. She whirled on the third, who came at her with a fist raised and rotting teeth bared, and punched him in the throat. The fourth grabbed her arm. She twisted, using her momentum and the Force to hurl him over her head, landing a blow to his jaw on his descent.

They all looked to be alive, but out cold. Better safe than sorry, though. Ventress relieved the guards of their blasters, then paused. Rhayme had asked her to kill only when needed. She set one blaster to stun, and gave the pirates a second shot.

Now to take over the *Steady On*—and make sure the item she'd been hired to safeguard was still on board.

Once Lassa told Jiro where Captain Rhayme's fleet was supposedly based, he, of course, decided immediately to take the initiative and send what ships were on Florrum to attack. Lassa encouraged him to send all his men, but he stubbornly shook his head.

"Hondo said he wanted the cargo unloaded," he insisted.

That was really too bad, but Lassa took comfort in knowing that she'd just sent all the intact ships on Florrum and every pirate but Jiro, those sprawled snoring on the ground, and the few unloading the *Steady On* off on a wild caranak chase. With gusto, Lassa spun outrageous tales of the terrors the "evil Captain Rhayme" perpetrated upon her hardworking crew, buying time for Ventress. Jiro swallowed it all, apparently having decided that since she had defeated a Jedi, Lassa was entirely trustworthy.

A movement caught Rhayme's eye. Ventress's slender, robed figure blended so well with the shadows that she was easy to miss. *She's very good*, Rhayme thought.

"So tell me more about this ale that your Captain Rhayme hoards all to herself," Jiro prodded, plunking down his empty cup and reaching for a refill.

"Ale? Oh no, it's Tevraki whiskey," Rhayme said, watching Ventress out of the corner of her eye while smiling at Jiro. "And a finer thing has never touched your lips."

Jiro leered hopefully at the implied invitation. Ventress made her way to the door and slipped outside. Lassa waited, continuing to exchange suggestive remarks with Jiro. She gave it a few minutes more, then unobtrusively placed both hands below the table, pressed a button on her bracer, and gave Jiro a bright smile.

"Well, I can't say this hasn't been fun, but I must be going." She indicated the cup of green liquid. "Thanks for the, ah... whatever that was."

Jiro's green eyes narrowed. "What're you talking about?"

"My ride should be here right about..." She cocked her head, and was rewarded by the unmistakable sound of a ship landing in the outside arena. "Now."

Faster than she would have given him credit for, considering the amount of alcohol he had imbibed, Jiro leaped over the table with a roar. Rhayme darted away, pressing the switch on the lightsaber. It activated with a *snap-hiss*, almost startling her with its speed. A sword was a sword, however, and Lassa Rhayme knew how to use one. Jiro grabbed for a blaster someone had left on the table, but Rhayme slammed the lightsaber down, slicing through both blaster and table with as little effort as if she were cutting through butter. Jiro

growled and threw a stool at her. Again, Rhayme waved the yellow, humming blade and cut the piece of furniture in half.

She laughed with sheer delight. What a glorious weapon! She swung it simply to hear the sound it made.

"Which of you is the Jedi?" blurted Jiro.

"Jedi?" came a smooth voice trembling with indignation. "In *my hall*? *Again*?"

Jiro and Rhayme whirled simultaneously to see Hondo Ohnaka silhouetted in the triangular doorway. He carried an electrostaff which sparked magenta at both sharp ends and stood like an aristocrat, head high, one hand on his hip, his duster billowing about him. The effect was spoiled by the Kowakian monkey-lizard perched on his shoulder. Hondo strode forward, fairly vibrating with offense.

"Jiro! You *imbecile*! What have you done? Where is my crew?" He completely ignored the woman holding the active lightsaber. Rhayme stared from one to the other, unsure whether to attack or to burst out laughing.

"Oh, hello, boss," Jiro said miserably. "This lady here came saying she wanted to defect from the Blood Bone Order and join us instead."

"Of course she does. Everyone knows Lassa Rhayme is a tyrant. Am I not correct? Hmm?" He peered alertly at Rhayme, expecting confirmation. She nodded wordlessly.

"And—she brought us—I mean you, boss—a Jedi she'd captured. Said we could hold her for ransom and—"

"Da-da-da-da!" Hondo cut him off with an imperious, irritated gesture. "I leave you alone for half a day—half a day!—and look what you have done. No more ransoming Jedi! That never ends well. Bad for business."

"But... it was like this beautiful fruit just fell, right into my lap!" Jiro pleaded.

Hondo sighed and placed two fingers to his temple under his helmet as if in pain. "How many times must I tell you, Jiro. You cannot trust such unexpected gifts. Fruit never falls into your lap *unless you shake the tree first!*" He looked at Rhayme, spreading his arms in a helpless manner. "You see what I have to deal with."

"I certainly do," Rhayme said, not without sympathy.

"Now, then," and he turned to her, "what do you *really* want?"

Rhayme sobered and drew herself up, meeting his eyes evenly. "To take back what's mine." She pointed the lightsaber at him. "You stole my haul, Hondo Ohnaka. You see..." and she smiled fiercely. "*I'm* Lassa Rhayme."

"You? The terrifying captain of the *Opportunity*?" He eyed her up and down. "Not what I expected. Not at all." He clucked his tongue and shook his head sadly. "Little girl," he said, "did you think I had come alone?"

And the hitherto empty chamber echoed with the sound of weapons being drawn.

Lassa smiled. "Did you think *I* did?"

Sudden perplexed cries of pain and anger came from the entrance area of the grand hall, followed by blaster fire. Hondo turned to look, and in that moment, Lassa sprang.

She brought the lightsaber arcing down, but Hondo recovered in time to block it with his electrostaff. His eyes narrowed behind his goggles. "This is a fight you cannot win, my dear. You may have the laser sword, but you don't have the Force."

Lassa brought the lightsaber arcing down, but Hondo recovered in time to block it with his electrostaff. His eyes narrowed behind his goggles.

"Don't need it."

He swung the staff low, but she leaped up and it sliced only air. A second jump brought her onto the table, and she swung with the lightsaber. This time, he struck it hard and the impact jarred her injured shoulder. Gritting her teeth, Lassa kicked out and up, and the electrostaff flew from Hondo's hands.

"Not bad," Hondo admitted. He recovered the weapon and vaulted up to join her, shoving one of the sparking ends of the staff like a spear. She parried, but let him drive her down the table, pretending to be unsure of her footing. A smile curved his thin mouth, and he feinted, dodging her blow and bringing the staff down. At the last second, Rhayme swerved and dove for a blaster someone had left behind. In one graceful movement, she grabbed it, fired at Hondo, and flung the lightsaber toward the doorway.

Ventress—don't fail me...

Ventress had been using a combination of the Force and the pirates' own blasters to methodically mow them down. It was almost too easy. She'd already incapacitated the half-dozen who had been unloading the cargo ship, and Hondo had brought only another ten back with him. There was an ample supply of things to hurl at them—pitchers, a crate and the sharp-edged tools it was filled with, mugs, stools, even the pirates themselves could be used to knock their fellows down. It was good exercise, and Ventress welcomed the chance to work up a sweat while fighting hated Weequays. Respectful of Rhayme's wishes, she didn't shoot to kill, but several of them were on the ground writhing in pain from blaster shots to their arms or legs.

Suddenly Ventress felt a quick, bright urgency in the Force. She whirled, looking toward the far end of the hall, and saw her lightsaber hurtling upward.

It turned end over end, still lit. Some of Hondo's pirates tried to grab it in mid-air, and paid with their fingers. Others, more wisely, dove out of the way. Ventress shot out her hand and the hilt smacked into her palm. She grinned as she sensed the tension in the remaining four pirates skyrocket. At that moment, she heard the sound of another ship landing outside, and felt the presence of two-dozen life forms racing across the landing field.

She grinned, and set to.

"Not so fast!" Hondo warned as Lassa turned to fire on him. He struck her full in the chest with the end of the electrostaff and Lassa gasped, flailing helplessly as the jolts surged through her. She crumpled, gasping, and tumbled limply off the table, spasming on the ground.

He leaped lightly down and gazed at her. "A good effort, my dear. I'm impressed. You almost lived up to your—"

Rhayme lifted the blaster and aimed it directly at his chest.

"—reputation," Hondo finished.

"It's set to kill," she warned him. "Throw away the staff."

"Surely we can work this out like two civilized pirates," he protested, but did as she ordered.

Lassa got to her feet, still feeling the effects of the staff, but forcing herself not to show them. "On your knees, hands behind your head."

Again, Hondo obeyed. "Come now, Captain Rhayme, let us not be hasty."

She stepped forward, placing the tip of the blaster between his eyes. "You mocked me earlier. I think you've changed your tune."

"Most certainly," he said. To his credit, his voice was completely calm.

"I'm taking what's mine."

She fired.

"Hondo was rather charming, actually," Lassa said, finishing her account as she and Ventress sat in her cabin aboard the *Opportunity*. On the table beside the bounty hunter sat a nondescript metal box about a third of a meter high. "Of course I wasn't about to kill him, but he didn't know that. It'll be fun to hear what sort of rumors he'll spread."

"Well done," Ventress said as Rhayme uncorked a bottle of aged Tevraki whiskey. "So... I've been wondering something."

"Fire away."

"You don't have any tattoos." She'd noticed it immediately upon meeting Rhayme. All the Pantorans Ventress had encountered adorned their faces with bright yellow tattoos. She wasn't sure what they signified—family affiliation, social rank, personal achievements—but they all had them.

"That's because I have no loyalties other than to my crew," Lassa said. "*They* are my family. Otherwise—I belong only to myself. I am my own woman."

Ventress nodded. She liked that. She thought of her own tattoos, and how much they meant to her. Rhayme's unmarred face obviously conveyed the same pride.

Rhayme raised her glass. "To success—and, perhaps, new friends."

Asajj was surprised at her reaction. She didn't have "friends." But she'd grown to admire Lassa, and the other woman had kept to every part of their bargain. And... she was good company. Ventress said nothing, merely gave a fleeting smile as their glasses clinked. The whiskey was delicious—a warm, slow comfort slipping down her throat.

"Much better than what they serve in the bars on Thirteen-Thirteen," Ventress said. "I could get used to drinking this."

"Why don't you?" Lassa said. "I can provide erratic but profitable income, bed and board, adventure, fair treatment, and the company of the woman who beat Hondo Ohnaka in single combat." She winked a golden eye.

It sounded good. Very good. And for a long moment, Asajj Ventress was tempted. But then she thought of all the company she would bring along with her, the shades of the dead, the remnants of dark memories, and a wariness that would likely never fade. Ventress would never trust anyone, not really, not even this remarkable woman with whom she had partnered for a brief time. She would always be alone, and she accepted that.

"While that's a fine offer," she said, "I must decline."

She sensed Rhayme's genuine disappointment, but the Pantoran recovered quickly. "If you ever change your mind, the offer stands."

"And if you ever need a bounty hunter, I'm not hard to find."

"Deal." They shook hands. "In the meantime," Rhayme said,"let's take a look at this item that's been so problematic."

Ventress glanced at the box beside her. "Part of the deal was that I don't look at it."

"You've worked pretty hard for your bounty this time, Asajj. Go on. You can always say you were making sure it wasn't damaged in the fighting."

Ventress considered that. "Sheb does strike me as a dealer who'd appreciate that concern."

The lock was easy to pick, and Ventress carefully lifted the lid. A small force field in the box itself prevented unauthorized handling. Ventress was seldom moved by beauty alone, but this time, even her eyes widened as Rhayme gasped softly.

The object that had given her so much trouble was no gem, or weapon, but a simple statuette. A sea mammal with four flippers and an elongated muzzle was caught in a moment of joyous freedom, its small gem eyes sparkling, its sleek body curled beneath it so its tail merged with the wave that formed the base. The stone from which it was carved was a breathtaking shade of blue. The entire image—its sense of action, of grace and power and playfulness, its delight in movement, even its hue—seemed to Ventress to be a reflection of the Pantoran woman sitting before her.

A pirate's life—but not for me, she thought.

"A pity you can't keep it," Rhayme said.

Ventress merely nodded. With unwonted gentleness, she closed the lid and locked it.

"I do my job," she said, and slid her glass over for a refill.

INBRIEF

WRITTEN BY **JANINE K. SPENDLOVE**
ART BY **JOSE CABRERA**

"I don't care what those rebels are blowing up! Howl's old scow is in orbit, which means Twilight Company is here and that scum is—" The door burst open and Governor Magé slumped forward over her desk. The comlink she'd been shouting into slid from her now limp hand.

"Good shot, Brand." Captain Micha "Howl" Evon ran a brown hand over his bearded chin as he strode into the opulent office. "Can't abide anyone making fun of my ship or my people."

He admired Brand's efficient handiwork and decided he wanted the recipe to whatever juice was on the dart sticking out of the Imperial governor's olive neck. The governor's long, dark hair had tumbled out of her tightly wound bun, and she was already drooling, as was her aide, who'd attempted to guard the door.

These backwater worlds always underestimated Twilight Company's efficiency and resolve. Captain Evon always felt sorrow at the unnecessary losses that resulted.

The noises from the battle outside in the hallways of the Imperial Headquarters were already dying down and the luxury of the governor's office explained a lot about why Twilight Company hadn't met much resistance from the locals when they'd dropped into Allst Prime to take out the Imperial outpost here.

"This'll do nicely for the recruiting interviews." He waved vaguely behind him with his right hand while he holstered his blaster with his left.

"Mind moving her over there?"

Not one for many words, his companion merely grunted in response, and gave the Governor's chair a shove, rolling it noiselessly away from the massive desk.

"And if Governor Magé is like every other Imperial leech with a taste for luxury..." The captain whistled as he pulled open a desk drawer. "Hope you like Nabooian whiskey. I know I do." He splashed the amber liquid into two crystal glasses, savoring the spicy smell. "Go ahead and grab a chair for yourself, Brand. May as well knock out your official inbrief, it's long overdue."

Turning around, Evon found himself staring down the front sight of a blaster.

Finally.

He extended one of the glasses out as a broad smile split his black and gray-bearded face.

"We can get to you collecting my bounty in a bit, Brand. Have a drink first." Evon took a sip from his own glass and smacked his lips in satisfaction.

Instead of taking the drink, a gloved hand reached up and tapped the release on the neck portion of the bounty hunter's mask. Metal and mesh peeled back to reveal the face of a woman. The faintest beginnings of age lines creased the dark skin near her eyes and mouth, though there were no laughter lines. Her blaster arm remained steady.

Shrugging, the captain set the rounded glass down on the redwood desk between the two of them.

"Suit yourself." He pulled up another chair, eased himself into the supple leather behind him, and took another sip of the amber liquid with a contented sigh. "This chair is wonderful. I think I may have to take it back to the *Thunderstrike*." Evon returned his attention to Brand and indicated the plush chair next to her. "Have a seat; if you were going to shoot me, you'd have done it by now, Lauren."

For the first time the bounty hunter's arm wavered and a glimmer of shock momentarily raced through her dark brown eyes. "What did you call me?"

Pulling a datapad from his vest pocket, the captain scrolled through it with calloused, brown fingers until he reached the screen he was looking for. He angled it toward Brand so she could see the photo of a youngling in a blue and orange checked dress, with colorful, beaded braids framing her face, and an infant boy wrapped up at her hip.

"Lauren Mel Coelho," Howl made sure to properly roll the R in her first name, and pronounce the "yo" sound in her last name. "Born approximately thirty-eight years ago on Tangenine. Mother, Remba. Father, Kelven. Brother, Julian, though you called him Ju-ju."

"Lau! Lau, come, please."

Lauren stood up and shaded her eyes as she looked down the row of norango bushes separating her and her father. Her basket was already half-full of sweet red berries, and she had only snuck a few to eat, so she couldn't be in trouble. Not this early in the morning.

Her father saw her worried expression and his mouth split into a wide grin. His perfectly straight teeth gleamed like white stars against his skin, black as the night sky. It was beautiful. Lauren wished she could smile like her father.

"Don't worry, little one, you're not in trouble."

Relieved, she hefted her basket over to him, careful not to squash a single berry. Inspecting her collection, he reached out a hand and fluffed up her braids.

"Ada!" she whined, pushing his hand off. "I am not a youngling."

Tucking a fist under his jaw, he eyed his daughter. "Hmmm, I think you're right. You are much taller now, and you have been doing very well with your chores." He turned to pick up a basket of berries beside him, revealing Ju-ju gurgling happily from his bound perch on their father's back. Ju-ju's eyes, round and green as a norango leaf, locked with Lauren's and he gave her a smile that mirrored their father's. Turning back to her, Lauren's father gently poured some of his norangos into her basket, topping it off. "Take these in to Ama, please."

Lauren looked across the sprawling berry field—past the workers filling baskets of their own with berries, toward the modest farmhouse in the center of it all—her home.

"Can't I stay here and watch Ju-ju? I promise I'm old enough now." She stood up straight, rising onto her tip-toes.

"Why do I think you just don't want to face what your mother has to say about your last school report?" Laughing, her father reached out to fluff her braids again, and Lauren quickly ducked under his arm.

"Ada!"

He sobered when he saw her serious expression. Reaching back, he unbound Ju-ju and set him down between them.

"My little Lau, what is the most important thing?"

"Family," she answered, without hesitation. Any youngling knew that.

"And so you, your brother, and Ama are more precious to me than anything else." He crouched and picked up a handful of soil before crumbling it between his fingers. "Without family, we are just dirt blowing uselessly in the wind." Then he took Lauren's smaller hand in his and guided it to the base of a norango bush. "Family is the root that gives the soil purpose and holds it in place. We are nothing without our families."

He placed both hands on her shoulders. "Someday you will have your own family to take care of, little Lau—"

"—and I will have to make sure they are pruned and tended to. I know, Ada." Lauren forced herself not to roll her eyes as she finished her father's proverb.

Three guards climbed out of the transport, carrying big blasters. Lauren frowned—that green-skinned Falleen, Annaz, was the only person who ever came to the farm with hired guns.

The whine of a fancy-sounding landspeeder cut off her father's response, and Lauren followed his gaze down the dirt road that led to their farm. Even from this distance she could see the dust plume it kicked up.

"Lau, take your brother and go to your bisáma's house."

"But, Ada—"

"Now, Lau!"

Without sparing her or Ju-ju a second glance, he ran across the norango field to join their mother. Ama was standing in front of the house, hands in fists on her hips, tall, strong, and unyielding as always.

"Come, Ju-ju." Lauren picked up her little brother and gently pried the black soil from his clenched fingers before he could shove the dirt in his mouth. "That is not for eating!"

Bending over, she set Ju-ju on her back and pulled his carrying wrap tight around her body, just as she'd always seen her parents do. Straightening, she could now see the landspeeder—flashy and yellow—pull up in front of her parents. All the farmhands had gathered around it, too. Three guards climbed out of the transport, carrying big blasters. Lauren frowned—that green-skinned Falleen, Annaz, was the only person who ever came to the farm with hired guns.

Captain Evon watched as Brand's full lips compressed into a thin line. "Annaz and her henchmen killed your parents, and all their workers, after your mother refused to pay a protection fee to the Malandro syndicate. You managed to get out with your baby brother, and lived with your gran for a few years, until a fever took her."

Brand narrowed her eyes and the finger on her blaster curled around the trigger, but he was still alive, so Howl pressed on. "Ju-ju took ill next. There was a cure, you just didn't have the money to pay Malandro for it. So you took a job. Boosted a speeder. Got caught. Landed in jail. By the time you got out, your little brother was dead."

Evon set the datapad on the desk and leaned back in his chair. "Lauren disappeared after that." He raised an eyebrow. "Have I missed anything?"

Brand tightened her grip on her blaster, Howl ignored it.

"A few years later the Empire showed up and tried to bring their version of order to Tangenine. They just didn't realize how deeply imbedded Malandro was. It's not unheard of, the Empire turning to bounty hunters, but it was a desperate move, and desperation sometimes breeds opportunity. That's about when Brand pops up, a bounty hunter who *took jobs almost exclusively* against Malandro." Giving her a wry smile, Howl waved lazily at himself. "At least until recently."

The Falleen jerked her head up in surprise. "Who let you in here?"

Brand raised her blaster. "Hands where I can see them."

"Wait!" Annaz froze in the act of pressing the comm button under her desk. "This is a place of business; you can't just barge in here—"

Brand lunged forward and jerked Annaz's arm out from under the desk. Holstering her blaster, the bounty hunter pulled out a long, black, serrated blade and buried it up to the hilt in the Falleen's green hand, pinning it to the desk.

She wasn't being needlessly cruel—which would be no less than Annaz deserved; Brand knew that the surge of pain would overwhelm any attempt the Falleen could make to release pheromones in an attempt to subdue her attacker.

Annaz shrieked and tried to pull out the knife with her free hand, but Brand's blaster was back out and trained on her. "Move, and you'll lose that arm for good."

"Who sent you?" Blood oozed from the Falleen's pinned hand, and she was gasping between her words. "What do you want?"

Brand tugged off her hood.

She regarded Annaz carefully, wanting to savor this moment. The Falleen stared up at Brand, her flint black eyes holding no hint of recognition.

"You don't know who I am."

"Should I?" The Falleen hissed through gritted teeth.

"I remember the families of everyone I kill." Brand fired a shot into Annaz's knee. The Falleen wailed incoherently as Brand aimed her blaster between the woman's eyes.

"No!" Annaz held up a shaking hand between the blaster and her face. "What do you want? Credits?"

Brand's gloved finger curled around the blaster's trigger.

"Please! Don't! I can give you anything! A new life even!"

"You already gave me that."

Captain Evon took another sip. Brand still had the blaster pointed at him, but if he was going to die, it might as well be with the taste of good whiskey in his mouth.

"If you wouldn't mind humoring me a bit longer before you shoot me, I've been wondering, once you got your revenge on Annaz, why did you keep picking up bounties?" He swirled the liquid in his glass before taking another sip. "Not to come off as maudlin, but why me?" Evon eyed the woman before him as she furrowed her brows, quietly considering his words.

It's not unheard of, the Empire turning to bounty hunters, but it was a desperate move, and desperation sometimes breeds opportunity.

To a casual bystander, Brand would have been mistaken for a vagrant on any world. Her gray trousers were loose and worn, with assorted bulging cargo pockets. But beneath her tattered old cloak, the simple black blouse under a maroon, hip length jacket in pristine condition gave the lie to Brand's carefully cultivated shabby appearance.

Brand spoke, drawing his attention back to her carefully neutral face.

"Things were turning sour with the Empire. I needed off planet, and this was my ticket." She shrugged, meeting his gaze fully. "It's just business; nothing personal."

"Well, you'll excuse me if I do take it at least slightly personally." Angling his face up, Evon gazed at the vaulted, marbled, ceiling. "You know what's amazing? Office like this for an Imp administrator," he jutted his chin at the snoring Governor, "on a back-world planet like Allst Prime, and there's a city full of half-naked kids just outside the gates, digging through trash heaps for junk to sell or trade so they can get a bite to eat.

"If you shoot me, Brand, you're siding with that system. And you know, as well as I do, the Empire is, at heart, no different than Malandro."

"You saying the Rebellion is?"

"I don't know. Maybe. I can't speak for the Alliance as a whole." The captain laced his fingers together in front of him, resting them comfortably on his stomach. "But you know Twilight Company is different. Besides, if you kill me, who'll take care of the new recruits?"

"Fresh meat's not my problem."

A large belly laugh rumbled from Evon as he swept his booted feet atop the desk.

The bounty hunter furrowed her brows together and the blaster wavered, just a little.

"I've been watching you ever since you joined us on Veron. Oh sure, you tried to keep your distance—at least at first—but when we picked up that load of recruits off Dorvalla, I noticed you hovered."

"I did no—"

Captain Evon raised a hand. "I don't mean like a momma bird with her chicks. That'd be too obvious for your liking. More like a nexu supervising her cubs on their first hunt. You only stepped in to keep someone from getting hurt. And before you say it was just part of your cover to get at me, why don't you explain what happened out there today?"

Brand tackled the Mirialan boy to the ground just as the All Terrain Scout Transport's bolt sizzled into the tree behind them, blasting it to pieces.

"Hey, Brand! I've been looking for you." Lylee Anaraku grinned as a shower of wood splinters rained over them.

Brand rolled off him with a grunt. "Seems to me like you should have been looking out for the walker."

"Pshhh." Lylee waved his blaster dismissively toward the maneuvering AT-ST. "That stalker doesn't have a chance with you around." The gleeful curve of his lips made the young man's black diamond cheek markings spread out across his yellow-green skin.

"That what we're calling scout walkers now? Stalkers?" Brand gazed back across the heavily forested battlefield before them, trying to reacquire her target. "What happens if I'm not around?"

"I heard Briala call them that." Peering up over the log, Lylee aimed his blaster at an approaching Imperial. "And of course you'll be around. You always survive!"

He aimed at another Imp and squeezed the trigger. "Speaking of Bria, she's got a card deck, and once we mop up here, we're going to play a game of Lifters back on the *Thunderstrike*—"

Brand jerked him back down as another blaster bolt singed by where his head had been just a moment before.

Lylee's eyes, green as a norango leaf, glinted with barely contained mischief. "Want to join us for a game?"

Grunting, Brand pushed past him and crawled farther down the log. She'd found her target.

"Come on, Brand, it'll be fun! We can be partners—work out hand signals to tell each other what other suits we have, how many tricks we can take..."

The boy's voice and the rest of the battle faded to the background. She raised her blaster and lined it up squarely on the backlit profile of Captain Evon, not twenty meters from her. He was bent over the body of Twilight Company's Forward Air Controller, Cait, yelling into the receiver as he called for fire, directing the X-wings to their target. The FAC stared back at Brand with lifeless eyes, a dried smear of blood across her ashen lips was the only evidence of her trauma.

"Brand!" Lylee's strangled shout was followed by a meaty thud. Brand whirled around, and shot the Imp towering over the boy.

Not another one...

She dropped to Lylee's side.

"You better not die on me, kid." She pulled off his cloth head covering to get a look at the blood oozing from the back of his head. "You owe me a game of Lifters."

Howl's boots thudded back onto the floor as he sat up.

"You're making me tired. *Please* sit." He indicated the soft chair next to Brand once again. "We need to discuss your position in Twilight Company. Now I was thinking—"

"I'm not joining the Rebellion." Brand's frown deepened.

"I'm not asking you to." Howl leaned over the desk. "I'm asking you to *actually* join Twilight Company this time."

Brand straightened her finger off the trigger.

"Of course, you'll have to renege on that contract the Empire's got on my head." Evon grabbed his datapad again, swiped the screen, and pointed at his own bounty.

"Ignore a payout and make an enemy of the Imps, just so I could be one of your subordinate commanders?" Brand shook her head. "You must be crazy."

"I would never ask that." He waved his hand before him as if the very idea was preposterous. "That's not who you are. I don't want you to change for us, Brand. *We* need you as you are. All I want is unswerving loyalty—not to the Alliance, and not even to me—but to the people out there, the ones you saved today. The ones you're gonna play cards with when we get back to the ship." Howl punctuated his words with a nod toward the door. "The ones who already *think* you're one of them. And in return we'll give you the same."

He could see her weighing the words and the offer, and what it must have meant to someone who'd been a hired blaster for so long—

Brand suddenly picked up the drink before her and stared at it for a long moment, mumbling almost inaudibly "*and I will have to make sure they are pruned and tended to,*" before downing it in one gulp. "Don't think this means I won't collect your bounty." Holstering her blaster, she took a seat, and held her glass out for more. "It's just not high enough yet."

Howl refilled both their glasses and raised his in a toast. "Welcome to the family."

TK-462

WRITTEN BY **SYLVAIN NEUVEL**
ART BY **DREW BAKER**

There's no blood on the ground. It just keeps pooling inside my armor.

When did it all start? For me, that's an easy answer. I remember that day like it was... Not true. Yesterday's a haze. So is the day before that, and the one before. I remember *that* day. I was twelve. My father was caretaking a farm of air scrubbers on Eriadu. Endless fields of vertical machinery cleaning the air while the mining industry pumps more toxic stuff into it. Most people have never seen a scrubber farm—they build these things as far from civilization as humanly possible. No one wants to be reminded that they're the only thing keeping the air breathable. And besides, they're really ugly. We didn't mind. To my sister and I, the farm was a playground, a forest, an army of droids. Whatever we wanted it to be. Mother was gone, and while our father worked, it was always just the two of us. We rarely went to town—dad said it was dangerous—and there was no one else around.

Xea had just turned eight when the rebels came. She wasn't feeling well that night, and I let her sleep in my bed. She liked that. Their ships were quiet, almost silent. I'm not sure how father heard them, but he did. It was the sound of his blaster that woke me. When I made it outside, the rebel ships already had tow hooks on two of the air scrubbers. I guess they thought they could just grab them and leave. Amateurs. After a lot of tugging, one of the machines finally budged, but it was still tethered by a power conduit. That big shiny cable ripped through the ground as the scrubber rose above our heads and into darkness. Father started screaming, firing at the fast approaching furrow instead of the ship. I just watched. I didn't understand. I should have—I had read enough of those science books my mother gave me. She loved science. "If you're gonna live in this universe," she said, "the least you can do is try to understand how it works." Those books were all that was left of her, and I knew most of them by heart. Tensile strength. Units of force per cross-sectional area. How much pull can a thing take before it breaks apart. Dad didn't know anything about physics, but he had fixed enough of these conduits to know it would put up one hell of a fight. Ship, power conduit, tow cable. One of them had to lose. When the ship ran out of leash, it came to a sudden stop, and the tow cable snapped. Half a second later, the scrubber reappeared in the sky. It fell through our roof and into my room, crushing my little sister into the ground.

When did it start? Right then. At that very moment, I knew I wanted to kill rebels.

That was the year Wilhuff Tarkin became Grand Moff. Things changed quickly after that on Eriadu. Rule of law. Crimes were punished, harshly. Some say too harshly, but there was nothing to fear if you had nothing to hide. I for one didn't mind if a few terrorists were made an example of. Lives were saved. We felt protected. You could walk the streets of Phelar without fear of being robbed or gunned down. Dad even sent me for supplies on my own a few times. I don't know if Xea would have lived had Tarkin been in charge at the time. I do know she would have liked to see Phelar.

I met him once, the Grand Moff. He came to the farm not long after it was attacked. I'd never seen my father so nervous. I don't remember what Tarkin said. To be honest, I wasn't paying any attention to him. All I could see was the shiny white armor of the men standing behind him. Strong. Placid. Unafraid of the world around them. They would never feel powerless inside that armor. I knew right away: I was going to be a stormtrooper. My father refused, of course. He'd lost a child to the Rebellion, he wasn't going to lose the other one to the Empire. It didn't matter. Nothing did. I enlisted as soon as I was of age. I snuck out in the middle of the night, left a note on the kitchen table.

Junior Academy was a breeze. It's meant to weed out the weak, but there simply weren't enough recruits in Phelar. Local authorities were more concerned about not sending their fair share of recruits to the capital than with any of us being unfit for duty. There were seven of us in my unit, and our instructors took great care to ensure that there were seven graduates at the end of the year. I was going to be a stormtrooper.

We were still in the lobby when I met my instructor, a clone by the name of Lassar. Everyone called him Jogan, like the fruit. I never found out where he got the nickname.

My father didn't attend the ceremony. He wasn't there when I left for the capital. It didn't come as a surprise—I never told him I was leaving—yet I found myself scanning the dock for a familiar face until our transport was well in the air. There were so many things I never got to tell him. I didn't want goodbye to be one of them.

The Imperial Academy of Eriadu. They say it isn't as large or prestigious as the one on Coruscant. I wouldn't know. It looked plenty impressive to me. The main offices were in the old part of town. Ancient, insanely ornate. Whoever made all those carvings lived a very wretched life. We were still in the lobby when I met my instructor, a clone by the name of Lassar. Everyone called him Jogan, like the fruit. I never found out where he got the nickname. I also never dared to call him anything but Commander Lassar. He hated me. No, that doesn't sound right. He was a clone, a perfect fighting machine designed and bred for a sole purpose. We were lesser things, flawed, just for being born. Rapid aging had made his kind obsolete but it was obvious he resented the idea of enlisted men taking his place, and he loathed all of us for thinking we could. To him, we were a bunch of house pets trying to act like veermoks. So start with that, profound resentment. Think of that as the baseline. He *hated* me. "You're short, farm boy. You'll be outta here in a week." That's how he introduced himself. He was right. I *was* shorter than everyone else.

Kidney shots. Why do they hurt so bad? That's how my first morning at the academy started. Lassar had my comrades pull my blanket over my head and punch me in the sides until I stopped moving. That's how every morning started for an entire year. I wasn't angry at the other

recruits. Every cry of mine was a stark reminder that it was best to stay on Lassar's good side. After about a week, I could tell they started pulling their punches, adding a little "ugh!" for dramatic effect. All the while, the commander just stood there and smiled. In his defense, he smiled all the time—literally. It might have been nerve damage.

Stupid as it may seem, being whaled on every day before breakfast only served to strengthen my resolve. The way I saw it, quitting after a day meant I'd taken a beating for nothing, the next day it was two beatings, then 50, then 100. After a year, I would have hit myself if it meant I could go on for another day. I was going to be a stormtrooper.

A new year meant a fresh batch of recruits. I hated myself for it, but I hoped one of them would be a bigger—how did he put it? Oh yes. A bigger "insult to the memory of the countless clones who gave their lives on the battlefield." No such luck. I was special. I don't know what they do to the suspected insurgents to make them talk. I only heard rumors. Whatever it is, I'm fairly certain it was done to me at some point or another during my training. I wouldn't break. Not then.

It was only a couple weeks before graduation. I can't help thinking that he timed it that way so it would hurt even more. It was a hot, sticky day, the kind of hot even a cold shower can't fix. We did a 5K run in full gear as a fitness exam. Before we left, Commander Lassar gave a little speech and offered a toast to those of us who had made it this far. It wasn't much of a toast since he was the only one with a drink. He downed the emerald wine and crushed the glass on the ground with his boot, as if part of some ancient custom none of us knew about. Then he asked me to remove my boots. I watched him put the broken pieces inside. The little ones worried me the most: the ones that burrow inside your flesh. I put the boot on. It wasn't courage. I did it out of spite. Spite ran out about 500 meters in. Focus and determination, that got me another three steps. After that, it wasn't me. Pain is an output from the brain, not an input from the body. Too many pain signals to deal with and the brain shuts down—parts of it anyway. All the things that make me *me*, my senses, my soul, or whatever you want to call it, all of that was gone. Whatever crossed that finish line wasn't me. It wasn't human.

I woke up in the infirmary three days later. They had reconstructed both my feet. I didn't know if I had finished the race. I didn't care. Every part of me had conceded defeat. I asked the nurse if I could speak to Commander Lassar. He found me lacking

on that very first day. Now that I had been measured, I felt I should be the one to tell him he was right. The nurse told me it would have to wait. The doctor had ordered two weeks of rest. Whatever I had to tell the commander, I could tell him after graduation. "You made it", she said, "You're a stormtrooper." Xea would have been proud.

I had made it. The elite shock troops of the Imperial Army. I was assigned to patrol district five in Eriadu City, the fashion district. The shock part was a bit of an overstatement, though plenty of shoplifters were genuinely surprised to see us. And some of them ran. We liked it when they ran. I had signed on with something slightly different in mind, but petty crime was still crime, and someone had to stop it. I was good at it. I liked watching people enjoy the sense of order and safety we provided. The way that people walk when they're unafraid, that careless stride, it was quietly rewarding. I wish it had been enough, but I could never quell the anger. After a year, I heard they were sending more troops to Lothal and I volunteered.

First time off the planet. Up until we left spaceport, I had held on to the notion that I would see my father again. I felt a knot in my stomach when the ship left the atmosphere, then I got really, really sick. It turns out I'm not built for space travel. Good thing I didn't choose the Navy.

The air on Lothal was different. Everything was different. People there had been through some tough times, and it showed. It also made them more genuine. I loved it there at first. The people in my unit were good men and women.

Our captain was raised on a nerf farm. He wouldn't stop talking about it. He could reduce just about every problem imaginable to some simple fact about farming. Crowd control? Think of it as nerf-herding. Hostage situation? You have to keep everyone calm—like assisting a nerf at calving. Terrorism? Well, imagine some of the nerfs contracted the Felucian flu. What do you do to save the herd? You put down all the sick animals, and maybe a few of the healthy ones they had been in close contact with. You have to act fast for it to work, but if it does, the rest of the herd will keep on grazing as if nothing ever happened.

I had a feeling it wouldn't be that easy. It wasn't. I've done things I… I'm not a military strategist. Hell, I'm probably not officer material. I realize I'm part of something infinitely bigger than anything I can fathom, and that the reason for everything might not be apparent for someone like me. Still… I've done things. Burning down a small village might indeed be for the good of the Empire. It might save lives down the road. But while you're doing it, it's hard to see the good of the Empire. It just feels like you're burning down a small village. We're the ones that have to deal with the screams, the crying children. I was doing exactly what I set out to do, I was hurting rebels. But I had always imagined it in black and white. Now I was swimming in a sea of gray. There were days when I missed grabbing petty thieves on Eriadu, the clarity of it. Still, I've never been squeamish about carrying out orders. I did my job.

Today, we went hunting for a stolen shipment of rare Kyber crystals. We were pretty happy with ourselves when we found it before lunchtime. There were check posts on every road in the area. Whoever stole that shipment obviously panicked and abandoned it near one of the resettlement camps. We grabbed a bite and headed there to find them. The captain told us how, when a nerf strays from the herd and gets lost, you smack one hard on the butt to make it wail. All the other nerfs will start bawling—some sort of natural instinct—and, with any luck, the stray will hear the nerf choir and find its way back. None of us had any idea what the captain meant, but he seemed pretty confident in his nerf-inspired stratagem, so we didn't ask. Apparently, it meant grabbing a Rodian shopkeeper by the throat and dragging him to the center of the town square before putting a blaster to his head. He said whoever stole the crystals had to the count of three to come forward, or the Rodian would die. He'd picked the wrong Rodian. No one said a word, even as he hit the ground dead. The captain grabbed a human next, a woman. He didn't bother explaining himself a second time and started counting down right away. As soon as he said "three," a man came out of the building to my left, holding a rifle. I shot him on the spot. You don't point a gun at a stormtrooper. You just don't.

A little girl—she couldn't have been more than ten—came out behind him and ran over to the body. She tried to get him up, shake him back to life. She really tried. One of the first things you learn in the corps is that bodies somehow weigh a million times more dead than they ever did when they were alive. It's like trying to pick up a sack of water. She fell back on top of him, then she just lay there, combing his hair with her hand.

It was chaos, blaster fire all around. Another trooper called for help. I turned my head for a second, and that's when she shot me. I didn't actually hear the shot, but I felt all my insides move away from the blast point in a nanosecond. There was no point in looking at it. She got me good. I just fell to my knees—that part happened all on its own—and I removed my helmet. It felt good. The breeze on my face, the smells, peripheral vision. And here we are. I'm dying.

I turned my head for a second, and that's when she shot me. I didn't hear the shot but I felt all my insides move away from the blast point in a nanosecond... She got me good.

She's still looking at me. Standing tall over her father's corpse, all four feet of her. That rifle is just as long as she is, but she's holding it straight. Her dad taught her well. She's not firing. She knows I'm done for, but it's more than that. I recognize that look. She's feeling something she can't understand yet. I know because I felt it the night my sister died. It's happening right in front of me. All that pain, that anger. It was too much to handle a moment ago, like a swarm of lyleks you just can't fight off. She's not fighting anymore. She's letting it in. Part of her just died, but what's left is feeling more alive than ever. She has purpose. There! Right now. She knows. She'll grow up to be a rebel. She's going to kill stormtroopers.

I wonder why I'm smiling. I bet you she's wondering too. What is it I'm feeling? It's not guilt. It should be, but it's not. Pride, maybe? Look at her! She's beautiful.

When did it start? For her, a second ago. When will it end? I'm coming Xea.

SCORCHED

WRITTEN BY **DELILAH S. DAWSON**
ART BY **JOE CORRONEY**

The moment Greer Sonnel finished chugging her drink, she knew something was wrong. Normally, she savored the scorching rush as it burned down her throat, hitting her belly like a bomb and practically smoking out her nose. To any pilot from Pamarthe, there was no better augury of triumph than an empty cup of Port in the Storm. But this time, the heat ripped into her head and touched down behind her eyes like a tornado, scrambling her thoughts and making her dizzy as her empty cup hit the bar.

Not again, she thought. *Not today.*

Surrounded by dozens of pilots who'd love to take her down, her grin didn't waver. She wouldn't show weakness. Not now, not ever.

As the other three clay cups slammed down on the rough wood, Greer held up her empty cup. "To the Gauntlet. If it's not me that wins, I hope it's one of you choobies."

"To we, the pilots of Pamarthe!" Torret shouted, clinking his cup to hers.

"To the bloody stone of Corellia. May we never taste it!" Bors growled.

"To the losers!" Vee crowed. "Which is everybody but us."

Her three fellow Pamarthens were talented competitors, and Greer could honestly say she hoped none of them died today. The Gauntlet was a mysterious and dangerous race sponsored by Han Solo himself, and everyone knew it was the chum pit from which elite young pilots were chosen to add to teams for the Five Sabers. That had been Greer's dream, ever since her parents had told her tales of flying for the rebels: to race in the Five Sabers and make them proud. With no war to fight, the fierce and restless children of Pamarthe had to be the best at something, and it might as well be the something with the biggest purse and the most reknown.

More and more bargoers noticed the time and hurried from the room until only Greer's table was left. They'd checked their ships down to the molecule, what good would worrying do? That wasn't their way. No one stood until the warning gong sounded, giving them ten minutes. Even then, Greer and her friends sauntered toward the hangar. They might run to their ships, one day—if there was ever a war worth fighting again.

At the open door, they parted to find their starfighters. Docking spots in the domed hangar had been assigned by lottery, the ships towed into place while the pilots waited. It was an odd set-up: Fifty ships in a circle, their noses pointed inward like the spokes of a wheel. Greer found her ship on the far side and didn't stop walking when an unfamiliar young pilot dropped a spanner as she walked by. With her hips naturally swinging in her slim-fit flight suit and her ink-black hair pulled back in a chignon, Greer was used to it. She valued skill over beauty and preferred the looks they gave her rear cam after she left their ships in the stardust.

A crude whistle drew her attention—and drew her hand to her knife. Turning slowly, as if she had all the time in the world, she gave the catcaller a dead-eyed stare that only went frostier when she recognized him. With a snort of derision, she continued walking.

"You can't ignore me forever," Karsted called from a shiny black TIE fighter.

"I can try," she muttered.

And who knew? Maybe her ruthless, narcissistic, cheating ex would crash his splashy ship and explode into a thousand pieces. That would be almost as satisfying as killing him herself.

She walked past two more ships and stood before her newest obsession: *The Ossifrage*. The Gauntlet released specs required of entrant vessels every year, and Greer had blown what was left of her savings on what only looked like a piece of scrap. The ship had begun as an A-wing riddled with scars from its time fighting the Empire, and despite Greer's extensive modifications, *the Oss* still wore its scorch marks like war paint. Greer climbed in, put on her helmet, and looked around the hangar, trying to puzzle out the race.

That was the thing about the Gauntlet: Every year, it changed. The previous year, it had involved dodging geysers over Cato Neimoidia's stormiest ocean. The year before that, the racers had slugged through an abandoned city half-buried in groundquake rubble and crawling with giant lizards. The pilots were given no clues other than specs for their ships and, at the starting line, a course map. After the final warning buzzer rang, a mechanized voice spoke into Greer's helmet.

"Welcome to the Gauntlet. This year's course is named The Evil Eye. Your map will upload simultaneously with the race's start. There are ten Eyes, and your score will depend on how many Eyes you can thread weighted against your overall time. When the countdown is complete, the race begins. Ten. Nine..."

Greer fired up the *Oss* and looked to the hangar door, but it was closed... and blocked by a green B-wing. Her heart kicked up a notch and her face went warm as she realized there was no way out. The floor appeared solid, and the dome didn't seem to be made of any material that would allow it to open or change shape. And that meant...

"Two. One. Go."

Light flooded the room as a circular hatch opened in the center of the dome's roof, and Greer knew in an instant what she had to do. Slamming on the throttle, she pulled back hard and left burn marks on the floor as she aimed straight up for that hole of sky surrounded by blinking blue lights: the first Eye.

The other pilots weren't as quick to catch on, and Greer allowed herself a moment of triumph from the other side of the hangar, watching the strangely polite dance to get out a hatch that could only accommodate one starfighter at a time. Two ships got greedy and collided in a fireball, slowing down the rest of the swarm. Enough time to gloat, now she had to fly.

The map sent her toward an icon of an eye, and she went for it at full speed, zooming far above the terrain of Corellia. Two other vessels were near, the rest following farther behind like crows trailing Pamarthen lions. It wasn't long before her goal appeared—a hoop of blinking blue lights set at a bizarre angle. She needed to go through it, to thread the Eye. As soon as she was through, the map revealed that the next one was just out of orbit.

So it was that sort of race, then? Swooping in and out of atmo? So be it. *The Ossifrage* could handle it, and so could Greer, who'd been performing such feats since she was old enough to "borrow" her mother's beat-up Y-wing and joyride across the stormy seas of Pamarthe. She shot upward into the clouds, determined to be the first pilot to hit the next target. The same two ships were close on her tail, Karsted's TIE fighter and another A-wing similar to hers but far more flashy, with modded fins and a metal coating that made it mirror-like. Far behind them, several dozen ships were catching up. She wasn't worried. They couldn't beat her—not once she hit space and had room to run.

"You guys okay?" she asked, already tuned to the agreed-upon channel shared by the Pamarthen racers.

"Bors didn't make it," Vee said. "Scraped off in the hangar. Alive but angry."

"Could be worse," Torret added. "At least he's already back to drinking."

"This is one hell of a course." Greer paused for the fizz of unexpected heat that shouldn't have accompanied hitting atmo and kept talking once she was in the black. "We're looking at an orbital shipyard for number two."

"Feeling generous?" Torret asked.

Greer chuckled. "Only because there's no way you can catch me."

Being in space always put Greer in a good mood. Something about the vastness, the possibility, the glittering stars—it was where she was meant to be. And during the most important race in her entire life, thus far? All the better. She forced herself to ignore the worries that surfaced along with sweat along her hairline. She was fine. There was nothing wrong. Really.

The other A-wing was creeping up as they neared the floating shipyard, abandoned and still. Only the Eye showed glowing lights.

"That little wedge looks like it's been in a trash heap since the Rebellion."

The voice in Greer's helmet was male and unfamiliar, and it sounded amused. Since only two ships were in her view and she had Karsted's channel blocked, the voice had to belong to the pilot of the other A-wing. Trash talk was nothing new, and she wouldn't let it vex her. But that didn't mean she was going to play nice, either.

"And yours looks like it was dipped in a droid bath. Let me guess. It's so you can see your reflection better? "

He chuckled. "It's not always about ego, kid."

"We're pilots. It's always about ego. Now shut up."

With an elegant swoop, she shot through the Eye, already on course for number four, which was back on Corellia. And, if she was reading the map right, underground.

"Nice flying," the man said.

She was going to block his comm and ignore him along with Karsted, but he copied her loop so flawlessly that she had to admit he had skills. "Just try to keep up," she said, as close as she'd come to a compliment.

Greer pushed the *Oss* through atmo and almost closed her eyes for another swoon before she realized that dozens of ships were headed in her direction, burning hard for the Eye she'd just threaded. Oops. She had to focus. With time to spare, she flew a wide spiral to maximize her speed and avoid the other pilots. Just behind her, the other A-wing kept pace.

"You okay?" the pilot asked.

She ignored him and looked for her friends among the throng.

"Kothan si!" Torret yelled as he shot past.

"Kothan si!" Greer repeated the traditional Pamarthen greeting, which roughly translated to *May you die at full throttle*. "Wait. Where's Vee?"

"Lost her in the first Eye," Torret said. "Skidded out. Probably alive."

"Blast. That's two out."

"With two left. Loser buys the next round!"

With that, he was gone, blazing upward. Greer aimed straight for the next Eye and savored the fall. She loved the mix of complete control and utter chaos, when the ship was half ruled by fuel and half by gravity. Her stomach flipped, a stronger wave of heat throbbing behind her eyes and making her hands shake with sudden chills. There was no choice but to ignore it, to push it down. She opened her eyes and focused on the horizon, breathing deeply.

"Is that you or the ship wobbling, kid? You buy some bad fuel or something?"

"I think I sucked another pilot into an engine," she answered, annoyed that the stranger had caught her moment of confusion.

After a few beats of silence, he asked, "So, why'd you help that guy, telling him about the next Eye?"

Greer snorted. He was breaking her concentration. It wasn't normal, talking so much to strangers during a race like this, even if they were capable flyers. And yet she didn't feel like he was trying to pick her up, as per usual. He sounded genuinely curious.

"He's from my planet."

"A friend?"

"If you mean I don't want him to die, then yes. Wait." She glanced at her comm. "How are you on our channel?"

"It's all open," he said, ignoring the fact that it was supposed to be private. "Would you prefer I go public?"

"No." He was entertaining and a decent pilot, and talking to him kept her from

That was the thing about the gauntlet: Every year it changed. The previous year, it had involved dodging geysers over Cato Neimoidia's stormiest ocean.

thinking about the fever or Karsted. She was completely certain that the blinking red light on her comm was his repeated attempt to hail her—and heckle her. "One annoying pilot is better than thirty-six annoying pilots, thanks. Now shut up. It's about to get tricky."

"Oh, good," he said. "I was worried it was boring you."

The next Eye was underground. Breathing deeply, she dove the *Ossifrage* between the red stone walls, dodging rock formations. The A-wing stayed behind her, but Karsted suddenly burst past them both, using what had to be an illegal mod. He nudged her wing, forcing her to do a barrel roll to avoid exploding against the wall. When the cave yawned around the next corner, she shot inside, her hands shaking as she zipped underneath Karsted's ship. If she was going to lose this race or die, it wasn't going to be because of him, and it wasn't going to be because of the mysterious illness that she'd been ignoring for months. Failure, like, victory, would happen on her own terms.

The A-wing pilot was quiet as she zoomed through the cave, turning sideways to zip between two stalactites and beat them both through the Eye, which hung upside-down from the ceiling. The tunnel immediately curved and spit them out of a basalt cliff over furiously pounding waves.

The next Eye was on an island's rocky promontory. The one after that was in a city, strung between skyscrapers. She almost clipped a wing on the ivy-covered Eye in a canyon, then swooped back up to a floating circle of blue lights anchored to a weather balloon.

If she'd been flying slowly, the course would've made a lovely tour of Corellia. As it was, she was pushing the *Ossifrage* to her limits—and her skills, too. The second time she swooped out of atmo and into space to head for an Eye floating in an asteroid field, the burning fever returned, so fast and hot that she blacked out for a split second and let go of the throttle.

"You slacking off, kid? Trying to let me win? Breathe through your nose and focus on the horizon if you have trouble with atmo jumps."

It was the guy in the A-wing again, and he sounded worried. And no wonder. Her speed had fallen off, and Karsted's TIE was almost past her. She slammed the throttle forward knowing full well that she'd rather explode against an asteroid than let Karsted win.

"I know what I'm doing. I just wanted to give the others a fighting chance," she said, swallowing down her worries and focusing on dodging asteroids. Six more ships were visible behind her now, including Torret's X-wing. The fever drained away as quickly as it had come, leaving her face cool and her hands steady, and that was all she needed to send her back into the zone, flying the *Oss* with the preternatural talent that had been her gift from day one.

"Nice," the stranger muttered as she slipped through the Eye, twirled around an asteroid, and raced back toward Corellia and the last eye.

"I couldn't hear you in my wake."

His response was another chuckle. "Let me know how mine tastes."

Although the shiny A-wing had lingered behind her, now Greer got to see what the mysterious pilot could do. He plunged through the Eye, executed a perfect flip, and caromed past her with impossible speed. She was so impressed that she forgot to be jealous for a moment.

"Did you add an extra engine?" she asked.

"A little something new from Novaldex. They call this ship the Double-A. This is a test run."

"Nice," she breathed, following him through atmo.

Once Greer was back in blue sky over Corellia, the *Ossifrage* shuddered. Her instrument panel went berserk, lights beeping and alarms blaring. This time, at least, the source of the burn surging through her veins was clear: rage. Karsted's TIE filled the screen. Her fist landed on the red comm button.

"Did you just shoot me?"

Karsted's laugh dripped arrogance. "Of course not. No weapons allowed—you know that. Must've been a chunk falling off that relic of yours—into your right thruster, say. Or maybe you're just not meant to be a pilot."

So he'd sabotaged her. And now her system showed something stuck in a thruster, causing her to veer right as she slowed down.

"Oh, no! Is the great Greer Sonnell about to lose?" Karsted taunted.

"Who's this joker?" Double-A asked.

Greer snorted. "My ex. If you have

guns, please shoot him down and take his ship for scrap."

"Forget him. Look, your right thruster is blocked. You need to power off for ten seconds and restart with the throttle on hot and your right stabilizer maximized."

It made sense to her, but she'd never heard of this trick before. "Why should I trust you?" she asked as Karsted shot past her, hurtling toward the last Eye.

"Because you know I'm right, and you know I could beat you if I wanted to. If you don't trust me, trust your gut. But do it now, or you're out of the running and that other guy wins."

Without a word, she powered off, the ship gliding forward as it lost altitude. Cold seeped into the cockpit, and Greer's stomach dropped out as she counted to ten, her breath fogging the glass. The Double-A slowed to pace her. When her countdown hit zero, she restarted and punched the right stabilizer as she pushed the throttle. The *Ossifrage* came back to life in a melee of alerts and jerked to the side as a tumbling sound ended with a loud bang on the right. The instrument panel went back to normal as the rest of the ships came into view in her rear cam.

The three craft raced toward Corellia. Greer had mere seconds to make her choice. A stranger she liked or a known quantity she hated who would only use her to beat her own time?

Greer exhaled in relief. "Where'd you learn that trick?"

Double-A chuckled. "I used to have a hell of a copilot."

"I owe you one," she said. "Both of you."

"Pay me back by beating the guy in the TIE."

Greer checked her map and her view. The last Eye was on the ground by the spaceport and larger than the others had been.

"This seems too easy..." she started.

The mechanized voice over her helmet, said, "For the final Eye, double points will be awarded for two ships passing simultaneously through the sensors."

"Still trust me?" Double-A urged.

Karsted had looped around, knowing that if he passed through alone, he had no hope of coming in first. Greer realized too late she'd neglected to close his comm.

"You'd fly with a stranger instead of a Pamarthen?" he broke in. "Whatever happened in the past, we're a good team. We're from the same town. I was

your first kiss. You know me. Let's fly through together."

The three craft raced toward Corellia. Greer had mere seconds to make her choice. A stranger she liked or a known quantity she hated who would only use her to beat her own time? If nothing else, two A-wings would slip through the loop more easily than the bulky TIE.

"I'm going with the A-wing," she said. Her fist slammed the red button as Karsted called her a rude word in Huttese.

"Okay, Double-A," she said. "I'll take top. You take bottom."

"Roger that. Let's do it."

Greer angled the *Oss* up, and a bolt of light shot past, barely missing her ship.

"That's your ex and his illegal guns again, isn't it? We need to lose him. Any ideas?"

Racking her brain, Greer came up empty. With no weapons and no shields, what could they do? Damn Karsted and his blasted ego!

"Wait. That's it!" she cried. "Double-A, can you use your ship to blind him?"

Double-A chuckled. "Good call, kid. You fly a loop and leave him to me."

Greer pulled back, shooting straight up and looping behind the black TIE fighter. The Double-A turned sideways and passed in front of Karsted, and Greer shut her eyes as the mirror-like A-wing aimed a bright white flash across the TIE's window. When she opened her eyes again, Karsted had slowed dramatically and veered off, and she dodged around him and back on course.

"See? It's not all about ego."

"We can debate that *after* we win the race," she said.

As they swooped into position, the Double-A slowed to match her speed, the ships flying across the grassland with less than a meter between the stranger's cockpit and Greer's hull. Her hands were steady, her head mercifully clear after the raging fevers and dizziness that she could no longer ignore. Her chin jutted out as they threaded the final Eye as smoothly as if they'd been flying together forever.

Greer's map changed, directing her back to the dome where the race had begun. She couldn't stop smiling. She'd won! Or if not won, tied. And even if ties weren't acceptable on Pamarthe, such skillfully coordinated flying infused her with triumph. When she got back home, she'd go to a medcenter and find the cause of her illness—and the cure. Flying like this was her everything, and she wasn't going to let some stupid fever slow her down. At least it wasn't bloodburn. It couldn't be. That was a weakness she would never allow.

"Nice flying, Greer."

"Nice flying, Double-A." Then she caught it. "Wait. How do you know my name?"

The other A-wing swooped in, side by side, the pilot saluting her from his cockpit. He'd taken off his helmet to reveal gray hair and a cocky, lopsided smile.

"The name's Han Solo," he said. "And I'd like to talk to you about joining my team for the Five Sabers."

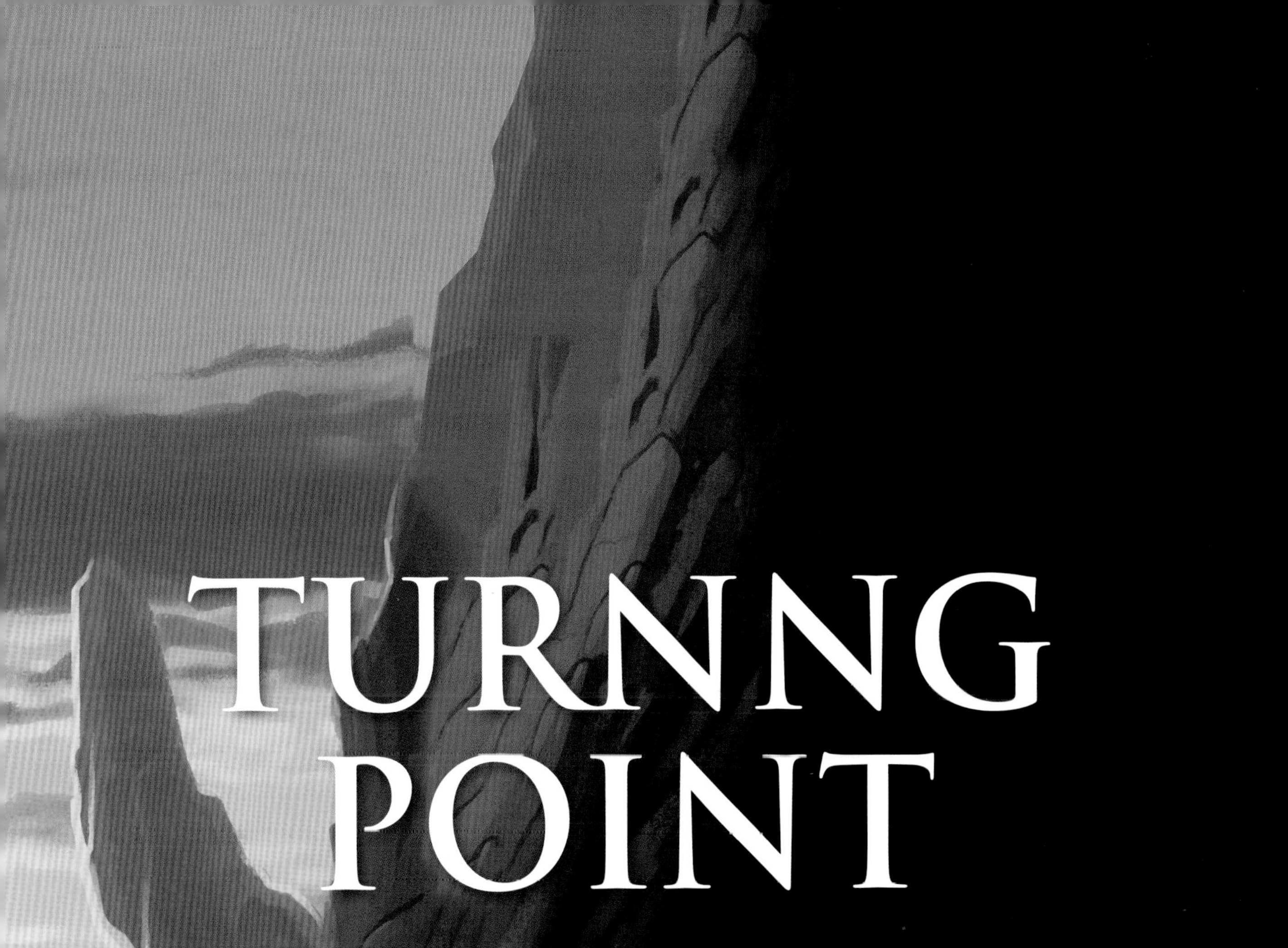

TURNNG POINT

WRITTEN BY **JASON M. HOUGH**
ART BY **CARSTEN BRADLEY**

Imperial stormtroopers are many things, but subtle they are not.

That morning I'd risen early, troubled, though I couldn't say why. Dawn had yet to break. I'd left Chloa and the kids to their dreams and done the only thing I knew would ease my mind: cleaned my gear.

Which is why I was in my workshop below the house, working grime out of the hinges of a trap, when I heard them.

I tracked them by sound alone, enjoying the mental exercise though it wasn't especially difficult. They moved at a brisk march, the sound of boots slapping against worn cobblestones. Four sounded identical and would have made a standard patrol for Tavuu's winding streets. Only there were three more pairs. Two, their steps fell heavier. More than a simple patrol, then, for they carried something. Bigger guns? That twisted my gut. Weapons of any sort were rarely needed in this quiet district of the city above the jungle. Tavuu was a big place, the capital city of Radhii. Plenty of crime and unrest in the darker corners on the eastern side to keep the garrison busy. Over here, though, on the western edges where the city abruptly ended at a monstrous cliff face, things were peaceful.

It was as if an unspoken agreement had been reached, long ago, among those of us who lived in this part of the city. We're cornered here; nowhere to go but over the edge, so we'll play along. We'll keep our heads down.

It was the last pair of footsteps that I focused on now. Lighter on the step, feet rolling slightly. Not subtle, perhaps, but not entirely unfamiliar with the concept, either.

They were beyond the alley, in the market.

I set the trap down, half cleaned, and laid the oiled rag beside it. My overeager ASP droid made a little *glomp* sound—*may I put that away?*—but I shushed it, my ears now fully pricked. Footfalls in the puddle-ridden alley. As their steps grew louder I grew nervous. Which one of my neighbors had earned Imperial attention? I should pay more attention to our neighbors. The only thing we shared was this row of old houses huddled together at the edge of the cliff. Beyond the wall at my back was a sheer rock face leading to the forest below.

The forest. Zoess, its ancient name, which literally meant *impenetrable*. My second home.

Chloa's voice, behind me. "Gorlan, dear?"

"Thought you were asleep."

She knew the art of subtlety. After all these years she could still slip up behind me—me!—and plant a kiss on the back of my neck, my first inkling of her presence being the static just before her lips arrived. "Do they come for us?"

Footsteps on the wooden stairs outside, answering her question. I turned, met my wife's eyes, and shrugged. "Let's find out."

They knocked hard enough to rattle the heavy door. I waited a few seconds, tried to make myself look tired. They liked to wake you. Draw you from bed.

Chloa stood beside me, chin up, as I creaked the door open a few centimeters. "Yes?" I said, with a touch of morning rasp.

"Gorlan Seba?"

"Yes?"

"May we enter?"

He wore no helmet, this one. Dark hair, sharp features, keen eyes. I knew little of Imperial rankings but the fact that he was in charge was unmistakable. "Have we done something wrong?"

The man's face tightened, ever so slightly, and I knew the answer to my question, plain as day. What I'd done wrong was not say yes to his request.

"On the contrary," he said. "We are here to hire you. We need a guide."

I said nothing. I couldn't think of anything to say.

"We need," he went on, "to visit the Zoess."

I stared, at a loss. Chloa gathered her wits before I could. "When?" she asked.

"Right now. This very morning."

"Impossible," I said automatically. "A proper expedition takes weeks to prepare."

"We don't have weeks," the leader said through clenched teeth. Then he glanced around, pointedly studying the curtained windows and balconies around us. Finally he held up his hands, palms out. "Let us in, and I'll explain."

I sat beside Chloa, arms folded across my stomach, and listened.

"There was an escape," the leader said. He'd introduced himself as Lieutenant Vrake and rattled off a bunch of numbers and classifiers no doubt impressive to someone who cared about such things. Only the subtext mattered. He had authority here. "Yesterday," he added, one eyebrow arched.

I realized he was waiting for me to speak. "Oh?" I said, and felt a little jab from Chloa's elbow. *Don't make trouble.*

"Any visitors last night?"

"No."

"Nothing out of the ordinary, then?"

My mouth opened on its own to say no, but memory held me back. I swallowed. "Well," I said, and felt Chloa tense. I pressed on. "Didn't think much of it at the time. Kids, I figured. Running around just after last bell. They raced up the alley and—"

Vrake leaned in. "You spoke with them? Aided them?"

A hint of accusation. I shook my head. "Only heard them. My hearing is pretty good."

"And?" Vrake asked.

"And nothing. They—whoever they were—were gone by the time I even sat up." It was the truth.

Vrake considered this. Then he explained.

Four soldiers of the Rebellion, prisoners, managed to escape a transport on the way to Segenka prison, all the way over on the east side of Tavuu near the Imperial base. Witnesses had seen the rebels descending the cliff eight hours ago, half a kilometer north of here, using one of the ancient stone ladders carved into the very rock. The reckless way. An act of desperation.

I sat there, staring at the man across from me and the two white-armored troopers behind him, weapons held angled toward the floor. It could just as easily have been four outlaws across from me, seeking a guide, if only they'd known to stop instead of running past last night. I wondered what I would have done. I cared about the Rebellion as much as I cared about Imperial rule. Which is to say, not much. None of my business. I had Chloa and the kids, and I had the Zoess. That was enough for me.

"We understand you have a lift," Vrake said. "And we know your reputation as a tracker. No one knows the forest as well as you. So I am asking you, Gorlan, to help us bring these criminals back."

Asking. Right. So easy to ask for something when you can just demand it if the answer is no. In fact, the only reason to bother asking at all in such circumstances was to give the person a chance to show their loyalty. I rubbed at my chin, pretended to consider the supposed request. Chloa put her hand on my arm and patted it. Get this over with, her gesture said.

I cared about the Rebellion as much as I cared about Imperial rule.

Finally, I nodded to the lieutenant. "You'll have to leave those blasters behind. And your communicators. Won't work down there."

"They've been specially hardened. With the extra shielding—"

My patient smile stopped him. "A common mistake that's caused more accidents down there than I care to count. Trust me, they won't work."

"Hmm." Vrake frowned. "Well, you are the expert."

"You want a good knife. Maybe a spear. I have a few extra. You're welcome to them."

One of his men leaned forward and whispered something to him. "Ah, good," Vrake said to him. He turned back to me. "It seems we may have an alternative."

Twenty meters from the base of the cliff, my lift came to a silent stop. Before we stepped off, I held a finger to my lips, a gesture acknowledged by Vrake. He and his squad stood perfectly still, waiting. They'd all left their helmets behind. None of the augmentations they offered would work once we descended below the canopy, which made them worse than useless: they'd hinder hearing and visibility, two things much more important than armor once in the Zoess. Still, I thought they might figure out a way to keep them. Gut their electronics, maybe. Something, if only to retain the fearsome edge their faceless uniform provided.

We all stared out at the vast bulbous carpet of foliage, alive with greens, purples, and yellows.

The forest hummed.

A low, undulating sound, almost like a pulse. Little more than background noise to those in the city high above, but down here the hum was a physical thing. It weighed on you. A pressure, wrought of the electrostatic build-up in the lightning trees that populated the forest. I gave the squad a moment to get used to it, while I listened for other things. Ghoma, and other, rarer, beasts. All quiet, for now.

"From here you do exactly as I say," I told them. The troopers looked to Vrake, who gave me a single, sharp nod.

We left the platform by a series of wooden steps that descended out to the edge of a small clearing, away from the trash and debris that had been dumped along the cliff's edge before Imperial law forbade the practice.

We hiked north, to the base of the stone ladder, a series of footholds carved into the face of the cliff ages ago, some so worn they were barely visible. I pointed out signs that people had descended here recently, just as Vrake's witnesses had said. Trampled leaves, newly exposed rubble. Those who had come down this ladder had gone straight into the heart of the Zoess. I had thought—hoped, even—that maybe they'd simply followed the cliff north all the way to its end. But of course that would have only got them captured, and the risks of the forest were clearly preferable to that. "What did these prisoners do wrong, exactly?" I asked.

"Rebelled," Vrake said, his tone closing off any further discussion on the topic.

Fine by me. I set the example after that, saying nothing. With this company I could only move at half the rate I usually would. I ducked under heavy blue fronds, dripping with slimy syrup that carried seeds away. I brushed aside thorny cavenna vines that hung in curling loops around our faces, probing, tasting the air. Harmless enough if you didn't let the little tongue-like tips get a sample of your skin.

The farther we got from the shadow of the cliff, the taller the trees became. Their bases grew thicker, and the domes their heavy upper branches made left my followers speechless as they stared up at the Zoess's

eerie green cathedral-like ceiling. Insects darted around us, leaving little blue trails of bioluminescence. Birds sang in the distance, mostly to the west, where sunlight had begun to creep over the city and reach the forest. By midday it would be sweltering.

And beneath it all, the hum of the lightning trees.

There was something else, too.

I dropped to one knee and held up a hand. The stormtroopers mimicked my position, weapons ready. Several held batons, one a long hunter's knife. The rest carried the "alternatives" Vrake had mentioned: modified bowcasters. Wookiee weapons, no doubt confiscated and then modified to only mechanically fire chargeless quarrels. I wondered where the garrison had dug them up. Had they ever been fired? *Not my problem*, I tried to tell myself.

The sound approaching us, *that* was my problem.

We'd been keeping to a game trail, same one the rebels had used. I gestured for my companions to move to one side, off the path. Some of them moved quickly enough.

Ahead, across the narrow patch of muddy forest floor, a fern exploded in a spray of green and blue. I saw only teeth and claws and the blur of motion before I rolled to one side and brought my knife up from its sheath. The beast, a deschene and a young one at that, galloped past me and slammed into one of the two stormtroopers who hadn't yet taken cover. The pair—animal and man—went rolling into the underbrush.

I barreled into the tangle of bushes and roots until I found the writhing pair. The trooper was on his back, hands clasped over his head, arms locked together in front of his face, as the deschene clawed at his white armor. Already there were gouges through the material, blood seeping through from the man beneath. Another few swipes and it would have him. I reached into a pocket and pulled out a device of my own design. A little black disk, its outer surface studded with small barbs.

"Down!" I shouted, and threw the device as hard as I could. Then I dove to the ground and covered my ears, hoping they'd heard.

With my arms clasped around my head, I could just see between my elbows. The throw had been true. It struck the six-legged animal on its middle flank. The barbs punctured skin and tangled in the fine hair. The impact caused the second feature of my device, a sphere within the sphere, to shatter. Chemicals inside mixed, creating a powerful electric current.

There was a pop I felt more than heard, and a brilliant white flash. Bolts of electricity snapped down from the canopy and struck the little device and the beast to which it clung. Another pop, this one ugly

and wet, resulted in a shower of smoldering meat and tough hide. I hid my face for that. I loved the animals that wandered the Zoess, even the predators.

I came to my knees, then stood. The stormtrooper on the ground lay motionless. Vrake stumbled past me and knelt beside his soldier.

"Alive?" I asked.

The reply came a few seconds later. "He'll be OK. Bring me a medpac!" This last command he shouted over his shoulder. One of the other troopers had recovered and complied.

Vrake looked at me. "What was that thing you threw?"

I shrugged. "My own invention. The trees' discharge is drawn to powered devices, I figured why not harness that?"

"Clever," he said, eyeing the suddenly pathetic bowcaster in his hands.

"Maybe, but far from subtle. If your rebels are out there, they know we're coming."

He snorted. "They're up against the Empire. They knew we'd come after them the moment they chose the wrong side."

I said nothing, a fact he seemed to notice. But Vrake ignored my slight and helped his stirring soldier to his feet. Soon we were moving again.

Hours passed. The forest sounds were occasionally tinged with the hollow growl of distant TIE fighters, patrolling the edges of the forest, maintaining a safe distance from the lightning trees. I stopped when we heard them the first time, and glanced at Vrake.

"You didn't think we'd risk letting the prisoners slip out the far side of the forest, did you?"

Half a kilometer later, as the day grew late, we came upon an ancient, petrified tree trunk in the center of a small clearing. The rebel's tracks were obvious, the ground trampled. "They rested here," I said.

"When?" Vrake asked.

"Three hours. Maybe four."

He let out a frustrated sigh. "We need to move faster, Gorlan."

"Why?" I asked. "Your patrols—"

"We need to get to them before this forest does."

"So you find their remains, so what? The forest does your job for you."

"No, it does not," he said through clenched teeth, patience waning.

in the knowledge they won't gun us down with blasters." He eyed the pouch at my belt. "How many more of your little inventions are you carrying?"

"Two," I said, regretting I'd let him see one at all.

He held out his hand. I hesitated, only just, and then placed the disks in his palm.

"Now," he said. "Move."

We marched until dusk. The forest grew cold and quiet, and we had no further encounters with the local wildlife. Luckily the rebels had taken a path that led to one of the few wide clearings in the forest, one I used frequently when my journeys required more than a day's travel. "We camp here," I said.

"We continue," Vrake snapped.

"No, we do not," I said. "Trust me. We cannot traverse the forest in the dark, much less follow tracks."

"They'll gain an entire night's march on us."

"Believe me," I said, "they'll have to stop, too. The Zoess is unnavigable after dark. Any light would trigger the trees, and a flame would bring the wrath of the wild ghoma. You haven't seen anger until you've seen one of them enraged by the sight of fire. Besides, this clearing offers some small comforts."

I went to the very center and lay down my gear on the ground beside a tall wooden post that protruded from the ground. Hooks poked out from a dozen places along its length. From my pack I removed an electric lantern, slipped it over one of the hooks, and reached for the on switch.

"What are you doing!?" Vrake shouted. He and his men leapt backward.

I turned the lantern on. A dim red light bathed the center of the clearing.

"Relax," I said, satisfied at their expressions I must admit. I indicated a circle of stones around the post, barely a meter in diameter. "The one place in the Zoess out of range of the lightning trees."

It took a moment before they regained their wits. "You should have told us," Vrake said. "We could have assembled a turret here. Or a sensor array."

"I had no idea their path would lead here," I explained. "And that kind of gear would have slowed us down."

"Won't the light alert our prey, or these ghoma, to us?"

"This hue calms the animals. I don't know why. And we only keep it on long enough to make camp, OK?"

I busied myself with the sleeping gear. Vrake and his men gathered a few meters away and spoke among themselves. When they finished, a pair of the stormtroopers sauntered off and began to patrol the edge of the clearing.

"I don't under—"

"We haven't interrogated them yet," he said, each syllable flat and sharp as a knife.

I held his gaze for a bit and then had to look away, to the ancient dead tree. *Interrogate*. What, I thought, had I gotten myself into? I should have never opened my door that morning. I shouldn't have gotten involved.

I studied the tracks around the tree trunk. There was a hollowed area at the base.

"If you wouldn't mind," Vrake said, sweeping one hand toward the direction the rebels had been traveling, "may we continue? I'd like to find them before they starve."

"You don't need to worry about that," I said.

"Meaning what?"

I moved to the gnarled, petrified wood and crouched. "They did more than stop here for a break. They had supplies cached here." I pointed to depressions in the mud within the hollowed trunk. "Three, maybe four packs, I'd guess. Heavy."

Vrake blinked. "What?"

"And another thing. Look at the tracks. There's more from here, leading west. Eight of them, now, I think. They joined up with others."

"Are you saying they *planned* this?"

At that I could only shrug. "I doubt it was a chance meeting."

"Don't get smart," he rasped.

"At least they're shouldering gear," one of the troopers offered. "Might slow them."

The lieutenant gathered his men. "Everyone stay sharp. Our escapees are likely armed. At least we can take comfort

We ate under the night sky. Those troopers not on patrol spoke in hushed tones. Soldier talk, old as time itself. I sat alone, weighed events. I stewed, as Chloa would say.

Something wasn't right. I just couldn't figure out what.

"Don't worry," Vrake said to me, suddenly.

I snapped out of my doldrums. "Hmm?"

"I know that wistful look all too well. Tomorrow we'll have them, and you can return to your family. The Empire will remember your aid to us here, I'll make certain of it."

I nodded. "You have kids?"

"Mm. Far from here," he said. "Now, rest. We've organized watches."

I wasn't tired, though. My body was, sure, but my mind still churned on the events of the day. I removed several items from my pack and assembled them, careful to attach the special battery last. Soon I had the holoprojector in one piece. I lay beside it, on top of my bedroll, the night pleasantly warm. Hands tucked behind my head, I stared at recordings of my children playing. Chloa, smiling shyly.

I'd learned, over the years out here. Soft light seemed to appease the forest. The Zoess had always left me alone, as if we'd struck a bargain. I wondered if I'd broken that bargain today.

Maybe so, because I woke some time later to sounds of violence.

Angry grunts of exertion. A shout of triumph or maybe rage.

A figure before me. Cerean, female, wearing prisoner's garb. Her face ghostly, lit by the flickering images from the holoprojector. I rolled as her spear came down. It slammed into the dirt where my head had been. She cursed.

Her companions were in a circle around the wooden post, each one standing over a bedroll, stabbing with spears, repeatedly.

"Something's wrong!" one of them shouted.

"They're not here," said another.

A boot slammed into my ribs, knocking me back to the dirt. I rolled and raised my hands. "I'm only a guide," I said.

"Be silent," she hissed.

"Yes," a voice called. Vrake. "Be silent."

The stormtroopers came in from hiding places around the perimeter of the clearing, forming a circle around the rebels who shifted from foot to foot, spears darting from one target to the next.

I shook my head. My ribs throbbed. Equal cries of "stand your ground!" and "do not move!" intermingled in the confused camp, as the stormtroopers closed in.

"We won't surrender," the woman beside me said.

Vrake began to pace. "Interesting venue, this forest. It puts us on equal footing. Our bowcasters," he said, and nodded toward the nearest rebel, "and your... what have you got there? Spears? Charmingly primitive—"

The woman beside me squeezed the weapon in her hands. There was a dull click, and then the tip of the spear shot outward. A harpoon. I should have seen it sooner, the length of wire coiled around each rebel's upper arm.

The tip of the weapon sprang outward at phenomenal speed, just missing Vrake's face, before whipping back and reconnecting itself into the barrel of the "spear."

Vrake's men raised their bowcasters. Everyone tensed.

My eyes were fixed on Vrake's hands. They were clasped behind his back, but he'd turned to dodge the attack and I'd caught a glimpse of what he held. The two small spheres I'd given him. I scrambled backwards toward the center of the clearing, to the marker post and my gear.

All of them—rebels and stormtroopers alike—shifted on their feet, adjusting their aim from one target to another. Sizing each other up. Deciding who to shoot first or which way to dive.

The air grew still. The forest, dead quiet. That strange instant of calm that always manifested before violence.

My hand bumped something. I turned, saw my still-flickering holoprojector, and my mind filled with grief and remorse. The idea that I might never see Chloa and the kids again.

One last glimpse, at least. I focused on the image.

And saw a stranger. Not my kids, not Chloa, but a woman with dark hair. It took my brain a few seconds to grasp who this was. No stranger at all. Far from it.

Princess Leia Organa stood there, holographically. The interruption of my own recording meant this was an emergency broadcast. She was speaking. I picked up the device, careful to keep it in the circle of stones lest the forest annihilate us all.

"He's got a weapon," one of the rebels barked, unsure. It didn't occur to me until later that he'd meant me.

"The tracker fights with us," Vrake said. "Or he'd better, if he wants to see his family again."

I'd activated the sound. I wasn't listening to them anymore, but to her. *Princess Leia Organa.*

"All of you, stop. Listen!" I shouted. Croaked, really. "Stop fighting. Something's happened."

I magnified the image until Leia seemed to stand, life-size, on my palm.

She was saying, "*The Death Star outside the forest moon of Endor is gone, and with it the Imperial leadership. The tyrant Palpatine is dead...*"

I stood there, the rest of her words unheard. Palpatine was dead. The Imperial leadership, gone. I glanced at Vrake, who stood frozen, trapped between disbelief and anger. I didn't know what to do, what to say. Somehow the only words that came to mind were the ones I'd just uttered.

Stop fighting.

THE VOICE OF THE EMPIRE

WRITTEN BY **MUR LAFFERTY**
ART BY **JASON CHAN**

Don't say a word. Stone-faced HoloNet News editor Mandora Catabe didn't say it out loud, but the message was clear. Calliope Drouth's eyes flicked from Mandora, seated at her desk, to the man standing behind her, smiling widely, hands clasped behind his back. Mandora's face was set, grim, her eyes fixed on Calliope's.

That's an Imperial smile. Calliope had hoped to be called in to hear about the promotion she'd asked for, but that hope died when she saw Mandora's face.

"Calliope, sit down," Mandora said, indicating the chair opposite her desk. "This is Eridan Wesyse. I wanted to tell you first: I'm retiring, effective immediately, and Mr. Wesyse will be your new editor-in-chief."

Where Mandora was small and shrewd, suspicious of anyone and everyone, Eridan looked as if he would always listen sympathetically, smile kindly, and report whatever fit the kind of story he wanted to tell; Calliope, knew the type.

She nodded. She'd seen the man around, doing Imperial PR. "Nice to meet you, sir," she said. "I've seen you at some events, haven't I?"

He nodded, smiling wider. "You do have good eyes," he said. "Mandora said you'd be my star reporter. Yes, I've done some work for the Empire, and I will continue to as Mondora's replacement. You see, the Empire wanted to have a tighter..." he paused, searching for the word, "*connection* to HNN. We'll want to keep on all of the loyal staff, though, so you shouldn't worry about your job."

Calliope couldn't help glancing at Mandora.

"No, I'm the only one leaving. I was already contemplating my retirement," Mandora said, her eyes indicating no such thing. "The Empire just made me an offer I couldn't refuse."

"How generous," Calliope said, her mouth going dry. "What plans do you have for HNN, Mr. Wesyse?"

"We're going to start by giving you a promotion!" he said. "We're promoting you to senior reporter and calling you the Voice of the Empire. We were so impressed with your work on the Wookiee threat."

Calliope froze. Her piece on the Wookiee "threat" had been heavily edited by Imperial censors, removing the main point of her story entirely and nearly causing Calliope to quit.

"Based on your noteworthy history with HNN," Wesyse continued, "it's obvious we want to promote you. It's quite an honor to be the one person on camera that countless citizens will watch to get their news!"

"That is an honor," Calliope agreed, using the smooth voice she used on sources she knew were lying. "Thank you for the promotion. I'm looking forward to the new direction you will take us in, Editor Wesyse."

She wanted to take Mandora aside and ask her what was going on, why was this happening, but Mandora's normally animated face was set, which scared Calliope more than anything.

"As our newly appointed Voice of the Empire, we're throwing you at your first story, actually," Wesyse continued. "You are to cover the Imperial Ball tonight. We got you an invitation, which was no easy task." He paused here, as if to give her a chance to thank him, but she pulled out a small keyboard and started taking notes, nodding for him to continue. "You are to go and interview the dignitaries, report what people are wearing, mention how good the food is, and so on. Your job is to show the Empire in

a way the public doesn't get to see it. Make it more accessible. By giving them the inside view, the Empire becomes *their* Empire. Understand?"

Before Calliope could protest that investigative journalism was her preferred area of news, Mandora pushed something across the desk at her. "I'm giving you Zox. I won't need it after I retire. It's yours now." She patted the little droid, an elderly X-0X unit about the size of her hand. "It's been very good to me, and I know it will serve you the same way."

The droid was dome-shaped, and its original color was probably red or orange, but it was hard to tell as the paint had worn off with age. It extended three spidery legs and rose from the desk, wobbled, and fell over on its side. It beeped plaintively until Mandora righted it.

"It will probably be better on your shoulder, now that I think about it," she said, smiling fondly at Zox and ignoring Calliope's confusion entirely.

"But X-0X doesn't transmit, it only records," Calliope said. "Why can't I take one of the newer droids?"

Wesyse frowned. "Unfortunately, the military did a recall of all of the transmitting droids reporters were using. Turns out there were some technical problems."

Calliope wanted to laugh, but her spine had turned to ice. Did he know how transparent he was being? Stifling the press by removing their ability to transmit video feeds would drive the press in a direction Calliope didn't want to go. She opened her mouth, but Mandora interrupted her.

"Anyway, I'm retiring and it needs a good owner. I know you will treasure it as much as I always have." She gave it another push, her steely blue eyes locking onto Calliope's. *Take the droid.*

Calliope's mind raced as she put her hand over the small dome. They were balanced on the edge of something very sharp now. "Thank you, Mandora. I'll treasure it."

Much of the HNN staff had plans to go to the terrace of the HoloNet News building to watch the Empire Day parade below. Thousands of officers and soldiers marched by, flanked by the Empire's machines of war. They were followed by small vehicles showing off the new Imperial TIE striker, designed for both suborbital flight and atmospheric flight, using state of the art technology in navigation and speed.

Calliope shook Mandora's hand, wishing she could talk to her and find out what was really going on. She waved to her coworkers and left during the parade. She was hardly dressed for an Imperial Ball, as she had been expecting an average day at the office, and had to rush home to change.

Calliope spared a look over her shoulder as the new TIE fighters were displayed to the crowds. She had hoped to do a story on them, but doubted she'd ever get the chance now if she were doing shallow interviews of famous people.

Calliope rummaged in her closet for her few pieces of fancy clothing. She had reported from the front lines of wars, from the bridges of starships, from high atop a tree as she reported a raid on a droid manufacturing plant. She'd endured a broken arm, several burns, and one cut on her cheek, which she refused to surgically remove, as it was a reminder to all about how seriously she took her job.

And now she had to pull out the ivory gown that she had worn to her sister's wedding. She had to admit it was beautiful, woven with smart strands of synthetic fiber that gave off shimmers of different colors depending on the angle of the light on the dress. The ivory contrasted well with her dark skin and delicate features, although accessorizing with a rusty droid would be challenging.

Finally dressed, she put X-0X on her shoulder. It beeped inquisitively at her. Its beep was more like a strangled chirp: this droid had been around for decades, and her boss had never replaced it.

"Why Mandora insisted I bring you, I'll never know," she said, and then stopped abruptly. X-0X whirred in a way that sounded much like the newer, sleeker droids, and its scratched ocular lens glowed. Had it been modified?

A hologram appeared in front of Calliope. Mandora paced within the small circle of X-0X's beam, showing finally the energy and fierceness that Calliope had expected.

"Calliope. I don't have much time. As of right now, the Empire is taking over HNN. I'm out, but you can still stay in. They will censor you. They will silence you. They will enrage you." Mandora stopped and jabbed her finger at Calliope, spitting out one word per jab. "*But I need you to stay where you are.*"

The hologram began pacing again, a few steps to keep within the ability of X-0X to record. "This will be my last message to you. I'm leaving Coruscant. The fight against the Empire is bigger than we ever expected, and I'm going to help them however I can."

"Against the Empire?" Calliope whispered. She'd found evidence of resistance while researching some of her stories, but Mandora had stopped every attempt to report on them. They didn't have enough to broadcast yet, she'd said.

Calliope kept watching the new man entering the room—tall, pale with a long white cape that shone in the light.

"You have a few choices. I'm sure if you do what Eridan Wesyse wishes you to, you will be rewarded. Voice of the Empire. The Empire does appreciate loyalty. But you're better than that. You're smarter than that. And my *friends* could use you. The second option available to you is dangerous and," she paused and smiled, "subversive."

Calliope listened to the second option, hope and excitement blossoming within her. This was the kind of reporting she could get behind.

X-0X clung to her gown, and she didn't even mind it crushing the fabric. It burbled and beeped at her as she approached the Imperial Palace. "What exactly did she do to modify you, anyway?" she asked. It remained silent.

Calliope walked past the dozens of Imperial guards, and then the helmeted troopers, who always made her shiver. She showed her press credentials and invitation to the stern-faced guard at the top of the staircase. He frowned, casting a suspicious eye on X-0X. "That a recording droid?"

"It is," she said, smiling. "It's vintage, mostly for show. It's here with HNN Editor-in-chief Eridan Wesyse's blessing." Recognizing the name, he gestured her through.

She thought of the impoverished people on far-off systems and wondered who among them would want to know which designer a diplomat from Alderaan would be wearing. But she went dutifully to find out.

Oddly enough, Alderaan had sent a junior diplomat who looked as if his suit was very uncomfortable. She joined him at the bar.

"You look like this is your first Empire Day," she said to him, smiling. "I'm Calliope Drouth, HoloNet News."

His pale eyes scanned hers, and he swallowed. "Pol Treader. I recognize you. And what you're really asking is why Alderaan sent someone so young to such an important day."

She laughed. "If you're going to succeed in diplomacy, you're going to have to be much less direct." She took the drink offered by the bartender.

"Diplomacy isn't my usual job title," Pol said, pulling at his waistcoat. "I'm here as a favor to the Organas. They couldn't make it."

That was interesting. "Why not?"

He shrugged and looked irritated at her. "They don't tell me things like that. I'm just an assistant in antiquities." He wandered away.

"Who did your suit?" she called after him, but he was gone. She stopped herself from chasing after Mr. Antiquities as someone new swept into the room. All eyes fixated on the newcomer, and some young Imperial officers at the bar began whispering in hushed tones. Calliope edged closer to them.

"I don't believe you," one said to the other. She was tall, nearly two meters, with the same dark skin as Calliope.

Her companion was shorter and pale, his cheeks ruddy from already enjoying the flowing alcohol. "Fine, don't believe me," he said. "Doesn't make it any less true."

"You were there, with him? For Project Celestial Power?" she asked.

He shushed her frantically, his head swiveling around to see who had overheard. Calliope kept watching the new man entering the room—tall, pale, with a long white cape that shone in the light. Everyone seemed fascinated with him, but he only gave attention to the high-ranking Imperials drinking from thin flutes in the corner.

"Yes, I was with him, now be quiet about it. If we're overheard I could be demoted!" He fingered his insignia of rank on his chest. "And I just got this."

"Yes, you said so. About five times," his companion said, sounding bored.

Calliope looked at their uniforms as if for the first time, and approached. The pale officer looked worried, but stood his ground.

"Calliope Drouth, HoloNet News," she said. "Everyone is impressed with that man who just came in, but I can't place him. Who is that?"

"That is Commander Krennic," the tall woman said. "He's the architect behind some of the Emperor's greatest projects."

"All classified, I would expect," Calliope said, smiling.

"Of course," the pale officer said.

"I would love to find out more about him, Officer..." she raised her eyebrows and waited for him to supply his name.

"Tifino. Officer Tifino," he said. He indicated his companion. "That's Officer Wick."

Officer Wick bowed, looking amused. Calliope decided she liked her.

"I'll get the next round," she said. "Incidentally, what do you two think of the fashion here tonight?"

Once she had the officers talking, Calliope managed to steer the conversation toward the various dignitaries flaunting themselves in the ballroom.

"Now, that is Ambassador Oaan from the third moon around Jaatovi," Wick said. The ambassador was tall and thin with long black hair cascading down her back, moving with grace through the crowd. She reached Commander Krennic and began speaking with him.

"She is so subtle she could step through a lightning storm and not get zapped," Wick said. "I'd watch out for her."

"Or interview her," Calliope said, winking. She took a testing step away from her new friends, and they began protesting.

"You can't leave, you just got here!" Tifino said. "You can talk to her later!"

Everyone likes the woman buying the drinks, Mandora had always told her, and she returned to them and got another round. If she could make these officers feel they owed her something, so much the better.

Calliope pointed to Tifino's mark of rank. "It looks as if you made an impression on Commander Krennic," she said, handing the bartender credits for the drinks. "It sounds like he's doing highly classified things. You could be heroes and few would ever know. What does that feel like?"

Tifino finished his drink in one gulp and focused on Calliope, blinking a few times. His eyes fell on the silent droid on her shoulder. "He's already a war hero," he confided. "I-I can't tell you why."

"Of course you can't," Calliope said, nodding. "That's not the actions of an officer who's caught the commander's eye. Speaking of which, where did he get that amazing cape?"

She'd guessed right, neither officer felt like following her lead about fashion. Wick brought up how she could be transferred to Tifino's ship.

"We need scouts more than anything," he said. "How's your tracking?"

Wick made a face. "I'm a pilot. I haven't spent time in any terrain but a city since I was a child."

"What do you need with scouts?" Calliope asked. "I'll bet the Emperor is looking for a place to spend a holiday!" She tapped on X-0X and frowned when it did nothing. Then she pulled her small keyboard from her bag and began typing. "Where is he looking to vacation?"

Tifino frowned. "No, it's not like that. Who'd want to spend time on Jedha for fun, anyway?"

"Who'd want to scout there?" Calliope said. She got another round of drinks. Tifino excused himself to visit the lavatory.

Wick sighed when he was out of earshot. "That guy. A screw-up through the academy. I carried him, you know. And then luck hit him and missed me, and he's under Krennic and I'm, well..." She looked down at her empty glass and Calliope gently removed it and put a full one there.

"I'm doing shuttle runs," she finally said.

"Shuttle pilots can scout," Calliope said. "You have a wider view of the terrain. You need to seize opportunity, tell them why they need you. You've got hot hands at the helm, right?" Wick nodded, realization dawning on her face. "You've got sharp eyes, right? Sharper than Tifino's?"

"Much sharper," Wick scoffed.

"Then you tell your superiors that shuttle pilots can be just as good at scouting as troops on the ground. Better. You can see lights, smoke, the movement of groups. The Empire needs you to look for hidden enemies."

Wick had been nodding fervently at her, and then frowned and stopped nodding. "No, they're not looking for enemies. They're looking for some kind of crystals. What were they called? Cyder? Kyber? Hyper? Something like that. Anyway,

Tifino's team just found a huge stash of them. That's what got him his new rank."

"And you carried that guy!" Calliope said, eyes wide with outrage.

"And I carried that guy," Wick said firmly, nodding. They clinked glasses and drank.

Tifino returned with a confused smile. "Wait, I want in, what are we toasting?"

"To Wick's future," Calliope said, raising her glass again.

"Who carried you through the Academy," Wick reminded him. "Who may just be the next hot officer to find the commander some of those fancy crystals!"

Tifino looked meaningfully at Calliope, who listed toward the wall and fiddled with X-0X, which was still unresponsive. Wick waved a hand, dismissing her. "She's as drunk as we are. Besides, her recording droid died a while back." She gulped and stood a little straighter, looking at Calliope. "You aren't going to mention this, are you?"

"Depends," she said. "Are you going to tell me who made the commander's cape or not? Because that's the story I'm chasing."

They laughed, and Calliope mock frowned at them. "No, really. If I don't report that, I'm going to get into serious trouble with my new editor. Everyone on Coruscant is going to want one!"

The officers laughed, and Wick launched into a very funny joke about bartenders on planets with high seawater content. Suddenly, X-0X gave a strangled chirp and tumbled off of Calliope's shoulder. It landed hard on its dome and bounced a meter away. Calliope went to retrieve it, and as she reached out, a black boot settled gently on the droid's still-rolling body and stopped it. She straightened and looked up into the face of Commander Krennic.

"Is this yours?" he asked, picking the silent droid up swiftly. Calliope groaned inwardly.

"Yes, it's not the most reliable," Calliope said, glaring at the little droid. She looked up and met Krennic's eyes, blue and searching. She held out a gloved hand and he looked at it for a moment, and then shook it instead of giving X-0X back. So she introduced herself instead. "Commander Krennic, it's an honor. I'm Calliope—"

He scrutinized the droid. "Drouth, yes, with HoloNet News," he said. "I was under the impression we would supply our reporters with better equipment."

"Actually we just heard the military recalled our newer droids. Anything to serve the Emperor's cause, but that leaves us with, well," she indicated X-0X's sorry state.

Calliope knew that if she protested too much, she'd make herself look suspicious. She glanced back at Wick and then looked meaningfully at Krennic.

"How old is this droid?" he asked.

"I don't know," she said. "It was a gift from my former editor. I keep it mainly for nostalgia purposes. And recording, when it works."

"Nostalgia and connections to loved ones," he mused. "Some would consider it a weakness."

"While others would consider it a comfort," she said.

He smiled slightly. "I would definitely think the inability to record things is a weakness for a reporter. You may just miss something that could make your career. Or you could be lucky enough to miss something that could destroy your career."

Calliope thought of the data that Mandora had sent her. She hadn't erased it from the droid yet, and now it was in Krennic's hands.

She smiled back at him. "I try not to rely on it too much."

"Then how will you gather your information to report on the Imperial Ball?" he asked. "Surely you're missing all of the gossip by fiddling with a broken droid."

"I'm getting gossip at the bar, sir," she said. "I just found out your tailor's name. Do you know that you're setting fashion trends?"

Krennic focused on the officers behind her, who were frozen at attention. "Tifino," he said. "Are you making the most of your shore leave?"

Tifino nodded, unable to speak.

"Good." He looked down at X-0X, held in his long, gloved fingers. "If you'd allow me to borrow this droid, Ms. Drouth," he said. "I know some tinkers who can fix it right up."

Calliope knew that if she protested too much, she'd make herself look suspicious. She glanced back at Wick and then looked meaningfully at Krennic. *Come on*, she mouthed. *Now's your chance.*

Wick swallowed and then lunged forward, stumbling slightly. "Commander," she stammered, putting a hand on his white coat and then pulling it off as if she just remembered herself. "Officer Ianna Wick, sir, and I wanted to make my case for joining your next mission."

Krennic frowned at her, and opened his mouth, but Wick forged on ahead, "I'm a shuttle pilot, best in my class at the Academy, and Tifino said you needed scouts—"

Calliope had no love for the Empire, but she'd developed a soft spot for Wick. She prayed the Imperial wouldn't blow it by saying too much in front of Calliope. Lucky for all involved, X-0X chose that time to come back online, its sensor glowing again and beeping in a confused way. It buzzed, vibrating in Krennic's hand.

"There you are," Calliope said, interrupting Wick. She reached up and took the droid from the distracted Krennic, who frowned at her. "He's working now, sir. Thanks for your offer, but you have more important things to do at this ball. Like listen to this young woman discuss her career with you." She made a play of looking around the room and focusing on the miserable nobody from Alderaan. "I see an ambassador I need to talk to, I hope you both have a lovely evening." She nodded to them both, passed behind Krennic, and then gave Wick a thumbs up. The woman smiled at her before making her case to the stern commander.

"She did carry Tifino, after all," Calliope muttered to herself. She put X-0X on her shoulder where it gripped her as tightly as it had before. "Let's circle the room once or twice and then get you home and into a good oil bath that will scrub you clean of *everything*."

Calliope faced the camera, smiling with experienced ease as the transmission to countless planets concluded. She deftly doublechecked the monitor to ensure her hands were still visible in the feed.

"We here at HNN hope you enjoyed your Empire Day. Last night, I was afforded an inside look at the elegance and finery of the Imperial Palace Ball." The monitors showed the footage X-0X had gotten before it had malfunctioned, panning around the room and focusing on the well-dressed dignitaries. "I can report that the fashion of Coruscant is going to be taking its lead from the attendees! From the sharply dressed dignitary from Alderaan to the elegant dress uniforms of the upper echelon of the Imperial Forces, these attendees showed more than their diplomatic and military might, but also their fashion sense. Our Imperial Forces are, well, a *force* to be reckoned with, both on the battlefield and in the ballroom! You can find some of the superstar tailors who dressed our dignitaries listed on your screen. You'd better get your call in soon! This is Calliope Drouth, your voice of the Empire."

The light above the camera died, and Calliope sat back and sighed, forcing her shoulders to loosen. Eridan Wesyse hurried up to her, beaming. "Even better than your script, so vivid!" he sang. "I'm going to put you on all the society stories!" He frowned. "I would have liked more interviews with the who's-who of the Empire, though."

"My droid malfunctioned halfway through the night," Calliope said truthfully. "I did what I could."

He clapped her on the back and rushed away to converse with another reporter. She finally unclasped her hands. *I got away with it.*

Now the question was, would anyone hear her true report? Mandora's message had included a file on code phrases and cyphers, which Calliope had used to carefully select the words in her transmission. The position of her hands during the broadcast would clue the subversives in to which algorithm to run on her seemingly vapid report. With any luck, they would be on their way to Jedha within the hour. Calliope didn't know what kyber crystals were, but if they were important enough for Krennic to go after, they had to be important enough to report.

If what Mandora said was true, Calliope was one of many spies, gathering information against the Empire.

She thought of Officers Wick and Tifino: possibly invisible "heroes" in the Empire's eyes. She knew how that felt now.

No one would ever know her work, not if she did her job right. No one but X-0X, which sat on her desk in her office, beeping quietly to itself.

She was growing fond of the little nuisance.

STAR WARS LIBRARY

STAR WARS: THE EMPIRE STRIKES BACK: THE OFFICIAL COLLECTOR'S EDITION

'STAR WARS: THE MANDALORIAN: GUIDE TO SEASON ONE

STAR WARS INSIDER FICTION COLLECTION VOLUME ONE

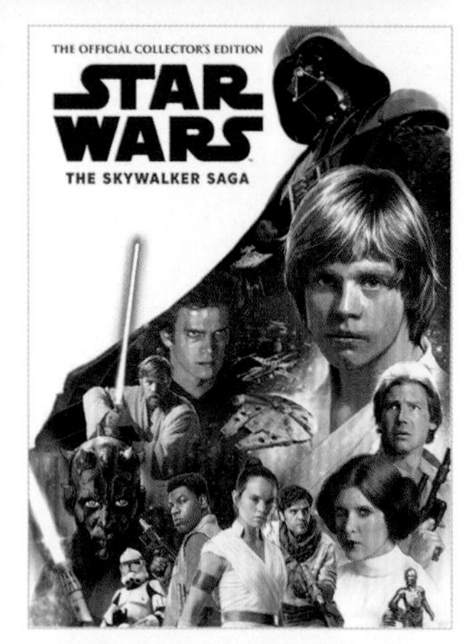

STAR WARS: THE SKYWALKER SAGA THE OFFICIAL MOVIE COMPANION

- ***ROGUE ONE: A STAR WARS STORY*** THE OFFICIAL COLLECTOR'S EDITION
- ***ROGUE ONE: A STAR WARS STORY*** THE OFFICIAL MISSION DEBRIEF
- ***STAR WARS: THE LAST JEDI*** THE OFFICIAL COLLECTOR'S EDITION
- ***STAR WARS: THE LAST JEDI*** THE OFFICIAL MOVIE COMPANION
- ***STAR WARS: THE LAST JEDI*** THE ULTIMATE GUIDE
- ***SOLO: A STAR WARS STORY*** THE OFFICIAL COLLECTOR'S EDITION
- ***SOLO: A STAR WARS STORY*** THE ULTIMATE GUIDE
- **THE BEST OF *STAR WARS INSIDER*** VOLUME 1
- **THE BEST OF *STAR WARS INSIDER*** VOLUME 2
- **THE BEST OF *STAR WARS INSIDER*** VOLUME 3
- **THE BEST OF *STAR WARS INSIDER*** VOLUME 4
- ***STAR WARS:*** LORDS OF THE SITH
- ***STAR WARS:*** HEROES OF THE FORCE
- ***STAR WARS:*** ICONS OF THE GALAXY
- ***STAR WARS:*** THE SAGA BEGINS
- ***STAR WARS*** THE ORIGINAL TRILOGY
- ***STAR WARS:*** ROGUES, SCOUNDRELS AND BOUNTY HUNTERS
- ***STAR WARS*** CREATURES, ALIENS, AND DROIDS
- ***STAR WARS: THE RISE OF SKYWALKER*** THE OFFICIAL COLLECTOR'S EDITION
- ***STAR WARS: THE EMPIRE STRIKES BACK*** THE 40TH ANNIVERSARY COLLCTORS' EDITION
- ***STAR WARS: AGE OF RESISTANCE*** THE OFFICIAL COLLCTORS' EDITION
- ***STAR WARS: THE SKYWALKER SAGA*** THE OFFICIAL COLLECTOR'S EDITION
- ***STAR WARS: THE MANDALORIAN:*** GUIDE TO SEASON ONE
- ***STAR WARS INSIDER*** FICTION COLLECTION VOLUME ONE
- ***STAR WARS INSIDER*** FICTION COLLECTION VOLUME TWO

MARVEL LIBRARY

THE X-MEN AND THE AVENGERS GAMMA QUEST OMNIBUS

MARVEL STUDIOS' BLACK WIDOW

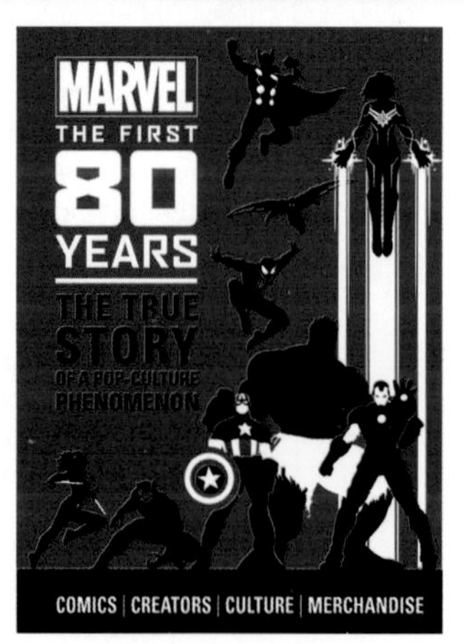

MARVEL: THE FIRST 80 YEARS

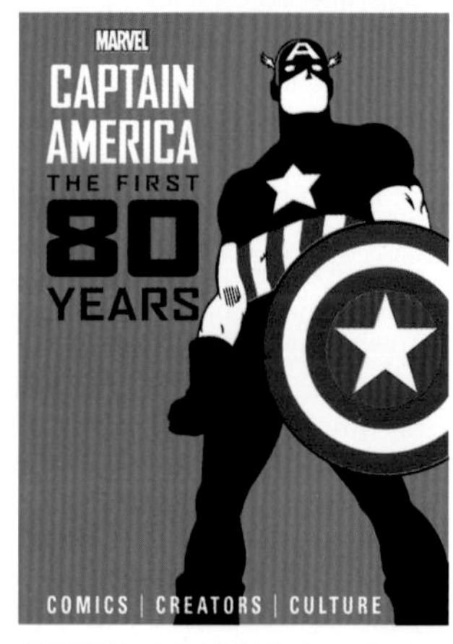

MARVEL'S CAPTAIN AMERICA: THE FIRST 80 YEARS.

MARVEL CLASSIC NOVELS
- **SPIDER-MAN** THE VENOM FACTOR OMNIBUS
- **X-MEN AND THE AVENGERS** GAMMA QUEST OMNIBUS
- **X-MEN** MUTANT EMPIRE OMNIBUS

NOVELS
- **ANT-MAN** NATURAL ENEMY
- **AVENGERS** EVERYBODY WANTS TO RULE THE WORLD
- **AVENGERS** INFINITY
- **BLACK PANTHER** WHO IS THE BLACK PANTHER?
- **CAPTAIN AMERICA** DARK DESIGNS
- **CAPTAIN MARVEL** LIBERATION RUN
- **CIVIL WAR**
- **DEADPOOL** PAWS
- **SPIDER-MAN** FOREVER YOUNG
- **SPIDER-MAN** KRAVEN'S LAST HUNT
- **THANOS** DEATH SENTENCE
- **VENOM** LETHAL PROTECTOR
- **X-MEN** DAYS OF FUTURE PAST
- **X-MEN** THE DARK PHOENIX SAGA
- **SPIDER-MAN** HOSTILE TAKEOVER

ARTBOOKS
- **MARVEL'S *SPIDER-MAN*** THE ART OF THE GAME
- **MARVEL *CONTEST OF CHAMPIONS*** THE ART OF THE BATTLEREALM
- ***SPIDER-MAN: INTO THE SPIDERVERSE***
- **THE ART OF IRON MAN** 10TH ANNIVERSARY EDITION

MOVIE SPECIALS
- **MARVEL STUDIOS' *ANT MAN & THE WASP***
- **MARVEL STUDIOS' *AVENGERS: ENDGAME***
- **MARVEL STUDIOS' *AVENGERS: INFINITY WAR***
- **MARVEL STUDIOS' *BLACK PANTHER* (COMPANION)**
- **MARVEL STUDIOS' *BLACK WIDOW* (SPECIAL)**
- **MARVEL STUDIOS'*CAPTAIN MARVEL***
- **MARVEL STUDIOS' *SPIDER-MAN: FAR FROM HOME***
- **MARVEL STUDIOS: THE FIRST TEN YEARS**
- **MARVEL STUDIOS' *THOR: RAGNAROK***

- ***SPIDER-MAN: INTO THE SPIDERVERSE***

AVAILABLE AT ALL GOOD BOOKSTORES AND ONLINE

TITAN-COMICS.COM | **TITAN**BOOKS.COM